THE BITTERSWEET ENCHANTMENT OF LOVE

She caught sight of Freddy and felt a glow of increased pleasure. Not that she would be able to dance with him, nor, in all probability, exchange a word with him. But he was there; it seemed the final happy touch to a delightful occasion.

She cast an occasional veiled glance in his direction, satisfied with a glimpse of the immaculately brushed hair, the bent profile as he talked with his elderly friend. When at length one such discreet glance was rewarded only by the sight of an empty table being reset for later guests she felt acute disappointment. Freddy was gone; the evening continued enjoyable but had lost some of its tang.

ANNE DUFFIELD
Come Back, Miranda

A BERKLEY MEDALLION BOOK
published by
BERKLEY PUBLISHING CORPORATION

BERKLEY MEDALLION BOOKS are published by
Berkley Publishing Corporation
200 Madison Avenue
New York, N.Y. 10016

BERKLEY MEDALLION BOOKS ® TM 757,375

Printed in the United States of America

Berkley Medallion Edition, FEBRUARY, 1974

SECOND PRINTING

CHAPTER ONE

A DRIVING WIND with squalls of rain lashed the docks; the boat train passengers hastened up the ship's gangway into the warm interior of the main deck where the usual chaos of embarkation was in full spate. People milling to and fro, crowding about the purser's desk, inquiring for mail, sending telegrams; stewards carrying baggage, answering questions, directing flustered ladies; a group of stewardesses in crisp cotton frocks alert in the background, a reassuring sight for those among the women passengers who were poor sailors. The weather threatened ominously, the Bay loomed ahead, but the calm-faced stewardesses would be on hand to help, comfort and see one through.

Mr Willison, an elderly Englishman resident in Portugal and returning to Lisbon after a business conference in London, stood in an angle by the companion-way and surveyed the scene with amiable eyes. The ship was a liner which in former days had not touched at Lisbon but was now combining its long routine run with shorter trips, allowing people to book for various ports hitherto bypassed and, for those who desired it, guaranteeing a passage home.

'A most accommodating arrangement from every point of view,' thought Mr Willison complacently.

His attention was presently caught by the voice of one of the clerks at the desk.

'Clayton? Sir Frederick Clayton—?' the clerk handed a couple of letters to the man who had inquired for them. Mr Willison stepped forward and touched the traveller's arm.

'Well, Freddy, where are you bound for?'

The other swung round.

'Hallo, sir! Been over on a spot of leave? Why didn't you give me a ring?'

'I merely flew over for a directors' meeting and am indulging in a comfortable journey back. Detest planes. I take it you are on holiday. Going far?'

'Not at all. Like you, I prefer the sea when there's no great rush. I am bound for your home town. And on a job.'

Mr Willison, an old family friend, looked astounded.

'A job? in Lisbon? My dear Freddy, what is all this?'

'I have been commissioned to write a series of articles on Portugal for a new publication that is to be launched in a few months' time. Travel magazine sort of thing.'

'Indeed? I knew you dabbled occasionally in writing but I had no idea your talent had been recognized to such an extent.'

Sir Frederick grinned. He was a man of thirty or so, with a face Mr Willison's wife had once described as 'nice-ugly'. It was, at all events, a decidedly attractive face, healthily tanned, the infectious grin revealing strong, regular teeth, the dark eyes laughing and a little quizzical. For the rest, he was tall, with good shoulders and a very easy bearing.

'The editor happens to be a friend of mine,' he explained. 'A bit of a wangle but I think my talent is adequate. An easy assignment, nothing political, just local colour and general chitchat. The point is, that it's a chance to get abroad for a decent period instead of the inside of a week on the idiot travel allowance. I'm frightfully lucky to have pulled it off.'

'Quite,' Mr Willison agreed, dryly. 'And meantime, the farm?'

'The farm is in better hands than mine. Waters, my agent, is an excellent fellow.'

'Thank you,' a harassed voice pleaded at this juncture. 'Thank you—' a second boat train had arrived and a laden steward was endeavouring to pass.

'We're blocking the traffic,' Sir Frederick said. 'I'll get along—see you later, sir.'

Mr Willison shook his head as the tall figure elbowed a way through the crowd and disappeared. Freddy was incorrigible. All this rushing about, this living solely for enjoyment—it was time and more than time that he pulled himself together, found a wife, settled down and looked after his own place instead of leaving it to the agent.

He had been a promising boy, doing well at school, his chief gift an exceptional aptitude for languages. His war record, too, was good; Freddy never talked about it but Mr Willison knew that, in due course, he had been selected for very special duties and acquitted himself with distinction. He had remained in the Army until 1948, attached as Liaison Officer to Headquarters in Germany. Shortly after his discharge, owing to the tragic deaths of his father and elder brother who were drowned when their racing yacht overturned, he succeeded to a baronetcy and a considerable fortune.

Like so many other ex-Army officers he invested in a farm, stocked it well and set about restoring the fine old Tudor farmhouse. And there, in Mr Willison's opinion, he should have remained; learning the way of the earth and its seasons, superintending and sharing the labours of his men, marrying some nice girl and starting a young family; living, in a word, the useful, wholesome life of a conscientious landowner.

This, Freddy had entirely failed to do. He kept on his London flat and continued his lively bachelor existence; he had a host of friends, drove a supercharged car, was always popping over to the Continent for weekends—no harm in any of it but life should not be one long pleasure chase. Well, it was his own business and he was a good lad in many ways. Despite his disapproval, Mr Willison was very fond of Freddy.

He went back to his corner by the companionway to watch the new lot of passengers embark and was suddenly conscious of the feeling that he, too, was being watched. He glanced from side to side and saw a young girl gazing intently in his direction, half smiling, her expression a mingled hesitancy and invitation. Her smile deepened; he noted how it slightly lifted her cheekbones and that a little nick, like a dimple, flickered in the left one.

'Upon my word,' Mr Willison said to himself, 'if I were thirty years younger I should be tempted to say she was making eyes at me.'

Modestly deciding that, at his age, such a thing was out of the question he averted his own eyes; he must be mistaken, it could not be at him she was casting that come-hither look. But the girl was now pushing forward through the crush; a moment later she stood before him.

'You *are* Mr John Willison, aren't you?'

'I am.' He regarded her with benevolent inquiry.

'You don't remember me but I was sure I recognized you. I met you and Mrs Willison several times when you were still living in London. I'm Charles Rendle's sister—' she spoke in a clear, unhurried voice, her words accented by the merest trace of flatness. An echo of Americanism; Mr Willison found it most engaging.

'My dear,' he exclaimed, 'of course I remember but you were in pigtails and pinafores in those days.'

She laughed.

'I was still at the convent and probably wearing the uniform.'

'Something of the sort. Now, let me see; you are Marion—Miriam—'

'Miranda.'

'To be sure. Miranda.' A charming name, and it suited her as names do not always suit their bearers. He gave her an interested scrutiny; dark hair, trimly netted under a tiny white hat; a pretty, somewhat contradictory face, the black-lashed grey eyes wide and appealing, the small nose a fraction tip-tilted inquisitive and gay, the curve of the red mouth denoting sweetness and, if Mr Willison were any judge, an impulsive temper. He liked especially her rather high cheekbones and that oddly placed dimple.

She stood without fidgeting, he approved further; she was wearing a little grey suit with white doeskin gloves and carried a large white handbag.

'Her mother over again, but let us hope with more stamina,' he thought, recalling the vivid, fragile American woman who had been Mrs Rendle. A lovely creature—Mary, his wife, had been devoted to her—but no staying power. Passionately in love with her husband, and when Colonel Rendle was struck down by a fatal heart attack she had never rallied from her grief. A few months later she, too, died.

'How friendly of you to come at once and make yourself known to me, Miranda,' Mr Willison continued, gratified that she had done so and amused by her precipitancy. Pushing through the crowd as if she couldn't wait—bless her little heart. 'Are you off to Lisbon to see your brother? Your aunt is with you?'

He knew that since her mother's death four years earlier she had made her home with an uncle and his wife.

'No, I am by myself. Uncle Arthur hasn't been well and he and Aunt Molly have gone for a trip to South Africa. So I wrote to Charles and suggested coming to stay with him and Sybil for a while. I'm crazy to see Portugal.'

'It is worth a visit, certainly. I take it—' Mr Willison's voice was a trifle dubious, 'that you have already met your sister-in-law?'

'Not yet. I was on a motor tour in Ireland when Charles came home on leave and met Sybil. Then, before I got back to England someone went sick and Charles was recalled. Sybil followed and they were married in Lisbon. But you know that, of course.'

Mr Willison did know, and had his own ideas on the subject.

'We must all see to it,' he said, 'that you enjoy your stay. Mary—she didn't come over with me this trip—will be delighted. She was so fond of your mother and Charles is a great favourite of hers.'

'It will be lovely for me, having old friends of Mother and Daddy there. I was so glad when I caught sight of you.' Her voice quickened a little. 'You were talking to someone. Funnily enough, he looked sort of familiar, too, although I only had a glimpse of his back as he went off.'

'That was Freddy Clayton.'

'Oh.' The grey eyes blinked.

'Do you know him?'

'Charles does, and I met him once or twice about two years ago. I haven't seen anything of him since. He is a friend of yours?'

'His father was one of my greatest friends. I saw a good deal of Freddy as a youngster and have always kept in touch. Mary and I generally dine and do a theatre with him when we are in London.'

'I suppose he is on a cruise? This is a sort of cruise ship, isn't it.'

'As a matter of fact, he is also bound for Lisbon. Some trusting editor has commissioned him to do a series of articles on Portugal.'

'Oh,' Miranda said again. For an instant she looked aghast. Her expression escaped Mr Willison who had turned as another passenger, a woman, greeted him.

'So we are to be fellow travellers,' she was saying.

'How are you, Mrs Sangster?' he responded. 'Enjoyed your holiday? Let me introduce Miss Rendle, Charles Rendle's sister who is coming out to visit him.'

'So this is Miranda, is it? Your brother has spoken of you and must bring you to see me. I don't make social calls but I am always at home on Thursday afternoons.'

'Thank you,' Miranda replied, amused by what sounded like a royal command. 'It is very kind of you and I shall certainly ask him to bring me.'

Mrs Sangster was a stout, middle-aged woman wearing a coat and skirt of substantial tweed and conservative cut, the skirt brushing her ankles, the coat more than three-quarter length. Her abundant, greying auburn hair was drawn back into a neat roll under a sensible felt hat and her shoes were uncompromising, heavy soled brogues. She had a brisk and capable air; her prototype could have been found in any English town.

Having exchanged a few commonplaces about the weather and what they might expect in the Bay she bustled on to her cabin.

'Who exactly is she?' Miranda asked.

'One of our institutions. A widow, whose husband was attached in some capacity to one of the Latin Embassies in Spain, a liaison post. When he died, she stayed on and when the civil war broke out she moved into Portugal. Likes the country and the climate and enjoys her position as an old established resident in these parts. A well-to-do woman; she owns a house in Lisbon and occupies herself with good works.'

'She looks it,' Miranda smiled. 'I don't mean that cattily but one can't mistake the type.'

'One cannot, indeed. An admirable type if sometimes a little exhausting. Gets a bee in her bonnet— dear me, these people have cut it very fine—'

Some belated passengers came hurrying in, chattering in some foreign tongue. The gangway, about to be lifted, had been held for them. They were a tall man of forty or so, a slender black-haired woman and a young girl whose blonde hair hung to her shoulders. A striking trio; all good looking and with an unmistakably aristocratic air.

'Hungarians, I fancy,' Mr Willison commented, 'and probably on their way to Portugal. We have numerous exiles there.'

The exiles, if such they were—they seemed very cheerful about it—went volubly past; Miranda took leave of her elderly friend and sought her cabin. She

12

closed the door, sat down on her berth and gazed with unseeing eyes at the opposite wall.

So it *was* Freddy. She hadn't really believed it when she caught that momentary glimpse of the tall figure. Her heart had given a little jump and she told herself not to be absurd; of course it wasn't he. But it had been necessary immediately to make sure; that was why she had approached Mr Willison in the midst of all the crowd and confusion instead of waiting until some more convenient moment.

Not only was it Freddy, sailing in the same ship, but he was coming to Lisbon. Of all wretched coincidences! There could be no avoiding each other; Charles liked him and would naturally want to see something of him, and they would inevitably meet at the Willison's hospitable house. Well, there was no help for it and Miranda could take it, but she had hoped never to set eyes on Freddy Clayton again.

She had first seen him at a fashionable charity ball to which Charles had taken her. It was her nineteenth birthday; she wore a frock of floating white tulle over a crinoline petticoat and had pinned the gardenias her brother had gallantly given her to the waves of her soft dark hair. During an interval in the dancing Sir Frederick Clayton had been standing not far from the sister and brother, inwardly debating as to whether he could unobtrusively slip away. He had come to the ball because a favourite cousin was making her début tonight and now, his duty done, felt he had had enough of the youthful affair. Suddenly, with the sense of compulsion everyone experiences at one time or another, he turned his head and looked straight at Miranda.

'Good lord,' he murmured inaudibly.

Something went *click* within him, as if a voice said

'This is it.' There was no accounting for it; she was by no means the most beautiful girl in the room but to him, in her ethereal frock, with the white flowers in her hair and her grey eyes shining like star sapphires between the wistful black lashes, she was irresistible. He saw that she was with a man he knew, Charles Rendle, and at once approached them, was introduced to Miranda and asked her for a dance.

He no longer contemplated leaving; they danced, and danced again. Miranda, for her part, went home walking on air, bewitched by a pair of laughing dark eyes in a brown, attractive face.

In the period that ensued they saw each other with increasing frequency. They did not meet at any more débutante parties for he moved in an older, more sophisticated set, but Miranda was allowed considerable freedom and Aunt Molly made no objection to Sir Frederick's taking her niece to a theatre, or to dine and dance. Miranda had other escorts, other suitors, but they paled in comparison with Freddy. They were boys, he was a man. A man of twenty-eight. It was not long before she was head over heels in love with him.

As for Sir Frederick, he had never cared very much for what he termed callow young girls nor did he, at that time, intend to involve himself with a girl of any age. He valued his freedom and found life as he lived it entirely satisfactory. But Miranda defeated him and he found himself becoming more and more involved.

Her contradictory face, with its appealing eyes and adorable tip-tilted nose, her gay spirits, tempered by the careful convent manners, the clear young voice with its piquant echo of her American mother's accent, enchanted him. He delighted in the way she moved, so quickly and so lightly in the ballet sandals she loved to wear; there was none of the gauche bearing and loping stride he deplored in his games-mad young cousins and their girl friends. Miranda was unique, a fairy child, a little angel drifted down from heaven. So he saw her, and during this period he found no occasion to modify his conception of her.

On a certain day he drove her into Gloucestershire to see his farm and charming old house. She was entranced with the house, entranced with everything. And Freddy had taken her hands, bending to look into her eyes and asked her if she could be happy here with him. She answered that she could, and he gathered her into his arms, holding her fast, then tipping up her face to meet his kiss.

Presently there had come a summons from the housekeeper; Sir Frederick was wanted on the telephone.

'Damn,' he said. 'How have they run me to earth?' And went in to answer the unwelcome call.

He returned to say that he had hoped to take Miranda to dinner this evening but something had cropped up to prevent it. She was sweetly amenable and he drove her home and left her at the door of her uncle's house.

'See you tomorrow, darling.'

'Tomorrow, Freddy.'

She went indoors in a state of almost unbearable happiness. Freddy loved her—he had asked her to marry him. She would say nothing about it, tonight, it was too precious a thing to be spoken of as yet.

Next morning—the very next morning at breakfast —her uncle had looked up from his newspapers and said:

'Frederick Clayton. Isn't he one of your young men, Miranda?'

'Yes, Uncle Arthur.'

'Well, you'd better drop him. There's too much of this sort of thing; decent people should take a stand and show these young blackguards what they think of them. Absolute menace; he'll be lucky if he isn't up on a charge of manslaughter.'

'What has he done?' Miranda's voice quivered with apprehension and indignation. An accident, of course, but anyone could have an accident—Uncle Arthur had no right to speak like that.

They were alone in the dining-room; Charles had gone back to his job with the engineering firm in Portugal and Aunt Molly was spending a few days with friends in the country.

Uncle Arthur, who had finished his meal, rose and handed his niece the paper.

'Read it for yourself,' he said and tramped out of the room.

Miranda looked at the folded sheet and a headline sprang out at her.

Wealthy playboy involved in crash after party at night club. Sir Frederick Clayton, well-known—

Miranda's heart plunged, stopped, beat again with heavy hammer strokes. Party—Freddy—*last night—*

At length she read the account, which was reported with considerable relish. An unsavoury affair; Sir Frederick Clayton, accompanied by an Oxford undergraduate and two girls, dancers at one of the more risqué revues, had with criminal recklessness caused an oncoming car to crash into a lamp standard and overturn. Three people had been badly hurt. The report did not state it in words, but the implication was clear

16

—that Sir Frederick and his companions had all been more or less under the influence of alcohol.

For a space Miranda sat frozen; then anger, like red-hot lava boiled within her. She possessed, as Mr Willison had deduced, an impulsive temper, a flame that rose and swiftly subsided and which, to do her justice, she seldom showed. But never before had she felt anything like this.

It wasn't the reckless driving, or the implied cause for it—that, she could have forgiven. It was the girls. The important thing that had cropped up, preventing his taking Miranda to dinner, had been a party with these two girls.

So this was Freddy, the real Freddy. He had done this; gone straight from her, from holding her in his arms and kissing her, telling her he loved her, to pick up his Oxford friend and the two 'lovelies'.

'How could he? How could he? But he did. Freddy did that.'

She was suffering from severe shock and, although she did not realize it, from acute jealousy. She would have scorned to admit jealousy but the scarifying emotion was there, and a passionate sense of insult.

While she still sat at the table, seething, tormented, the telephone bell rang. Automatically she ran to answer it and heard Freddy's voice.

'Miranda? I suppose you have seen the papers?'

'Yes, I have seen them.'

'I'm frightfully sorry—it isn't as bad as it reads—may I come round now and explain?'

'There's no explanation so far as I am concerned and I don't want to see you, ever again.'

'Miranda! Darling. I know you're upset but don't be ridiculous.'

'I am not being ridiculous. I mean it, Freddy. I have finished with you.'

'The devil you have. Look, angel. I'm coming. I'll be there in fifteen minutes.'

'You can save yourself the trouble. I won't see you.'

'You refuse to give me a hearing?'

'I do. I have told you. I'm finished with you.'

At the other end of the line, Sir Frederick's face went pale; he had a temper of his own. His voice, hitherto affectionate and a little rallying, crisped.

'Are you serious, Miranda?'

'I couldn't be more so.'

'I thought you—cared for me.'

'I thought I did, but I didn't know you then. Now I know what you really are.'

'And what am I?'

'A man who asks a girl to marry him and the very same night goes off on a party with—with—'

'That is just what I want to explain to you.'

'You can't explain. You did it.'

'All right.' Freddy's patience snapped. She was hopelessly unreasonable and if she thought she could dictate his behaviour—

'All right,' he repeated. 'I did it. Now listen, Miranda. Once more, and for the last time, may I come? I won't ask you again, believe me. Will you see me?'

'No.'

'You mean—this is the end?'

'I mean it. And I am only thankful I found out, in time, before I—I—'

'Very well,' he interposed. 'I, too, am glad to have found out, in time, that the girl I hoped to marry is such a stupid little termagant. Goodbye, Miranda. We'll call it a day.'

He made no further *démarche* in her direction. If she had been shocked, so was he, and wholly disillusioned. His fairy child, revealed as a stupid, vindictive little shrew. It took a bit of getting over for he had been very much in love with Miranda, but the affair, after all, had been of the briefest, a sweet and foolish interlude, an aberration on his part. She had proved, in the end, a mere figment of his imagination and he was well rid of her. If she were like this now, what would she be in ten, in twenty years' time?

He revived from his disappointment, put her out of his mind and went his usual way. Their paths in London never crossed and he saw no more of her.

As for Miranda, when the first stunning effects of her hurt and rage had worn off she began to regret her hasty action. She was still outraged by what he had done but she found herself watching for some letter from him, listening for his ring on the telephone. As day followed day and he neither wrote nor telephoned, she was forced to acknowledge the fact that Freddy had accepted dismissal and bowed himself out.

Pride came to the rescue then. She would make no move on her own part. He had been the one in fault and her anger fully justified. She would cease to think of him, she would forget that such a person as Freddy ever existed.

She didn't quite forget but time worked its normal cure. Since she never saw him and he had not been a member of her particular set there was little to remind her of him. Charles, who knew him only slightly, on one of his Christmas leaves mentioned having fallen in with Freddy and their lunching together, and the name of Sir Frederick Clayton appeared now and then in the society gossip columns. He had been seen here or there, escorting this or that fair lady—Miranda read the silly items with scornful eyes. Playboy was the word. By the time six months or so had passed she had, or would have sworn she had, completely recovered from what she now called a childish infatuation. But the episode had left its mark upon her; she did not fall in love with anyone else.

CHAPTER TWO

THE SHIP stirred, a barely perceptible movement, and the walls of the cabin creaked faintly in response. Miranda sprang up from her berth; they were off, moving downstream, and the first stop would be Portugal, the country she was 'crazy to see'. If only—but she wasn't going to let this maddening coincidence of Freddy Clayton spoil things. With a little grimace she said to herself: 'It's as maddening for him as it is for me and there's a funny side to it.'

When she went in to dinner she found herself placed at the First Officer's table where Mr Willison and Mrs Sangster were also seated. She cast a quick glance about the saloon and saw, some distance away, a pair of shoulders and a russet-brown head that she had recognized. He sat with his back towards her and his companions were the interesting-looking people who had hurried aboard at the last moment. Later, in the big lounge where she was drinking coffee with Mr Willison and the English lady she saw him come in with the exotic group. They sat down in an opposite corner; Freddy signalled a steward.

'It hasn't taken him long,' Mr Willison chuckled. 'Trust Freddy.'

The young man looked idly in their direction, nodded smilingly to his old friend, then his face changed. He stared with an expression of rueful astonishment. A moment later, with a word of excuse to his companions he rose and crossed the room.

'Well, Miranda,' he said, 'it is Miranda, isn't it? You girls grow up so suddenly without fair warning—'

'Hallo, Freddy. Yes, it is me. You know Mr Willison? Mrs Sangster, this is Sir Frederick Clayton.'

He bowed to the elder lady.

'Are you on a visit to your brother?' he continued. 'I am also on my way to Lisbon.'

'Yes, I am going to stay with Charles and his wife.'

'Married, is he? I hadn't heard—'

'He got married last year.'

'Good show.'

'Who are your new friends, Freddy?' Mr Willison inquired. 'They look remarkably like Hungarian emigrés to me.'

'They are. A Count Radizlo and his wife. The fair-haired one is Princess Tamara something-or-other; all her people killed, apparently, and the Radizlos are bringing her out with them. Picked her up somewhere en route. They had thought of settling in England but it didn't work, so now they are joining a colony of compatriots in Portugal.'

'Travelling first class,' Mrs Sangster said, shaking her head. 'Typical. Sold a few more jewels, no doubt, and squandering the money this way.'

'As to that,' Freddy rejoined, 'I wouldn't know.

They may have money invested abroad. They don't strike one as worried about it.'

'They never do worry, that class. Utterly irresponsible, living for the day—'

'Mrs Sangster takes a great interest in all refugees,' Mr Willison said. 'Helps them in no end of ways—badgers—' he twinkled at her—'badgers the consular authorities about granting them visas for the Americas, always their ultimate goal, their Shangri-La—'

'How good of Mrs Sangster.' Sir Frederick's eyes rested for a moment on the English lady's face with its freckled skin, prominent blue eyes and large, flexible, pale-lipped mouth. 'Well, I must get back. Nice to see you again, Miranda.'

She smiled, with a flicker of her black lashes.

'So nice to see you, Freddy, after all this time.'

Each meant exactly the reverse as their glances, crossing for an instant, informed one another. But they had preserved appearances and carried off the unfortunate situation with mutual aplomb.

As he returned to his table Sir Frederick reflected that Miranda had, in truth, grown up during the last two years. The dewy freshness and starry-eyed quality were gone, nor was she any the worse for that. Her pretty face had taken on a more definite outline, the convent manners which had aroused in him a tender amusement were crystallized into a natural poise. She even showed signs of having developed a sense of humour; she had possessed none at the age of nineteen. Grimly, he wondered whether her temper were now under better control; for the sake of Charles and his wife it was devoutly to be hoped so.

As Sir Frederick departed, Miranda drew a breath of relief. She had been nervously dreading their first encounter but it had taken place with far less discomfort than she feared. He had done the correct thing—she had to grant him that—making it very easy for her and setting the casual note of their future meetings. She might have spared herself the worry; Freddy had always known what to do.

'He hasn't changed,' she thought with an involuntary little pang, not for Freddy but for the memory of a lost first-love, for something she had innocently and ardently believed in and found to be dust and ashes.

She went early to her cabin, sleepy from the effects of the sea air. Snuggled into her berth, she listened drowsily to the familiar—but all new to her—sounds of a passenger ship; people walking along the corridor, exchanging goodnights; bells ringing for stewards and stewardesses, the clink of curtain rings, baggage being opened or snapped shut; the rhythmic faint creak of woodwork and the throb of engines like a rumbling bass.

'I adore it,' she thought. 'I'm so glad I came by sea.'

Child of an air-minded age, although she had been several times to France, and to Ireland, this was the first time in her life that Miranda had been on a ship. She became conscious of more movement; the berth was rising and falling, she was being rocked, and was presently rocked to sleep.

She was being more than rocked when she opened her eyes next morning. The ship was not only going up and down, it writhed from side to side in a most disconcerting fashion. To her intense chagrin, Miranda found that getting out of her berth was not to be thought of; she was proving, what she had never expected to be, a very poor sailor.

She did not appear again until the evening before they were to make Lisbon; the storm had blown itself out and they were in comparatively calm waters. She came in to dinner pale and shadowy-eyed but otherwise restored. Her two elderly friends welcomed her with kindly concern; they had coffee together in the lounge, then Mr Willison repaired to the smoke room, Mrs Sangster retired to her cabin and Miranda, drawn by the strains of music, made her way to the ship's ballroom.

There were a number of young holidaymakers on board, including a sprinkling of American servicemen; better sailors than the unfortunate Miranda they had forgathered while she lay stricken and were now indulging in a gala eve-of-landing party. Rather forlornly, knowing none of them, Miranda sat down to watch; if only she hadn't been so absurd as to get seasick, she could have made friends, too. She loved to dance, the band was an excellent one, her feet in their little ballet sandals were restless. She saw the blonde Hungarian child dancing with various lithe young partners who executed all manner of intricate steps which she followed joyously, her face rose-flushed, her curtain of golden hair swinging at every step. Her two compatriots were not in evidence, nor was Sir Frederick Clayton.

They would doubtless presently appear; Miranda wondered whether Freddy would introduce the Radizlos to her and, himself, ask her to dance. He could hardly help doing so, seeing her all alone. She had no desire to dance with Freddy but she did, very much, want to dance with someone. The music was so beguiling—she had been lying still for two long days. The count, if introduced, would probably ask her to dance and he was certain to be a skilled performer. . . .

Then she shook her head. It wouldn't do. She couldn't be discovered here, by Freddy Clayton, as if she were waiting . . .

She decided to return to her cabin, finish her packing and go to bed. They were docking next morning and she wanted to be up early in order not to miss the approaches to the unknown coast.

She was roused more than once during the night by shouts of laughter and noisy chatter; the young people seemed to be keeping it up until the small hours. But she wakened early, as she had intended, and hurried out on deck. To her disappointment the ship was shrouded in a light mist; there was nothing to be seen as yet but the sun promised to break through and she sat down to await it.

The deck was empty save for herself but she had been there only a few minutes when someone came with rushing, stumbling steps and flopped in to the chair beside her. It was the Hungarian girl. She looked at Miranda, breathing heavily, and smiled, a radiant smile disclosing small milk-white teeth.

'Oh—my,' she gasped, in a tone of weak hilarity.

'You are Princess Tamara, aren't you?' Miranda said. 'Is anything wrong? Can I help you?'

The girl drew a succession of shallow, labouring breaths.

'You've had too much to drink,'-Miranda deduced.

'Yes, I think so,' the other assented.

'It's rather early to begin, eight o'clock in the morning.'

'Yes, I think so,' the princess agreed again, sweetly. She got unsteadily out of her chair, 'Oh—my—'

Miranda was just about to spring up and do something about this when Sir Frederick Clayton appeared.

'Is Freddee,' Tamara announced, and took a swaying step towards him. He caught the two little outstretched hands, steadying her.

'What's the matter, Mara? Got a hangover?'

'Yes, I think is hangover. I feel not well this morning and I meet Johnnee and he say I must have *hairadog*. So he give me hairadog—I feel lovelee—but I think I come out in the air—'

'I see. The fresh air knocked you. I'd better—oh, good—'

A stewardess, carrying a tray that held someone's early tea came along the deck. Freddy beckoned her.

'Will you take this young lady to her cabin and—'

'See to her? Certainly, sir.' The experienced woman had grasped the situation at a glance. She set the tray down and took the girl gently by the arm.

'Can you—fix her up?' Freddy asked. 'She's getting off at Lisbon.'

'I've fixed up a considerable number in my time,' the stewardess returned with asperity. 'Some strong black coffee with a tablespoon of lemon juice to start with—I'll have her right as rain by the time we dock, though probably feeling sorry for herself. I must say, it seems a pity, a girl of her age who's very likely never tasted spirits before. There's nothing clever in making a young person tight.' With which parting shot and a severe look at Sir Frederick she led the princess away.

'That was a nasty crack,' Freddy said with a grin. 'The good lady appears to hold me responsible.'

'Aren't you?'

'I?' He stared down at the slender figure in the long

26

chair. 'Are you actually suggesting that it was I who made the young person tight?'

'I am only suggesting,' Miranda replied in her clear, unhurried tones, 'that as you and she are evidently on intimate terms, you might have taken better care of her last evening.'

'I had nothing to do with it. I was playing bridge all evening and did not see her at all. She must have got in with the American lot—they were hitting it up—'

'Why didn't the others, the count and his wife, look after her?'

'I don't suppose it occurred to them. They were playing bridge, too, and she was dancing. They could hardly foresee—and in any case there's no great harm done. Mara had a little too much to drink last night and some misguided young fool gave her a whisky or a brandy first thing this morning. She'll get over it.' He shrugged, dismissing the subject. 'I understand,' he continued civilly, 'that you have had a rough passage. Bad luck. Are you breakfasting on deck? Shall I find a steward for you?'

'No, thanks. I am quite recovered now. I just want to wait here until the sun breaks through.'

'Right.'

He gave her a little nod, indifferent rather than unfriendly, and walked away.

CHAPTER THREE

THE SUN was taking its time, the ship nosing steadily through the thin veil of mist. Miranda reluctantly left the deck and went below.

'I can't wait for ever, I must finish everything in the cabin, and get some breakfast—'

When she presently came back again she was dressed for going ashore in her trim little suit and white hat and small white shoes with the flat heels to which she was addicted. The fog had cleared at last and she made her way forward to where a number of people were looking out over the ship's bows.

Frederick Clayton, standing in a group among whom were Mr Willison and the Hungarian trio, saw her coming, walking with that peculiar lightness which once had enchanted him. Fairylike, elusive, he had called it. She still retained an elusive quality; Freddy wasn't given to flights of fancy but he had a momentary vision of dark-haired Miranda moving silently through dim, deserted rooms, her face intent, her grey eyes glimmering palely—he gave his shoulders a quick shake. What on earth had conjured up so improbable and spectral an apparition?

'Gaga,' he told himself.

There was nothing spectral in Miranda's eager figure, pressing against the rail as the others made room for her, not in her enraptured face as she gazed at the city across the wide bay. A city rising placidly from the green-brown river that swept in a great arm to the right.

'That's the famous Tagus,' someone said instructively.

Miranda had no eyes for the Tagus, or the busy little ferry plying from a distant wooded shore and the various shipping in the harbour. She saw only Lisbon, very still, clear cut in the sunshine under a sky whose luminous blue was like no sky she had ever before seen.

'Love at first sight, Miranda?' Mr Willison asked, amusedly.

She turned to him, nodding assent.

'Is it as lovely as it seems?'

'More so. You can't see the colour from here. You are lucky today in your first impression; the fog has its uses. One is generally blown off one's feet crossing this harbour.'

'But that would be too much,' the Countess Radizlo cried with animation. 'To arrive in a gale of wind, after leaving that so cold and stormy England. *Brrrr*—not once was I warm—a terrible country. But I should perhaps not say so—' she sent Miranda a laughing, apologetic glance.

'Miss Rendle will agree that England has had an unusually drastic spring,' Mr Willison said. 'By the way —I don't think you have met—' he introduced them. 'And this is the Princess Tamara.'

'Already we have met,' Tamara said, coming to stand beside the elder girl. 'Such a foolishness, I do not know what you think of me.'

'Nothing very bad,' Miranda replied, smiling down into the eyes that were raised to hers. Eyes like brown pansies, and in charming contrast with the bright golden hair. 'Are you feeling all right now?'

'Yes, thank you. The stewardess—oh my, what she make me do—I think I will not again have hangover.' She made a mischievous little grimace, and continued, 'Do you leave the ship at Lisbon, Mees Rendle?'

'Yes. You, also, I understand.'

'It is so. Bela and Olga have friends, who meet us and take us where they live. Again some new place, and this time where is warm and sunnee. Do you come as *touriste*, for holiday?'

'I have a brother here and am staying with him.'

'Is good to have a brother and to arrive at a home,' the princess said cordially. She spoke in the polite, impersonal fashion of one making conversation with a casual acquaintance; there was no hint of self pity in her voice. But the words went to Miranda's heart; poor little homeless waif. And not less in need of compassion because she herself bore out the truth of Mrs Sangster's pronouncement; utterly irresponsible, living for the day. Tamara dancing so joyously last evening, gaily amused at her predicament this morning, going to 'some new place' and happy because it was a warm and sunny one, giving no thought as to what might happen next. Insensitive, Miranda concluded and, all things considered, perhaps fortunately so.

There was a stir along the deck, the ship was drawing in. Countess Radizlo called:

'Come, Mara, it is time—'

'I come, Olga. Goodbye, Mees Rendle, or au revoir. Maybee I have pleasure some time to see you again.'

The bustle of disembarking was over, the customs cleared; Miranda's excited eyes searched the shifting crowd. Where—where—

Two hands grasped her shoulders, she was swung lightly round.

'Oh, Charles—*darling*—'

'Well, poppet,' her brother kissed her warmly. 'Had a good trip?'

'Dreadful. I was sick for two solid days. Not that it matters; I'm so thrilled to be here and to see you. It's been such ages, and as you said you wouldn't be coming home this year I couldn't resist the chance. You *didn't* mind my inviting myself, did you?'

'What do you think?' He looked affectionately at the young sister who had always been his special pet. She laughed.

'I wasn't really worrying about it.'

Charles Rendle, a young man over six feet in height was dark-haired and grey-eyed like Miranda. Broad-shouldered and thickset, he had none of the debonair charm that marked Sir Frederick Clayton but there was something very pleasing in his appearance, something disciplined and dependable. Miranda, who had adored him from babyhood, always thought of Charles as gentle and strong; she could still remember the happy security, after some childish fright or tantrum, of being held and comforted in those strong and gentle arms.

One of those arms was encircling her now; she snuggled her head against his shoulder. As she did so, she felt him stiffen as if something had startled him.

'Who is that?' he said abruptly.

Miranda followed his gaze and saw the Princess Tamara, standing apart from the chattering, gesticulating group of her compatriots. She was only a few yards away from the brother and sister and was watching them absorbedly. She smiled as she caught Miranda's glance, and kept on smiling, but the pansy-brown eyes widened and brightened and two big tears welled up and ran down the princess's cheeks. Instantly, with a quick and careless gesture that defied anyone to believe they really were tears, she brushed them away.

'Oh—the poor little soul.' Miranda swiftly disengaged herself. 'She's a refugee—I'll tell you later—I'll bring her over—' She went across to the girl. 'Will you come and meet my brother, Princess? And we can give each other our addresses, I would like so much to see something more of you.'

'Thank you, I shall be glad—'

Charles came forward and his sister presented him. He took the small extended hand in his big warm one and smiled down at the heart-shaped face with its velvety eyes whose lashes were still wet. Bravely, for she was obviously in the clutch of some strong emotion. Tamara smiled back, the red lips parting over the little milk-white teeth.

'Is pleasure to meet the brother of Mees Rendle,' she said. 'And your sister has been so kind as to say we shall give each other our address—'

'Yes, will you write it down for her, Charles, and the telephone number?'

'I will.' He released the hand he had been holding in his reassuring clasp and took a notebook and pencil from a pocket. The addresses were exchanged; once again the countess called to her young companion.

'I must go,' Tamara said. 'But you will not forget, we shall meet again, Mees Rendle?' She spoke to Miranda, but it was at Charles she looked and it was he who answered.

'We shall certainly not forget.'

'So. Is good.' She flitted away.

'Now, poppet, we'll get along.' Charles signalled the porter who was patiently waiting with Miranda's luggage. As they followed him, they were intercepted.

'How are you, Rendle?'

'Hallo! You, Clayton?'

The two men shook hands.

'Miranda tell you we were shipmates?'

'I haven't had time yet, Freddy.'

'Good chap, Clayton,' Charles commented after Freddy had left them. 'I'd like to show him around a bit if it's his first visit but I suppose his stay will be short. The allowance doesn't extend far and no doubt he has made his own plans.'

'He's on a job,' Miranda replied, and explained the nature of it.

'What an extraordinary thing to do. I thought he was farming. Well, all to the good. Here we are—' They had reached the parked car; Miranda's bags were stowed away and they set off.

'Tell me,' Charles continued, 'who is the young princess?'

She told him the little she had learned.

'I have no idea as to whether she has any money, or what she expects to do—or has been doing. Freddy Clayton may know, he made friends with them at once. So did Mr Willison; he was on board, too. But I was *hors de combat* until last night.'

'Poor child.'

Charles concentrated on his driving and Miranda gazed eagerly out of the window.

She could take in very little during this first drive but she saw the colour; façades painted in pastel shades or covered with small tiles glinting blue and green and pink, grilled iron balconies, their shadows etched behind them, a glimpse of mellow ochre walls and beautiful old roofs. Then they traversed a succession of side streets, in the last of which they stopped before a large, rather shabby but fine old building which looked as if it might once have been the mansion of some highly prosperous merchant. The roadway ascended steeply and the house stood at the crest of the rise, its top storey well above the modest roofs on the opposite side of the street.

'Not a very grand locality,' Charles said as he opened the door of his car for his sister, 'but that's one thing that couldn't matter less, in Lisbon. I was lucky to get a flat here; big rooms, good view and we have the whole top floor. Sybil doesn't altogether like it—' he broke off to direct the Portuguese caretaker who had come out to collect the luggage.

Miranda experienced a slight shock. It had been a full morning, incident following upon incident, and what with one thing and another—Tamara, Freddy, the joy of seeing her brother again and the thrill of her first glimpses of the fascinating city—she had, as near as made no matter, forgotten Sybil. She was conscious of a guilty wish that Charles were not married and she herself arriving to keep house for him, but she hastily disowned so selfish a thought. Darling Charles, as if he didn't deserve a wife, and the best one in the world.

He had done so well and worked so hard, continuing his studies and receiving his degree after the war, and then obtaining this job with the engineering firm in Lisbon where machine parts of all description were assembled after being manufactured and shipped out from England. Already he had risen to a responsible position. There had been scant leisure for girl friends during all these years and his sudden marriage had astonished but, on the whole, pleased his relatives. It was time he had a wife and a real home.

They entered the house and Charles conducted Miranda into an automatic lift that slowly and asthmatically ascended. When it stopped with a grunt they crossed the landing to a door that opened upon a long passage, from the other end of which poured a flood of light.

'Sybil,' Charles called.

'In the lounge,' a voice responded. 'What a time you have been.'

'The ship was delayed by fog. But here is Miranda, safe and sound.'

For a moment, coming into the sun-flooded room Miranda was dazzled and could distinguish nothing clearly; she went swiftly forward, took Sybil's hand and bent to kiss her.

'I am so glad to meet my new sister at last,' she said. 'And it is so good of you to have let me come.'

'That's quite all right,' the other answered, a choice of phrase which surprised Miranda. 'Come and sit down. I have coffee ready. Unless you would prefer to see your room first.'

'No, I'd love a cup of coffee right now.'

'You've got an American accent,' Sybil observed, seating herself at a gate-leg table. 'But of course your mother was an American, wasn't she?'

'Yes.'

Miranda's vision had cleared; she sat down, unbuttoned her jacket and took stock of her sister-in-law.

Sybil was a small woman, not exactly dumpy but showing a tendency in that direction. She had a round head with brownish hair worn in a tight poodle cut. She was short-necked, and her ultra-fashionable high-collared jersey gave her a somewhat froglike appearance. But her face was very pretty, the dark blue eyes especially so, fringed with very thick curling lashes. She had a thin nose, a tiny mouth and rather thrusting little chin.

Her hands were ugly, stubby-fingered with incredibly long, pointed, crimson-painted nails; when she turned a hand palm upward they curved in and looked like parrot's claws. They made Miranda feel a trifle sick, but she hastily reminded herself that Sybil was only following a regrettable fashion.

Sybil, meanwhile, as she poured the coffee was taking stock of Miranda. She had not been prepared for anyone like this. Charles, with brotherly under-statement, had said that Miranda was a good kid, easy to get on with; nice-looking, yes, and left it at that. His wife had drawn her own conclusions. The girl could hardly be attractive; she must have made her début at eighteen if not younger, she belonged to a well-known, old established family and had money in her own right, inherited from the American mother. Yet she was neither married nor even engaged.

When Miranda's letter arrived proposing herself for a visit, Sybil had offered no objection. She rather liked the idea of chaperoning and patronizing Charles's sister; it would cement her own position in her husband's family and add to her social value. Now, however, she found herself confronted with someone very attractive indeed, someone who did not look as if she would be easy to patronize, and Sybil's expression became a trifle aggressive.

The coffee was excellent, and there were meringues filled with thick cream.

'A speciality of the cook,' Charles said.

Miranda expressed her appreciation and then, looking about her:

'What a lovely room this is.'

'You like it?' her brother smiled.

'Adore it. So different from anything at home—'

The room was long and fairly wide; this had been the attic storey and the low, but not too low ceiling preserved its attic shape. There were deep casement windows and a pair of French doors giving upon a balcony. In the centre of the inner, cream-washed wall was a fireplace, with bookshelves extending the entire length of the wall on either side. Pewter plates and bits of bright pottery stood on the topmost shelves. The floor was covered with fine, corn-coloured matting upon which were strewn a few small rugs. The furniture was sparse; two large, highly-polished old oaken chests, some straight-backed oak chairs with straw seats, a table or two of the same dark, polished wood and three or four more comfortable chairs with flowered cotton loose covers, matching the curtains at the windows. The effect was one of simplicity, freshness and dignity. Miranda's opinion of her sister-in-law, as yet less high than she could have wished, began to rise. If this were Sybil's taste—

Sybil at once disabused her.

'It's the Portuguese idea,' she said bitterly. 'Charles bought the furniture and fittings, just as they stood, from the last tenants.'

'They do suit the room,' Miranda ventured. 'It is such a quaint, atticky room—'

'You're telling me. There's no disguising it. Sloping ceiling and plastered walls and matting on the floor— I ask you. *Matting.*'

'It is very beautiful matting. I have never seen any in the least like it.'

'Oh, it's good quality enough. But I like a fitted carpet, and wallpaper, and proper three-piece suites, not a lot of wooden chairs with straw cushions. The sort of thing you'd see in a farmhouse kitchen. If only I had been consulted, but Charles took the wretched place on his own before I got here.'

'Flats aren't easily come by,' Charles said mildly. 'If I hadn't snapped this up—'

'You should have got one of the modern ones near the Avenida da Liberdade. It isn't as if we couldn't afford it—'

'We've been into all this, Sybil. Don't let us discuss it now.' Charles stood up. 'I must get along to the office. If you want to take Miranda out this afternoon, call the hire-car people. I expect she'd like to do some sightseeing at once.' He patted his sister's shoulder, smiled pleasantly at his wife and departed.

'Will you have some more coffee, Miranda?' Sybil asked.

'No more, thank you.'

'Then I'll show you your room and the rest of the place, such as it is.'

The other room had the same delightful ceilings and were furnished with the same simplicity as the drawing-room. In the kitchen two Portuguese maids beamed at the visitor. When the tour of inspection was over the sister-in-law adjourned to Miranda's bedroom.

'Where I blame Charles,' Sybil said, seating herself by the window while Miranda attacked her luggage, 'is that he simply hasn't any ambition. Socially, I mean. Living in this quarter when he could have a flat, or even a house, in the Liberdade or Park Section. The way we live, nobody would guess that Charles has private means, and plenty of them.'

'You can always tell people that he has,' Miranda suggested in a gentle, guileless tone.

'Well, of course, but why not *show* it. Charles has such idiotic ideas—'

'Such as—?' Miranda pulled a dressing-gown from one of her bags and took out her toilet articles.

'He insists that for a junior in the firm to make a splash, live in the same style as, say, the tiptop director, wouldn't do. Bad taste or something.'

'How like Charles. He *would* feel that way.'

'He does feel that way. And it makes me so wild—'

'Well,' Miranda spoke carefully now. She did not want to begin her visit by antagonizing her sister-in-law, far less to appear as siding with Charles against his wife. 'I can see how annoying it must be for you, but that's Charles. He has certain fixed standards and nothing can budge him. I haven't been his sister for almost twenty-one years without learning that,' she finished gaily.

'Stubborn as a mule,' Sybil agreed.

Miranda had taken off her hat and suit and donned the dressing-gown. She lifted the net from her head, drew out a few pins and the hair fell in a smooth coil about her neck.

'You still wear it long,' Sybil exclaimed. 'I hadn't realized—with your hat on—'

'I don't like it hanging over the collar of a coat so I pin it up when I'm wearing a suit.'

39

'You ought to cut it. Like mine. It's ever so much smarter, you know.'

'I know it is but it would be all wrong for me. Can you imagine a girl called Miranda wearing a poodle cut?'

'I don't see what names have to do with it. You might be a Portuguese or Spanish girl with that old-fashioned do.'

'Well, I have a Spanish name.'

'So you want to look like a foreigner—'

Miranda cast a glance at her reflection in the mirror. Anything less like what Sybil deemed a foreigner would be hard to find. She smiled, her single dimple flickering in her cheek.

'I want to look like—Miranda.'

Conceited little madame, Sybil thought. So pleased with herself.

'Is that a scar?' she asked of the dimple. 'What a pity.'

'This? No. I was born with it. I don't know why there is only one.'

'Funny,' Sybil rejoined. 'Makes you look a bit lop-sided.'

'And that,' Miranda said to herself, 'ought to hold you, my dear.' She was amused by the other's thrusts, but less amused by Sybil's revelation of herself. Why, why, why had Charles married this woman? What madness had possessed him?

'I'll leave you to finish your unpacking,' Sybil said. 'I want to speak about lunch; you have to stand over these Portuguese maids.'

As she left the room, Miranda's eyes followed her with a look of distress and perplexity. A second-rate, bumptious woman; a nagger, if ever Miranda had seen one; older than Charles, too.

'I've never been so shocked in all my life,' she said to herself.

She did not, however, regret having come; not even Sybil could spoil the joy of being with Charles, of the delightful adventure of visiting a country hitherto unknown to her.

'I'll manage, I'll keep the peace with her, and there'll be plenty of other people; the Willisons and all their friends—Sybil doesn't really matter.'

But suddenly she blushed, as she recalled that one among those other people would, inevitably, be Freddy Clayton. Not that he mattered, either, but she shrank in spite of herself at the thought of Freddy being presented to her sister-in-law. He would be all that was correct, of course, but what would he think? Think of Charles?

'Oh Charles, darling, *why* did you do it?'

Oddly enough, it was Freddy himself who, on the evening of this same day, was supplied with a clue to Charles's inexplicable behaviour.

He had dined with the Willisons; shortly after dinner a confrère of his host had appeared and the two elder men had presently excused themselves and retired to the study to discuss some business matter. Freddy was left with his hostess, to their mutual satisfaction. They were great friends, despite the difference in their ages.

Mary Willison was a tall, slender woman with black hair becomingly streaked with silver, and mischievous hazel eyes. Her husband's junior by a number of years, she was intelligent, lively, at times indiscreet and no sufferer of fools, but she was also generous and warm-hearted. Childless herself, she was very fond of young people and invariably kind to them.

They discussed Freddy's venture which Mary, unlike her husband, thoroughly approved, declaring that there was plenty of time later on to stagnate on a farm in that awful English climate and Freddy was perfectly right to seize this chance of coming to a warm, sunny country and enjoying himself. As for the articles, of course he woud make a success of them; Portugal simply clamoured to be written about with all its local colour and the international exiles and so on. This led naturally to his telling her about his Hungarian acquaintances; he mentioned also Mrs Sangster, saying that he understood she was active in welfare work among the refugees.

Mary laughed.

'Active is putting it mildly. She wears us all out—but she does do good work that no one else would bother about. She enjoys it, of course, loves being the *dea ex machina.* Did she inform you that she is at home on Thursday afternoons?'

'As a matter of fact, she did. Must one go?'

'Everyone goes, at one time or another. I'll take you, you'll meet all sorts of people, not only British. And her house is worth seeing. By the way—' Mary dismissed Mrs Sangster. 'John tells me that Charles Rendle's sister has come out to stay with him. You met her, of course, on board?'

'I had met her before, about two years ago. Haven't seen anything of her since. And on board she was confined to her cabin after the first night.'

'I knew her mother well in the old days,' Mary said.

'I haven't seen the girl since she was a child but we see a lot of Charles. You know him, too?'

'Yes, slightly. Good type, I've always thought. I was surprised to hear he had married; last summer, wasn't it?'

'Last July.'

'I met him, in July,' Freddy said, 'at the airport. He was rushing back to Lisbon. He had a drink and a chat —he never gave me a hint that he was married, or on the eve of being so.'

'I don't suppose he did,' Mary returned. Freddy cocked an eyebrow.

'Why not? Something fishy about it?'

'No, I just meant—' Mary paused.

'Come on,' he urged, 'tell me. What is the wife like?'

'She—I'll leave you to judge for yourself.'

'I gather you don't care for the lady. Anything in her favour? Has she got looks?'

'Most people would call her pretty. Her eyes are lovely, with enormous curly lashes. A very small woman—she's put on a lot of flesh lately but she was a tiny creature a year ago, which probably appeals to big men like Charles.'

'Who was she? Where did he meet her?'

'She was on the ship when he and John went home together last year; Charles on leave and John going over to settle up an estate. John had to go first on business to Barcelona, and because he was a bit fagged and wanted a sea trip, he was sailing from there. Charles likes the sea, too, and had never been into Spain, or seen Gibraltar, so he decided to go with him. They took one of those cargo boats that don't hurry and carry only a few passengers: it was a Spanish line and they and Sybil—her name is Sybil—were the only British people on board.'

'What was she doing on a Spanish cargo boat?'

'She had been with some English people in Barcelona as secretary or some such job. Apparently they had treated her very badly and she had left them and, having very little money, was coming home by the cheapest route. She was overjoyed to find two Englishmen aboard and attached herself to them like a frightened kitten and poured out a long tale of slights and insults. John wasn't in the least impressed but Charles took it all as said and was highly indignant and sympathetic. He's an extraordinarily kind person, as big men so often are, and anything small and hurt rouses him at once.'

Anything small and hurt, thought Freddy, recalling a scene he had witnessed on the dock this morning. Tamara standing wide-eyed and forlorn, Charles's concerned face as he caught sight of her, the subsequent introduction. Freddy had not missed the kindly, reassuring smile and compassionate gaze as Charles looked down into the tear-wet eyes, and the gradual relaxing of the young girl's tense figure as if she drew strength and comfort from the clasp of his firm hand. A thought, half formed, had crossed Sir Frederick's mind: 'There is a man who could be a good friend for Mara.'

Now, he said:

'Yes, Rendle is like that. And the Sybil person being small and—according to her own story—hurt—'

Mary nodded.

'She played upon his sympathies, of course, and—well—you know how it is. Summer, a calm sea, moonlight—'

Freddy grinned.

'I know. I've been there myself.'

'So have I, in my time. And then goodbye and no harm done and no hard feelings. I am perfectly certain there was no more to it than this on Charles's side and that he gave her no earthly reason to believe him serious. I know him too well. And when they reached England he went straight on to pay a duty visit to relatives in Scotland; he said to John that as his sister and uncle and aunt were in Ireland at the moment he'd save London until they returned. Ten days later his immediate chief and another member of the firm were injured in a car accident and Charles was recalled; you met him, rushing back. I saw him a day or so after he arrived and nothing was said of any engagement; Sybil's name wasn't so much as mentioned. Yet the next thing we heard was that she was coming out to marry him. And out she came.'

'Good lord,' said Freddy. 'You mean—uninvited?'

'I am only telling you what happened. One couldn't, naturally, ask Charles.'

'It's pretty obvious, isn't it? A try-on—but why was he such an idiot as to let her get away with it?'

Mary shrugged, spreading out her fine white hands.

'Why, indeed. I could take him by the scruff of the neck and shake him. But that's the way Charles is made. If she gave him to understand that she believed him serious and herself engaged to him, he wouldn't let her down.'

'He would probably have found himself involved in a breach of promise case if he had,' Freddy commented. 'She sounds a lady who is all there, clever—'

'Not clever,' Mary snapped, 'cunning. Yes, she is quite capable of having brought such a case although she couldn't possibly have won it.'

'But not very nice for the Rendle connection.'

'No. I don't imagine that occurred to Charles, however. He just felt he had led her astray and had to make the only possible amends. If it *did* happen like that,' Mary added hastily. 'I am only telling what I actually know and what I conjecture. *Shh!*—here comes John. Don't say anything about this or he'll declare I've been gossiping again. So I have.'

As he made his way back to his hotel which was situated not far from the Willisons' house, Sir Frederick reviewed the story he had just been told. Poor Rendle—a quixotic fool, of course, but a man is as he is. He wondered how Miranda was making out with this redoubtable sister-in-law, and confessed a mild curiosity to see the good lady for himself.

But as he presently turned in at the gates of the hotel he was thinking no longer of the Rendle ménage.

'Thursday,' he said, half aloud. 'Yes, I'll get Mary to take me, on Thursday.'

CHAPTER FOUR

TAMARA PLACED a straw cushion upon the floor of the balcony and knelt down, her elbows resting on the iron railing, her chin in her cupped hands. The morning was clear and sunny; she wriggled her shoulders like a satisfied kitten as the warm rays fell upon them, and gazed with absorbed brown eyes at the street below.

It was a narrow street, cobbled and steep, the small houses descending into two lines of dazzling white-washed walls, painted doors, and scarlet geraniums spilling from every window sill. The roadway was filled with cheerful humanity; elderly men in stocking caps gossiping in open doorways, women carrying tall water pitchers, sturdy old crones bearing baskets of oranges or silvery sardines. Here and there on a doorstep a black-eyed little girl with a toddler or two at her feet, sat fashioning bright paper flowers.

In this colourful thoroughfare the friends of the Radizlos and several other exiles were established; they had been fortunate in procuring a modest dwelling at the upper end and lived there communally in a state of lighthearted confusion, physically and financially, which would have driven any Englishman to the verge of madness.

Tamara had been accepted by them with off-hand good humour; she was the Radizlo's protégée and they could find room for her. She had, in fact, been so lucky as to be given a room to herself, a cubbyhole just large enough to contain a bed, a table and a row of wall hooks for her clothes. But it was her own, and it possessed this private balcony.

'I hope I shall stay here,' she said to herself now. 'Lisbon is good and there are nice people. That so *affairée* but hospitable Mrs Sangster who has invited us today, and Freddy and Mees Rendle and—and the brother of Mees Rendle—yes, I think I may find Lisbon the best of all the places I have known since I left Hungary.'

Of Hungary, the house in Budapest and the several country estates belonging to the prince, her father, she remembered nothing very clearly. When she looked back it was through a roseate haze in the centre of which flitted her own small figure. So small, but so important. Cherished, petted, Mama's Pink Peachblossom, Papa's Tiny Sweetheart, Laszlo's Little Mouse.

There had come a day when she found the princess and the old nurse superintending the packing of trunks. To her interested inquiries Mama had replied that they were going on a journey. Even at her then very tender age, Tamara was always ready to see life and welcomed the news with enthusiasm. Later, she was upset to find that neither Papa nor her big brother Laszlo were to accompany Mama and herself. The princess, too, was upset and bitterly opposed to leaving but the prince declared that the situation was deteriorating—whatever that meant—and she and the child must get away while the route was still clear. So the mother and daughter departed and in due course arrived in Switzerland.

Switzerland for a considerable period proved far from amusing. The princess took a flat in a quiet, unfashionable quarter of Geneva and lived secluded there, keeping Tamara close at her side as if she feared this last precious possession might be snatched from her. Except for the Swiss woman who cooked for them and did the housework and the manager of the bank where Mama drew her money, they spoke to no one. Tamara's sole recreation out of doors was to go for walks, her hand held tightly in her mother's; indoors she played with her dolls and Mama read fairytales to her. These were in French, but French was a second language in that family.

As the child grew older she learned why it was they had left their home and learned, too, that after a time there had come no word from Papa and Laszlo. They might be prisoners; they were more probably dead. The princess's sorrow and loneliness told on her health; she became increasingly frail. Tamara sorrowed, too, but she had the resilience of youth and, in any case, Papa and Laszlo had retreated into shadowy figures.

In other respects, matters began to improve so far as the little girl was concerned. They were not, like so many other emigrés, straitened for money; if they lacked the luxury they once had known at least they lived in perfect comfort. Tamara did not know, nor did it ever enter her head to wonder, how this was achieved; she took it for granted as she took for granted each aspect of her life.

A Mademoiselle presently appeared, arriving daily to give Tamara lessons, and eventually, yielding to the kindly persistence of certain interested people, the melancholy princess acquired a small circle of acquaintances. Later, to her delight, Tamara was enrolled as day scholar at a select establishment where she was taught, among other accomplishments, deportment and dancing. The language of the school was French, but several American girls were boarders there; they took a great fancy to the exiled Hungarian girl and from them, parrot-wise, she picked up her fluent, if broken, English, in addition to lessons in reading and writing it.

These school years were a time of unclouded enjoyment to Tamara. Her mother, to older eyes, was visibly failing but youthful observation is less acute and the little daughter saw nothing seriously amiss.

Then Bela and Olga Radizlo descended upon them. They were old friends, although considerably younger than Tamara's parents, and Bela had formerly been in charge of the prince's famous stud farm and racing

49

stables. They had remained in Hungary during the German invasion and Russian liberation of their doubly afflicted country, reduced to a wretched, furtive existence. At length they had escaped—happily with some valuable family jewels—and after the usual routine detention had made their way to Switzerland where they knew the princess to be installed. They confirmed what needed no confirming; that the prince and Princess Laszlo had been murdered.

The princess was pathetically glad to see them, almost hysterically so. Her own people; she could speak once more in her own dear tongue. She had long private interviews with Bela, she took him to meet the manager of the bank; a number of papers were drawn up and signed. When all this had been effected, as if now she could go in peace to join her husband and son, quietly and without apparent suffering she died.

Tamara was shocked, grief-stricken and frightened. Mama had left her, she was alone in the world, what would become of her?

Count Radizlo supplied the answer. The princess had confided her daughter to his care, he and Olga would look after her, she had nothing to fear. He furthermore informed her that there was a small amount of money which would be paid to him to administer on her behalf. She would not be entirely beholden to Olga and himself; there was sufficient to keep her in clothing and to pay her share of board and lodging. Tamara had not been considering the financial side of the matter and gave it no further thought now, realizing only that she wasn't going to be left alone. Just seventeen, possessed of a buoyant nature, she soon recovered from the stunning effects of her grief. Olga and Bela were kind to her in their careless fashion; they were not tender and she didn't love them but they were cheerful and unexacting companions. Occasionally, she was swept by the recollection of her insecure state, bereft of all her kin, homeless. But this feeling, subconscious rather than conscious, seldom rose to the surface to trouble her.

The princess had died in the early summer and the Radizlos decided to stay on for a time in the flat. Good-looking, gay, well-bred and speaking both French and English, they were taken up by Geneva's international set. Despite her loss, Tamara enjoyed her summer; Olga was not the type to play duenna and the young girl was accorded the freedom she would never have been allowed under the chaperonage of the princess.

When the cold, damp Swiss autumn began, the Radizlos moved on to Paris where they spent the winter in a *pension* on the Left Bank with a group of people in the same circumstances as themselves. It was very different from Geneva and Tamara did not like it at all; she hoped that in the spring they would return to Switzerland. But in March they crossed to England where the count had an idea of permanently settling.

England was undergoing a penitential season; for three months they shivered in the grim private hotel in the Cromwell Road while Bela looked about and contacted this person and that. Finally, to Tamara's infinite relief, Olga informed her that they had decided to go to Portugal; they had friends in Lisbon, living was less expensive and, above all, they would find warmth and sunshine in place of bitter winds and ceaseless rain. So here she was, on this bright morning, kneeling upon the straw cushion and hoping that this time Bela and Olga would 'stay put' as the American girls used to say.

'I don't believe it,' Freddy Clayton said in an under-tone. 'There just isn't any such room.'

Mary Willison smiled.

'I told you it was worth seeing.'

They stood together in Mrs. Sangster's drawing-room while their hostess, having welcomed them, was greeting other arriving guests.

They had driven, in Mary's car, to the old Alfama quarter and because the street they sought was so nar-row they had parked the car in a convenient garage and continued on foot.

'Where are you taking me?' Freddy demanded as they picked a precarious course beneath overhanging balconies, among baskets of fruit and fish, wine bar-rels, brown nets being mended by gnarled old men, vendors of water-melon seeds, women bringing water from the fountain, scrambling children and whisking cats. 'Our good friend surely doesn't live *here*?'

People live anywhere in Lisbon. Addresses don't matter. As for her house, you'll find others like it in this section, some of them still occupied by old noble families. When they do come into the market, one can usually get them for a song. Here we are.'

They had come to an imposing façade pierced by heavily grilled windows and bearing a stone coat of arms above the doorway. A maid-servant admitted them into a dusky hall and thence to the drawing-room. This was a vast apartment, reminiscent of a ban-queting hall, as in truth it once had been, and every inch of it, at first glimpse, appeared to be filled.

At one end was a fine Italian marble fireplace, the low mantleshelf crowded with pieces of Dresden china. Above the mantel, between branching wrought iron candelabra hung a large and beautiful Florentine gilt mirror, and above this again a religious triptych. Below, on either side, were single panels of painted wood and a collection of miniatures. The other walls were crammed with oil paintings, water colours, flowered porcelain plates, antique plaster plaques, whose greens and gold and scarlet were still vivid, and more mirrors.

The furniture was correspondingly varied. A delicate Chippendale cabinet soared airily on one side of the room, faced and intimidated by a cabinet of equal height in heavily embossed black oak. This in turn was outmatched by a massive black oak settle, carved and scrolled to the last degree, which looked as if it might have once have graced some monastery, as did the great throne-like chairs that flanked it. At intervals along the walls stood other stately pieces of furniture some of which Freddy, who loathed it, identified as as buhl.

The main part of the room provided light relief. Fragile *bibelots* of china and crystal and old enamel were displayed on tables of various size and shape, two with hinged glass tops, and scattered among the tables were a number of little fat, round-backed chairs with gilt rims, covered in *petit point*. Freddy's fascinated gaze took in also a yellow satin love seat, a saddlebag chair and one on rockers. The long windows were draped in pelmeted crimson velvet, their panes hidden behind white lace.

'Well?' Mary murmured when her companion had looked his fill.

'No use,' Freddy said. 'I still don't believe it.'

'Who could? It's very funny and quite frightful—although some of this stuff is extremely good. Dear soul, she's so proud of it and it's exactly her setting.'

'Is it?'

'But of course. Thoroughly mid-Victorian—she isn't old enough for that but she has a mid-Victorian mind. They were magpie collectors and cluttered up their rooms like this—more money than culture—I'm not being nasty. I delight in this drawing-room.'

'It is hardly *your* setting.' Freddy smiled, with a glance at the elegant *mondaine* figure.

'Nor anyone's, except its owner's. People always look out of place and afraid of knocking something.' She broke off. 'Here is some one who really does fit in and won't knock anything over. What a lovely girl and how beautiful she walks.

The girl in question wore a summery frock with a rather long full skirt; her dark hair was waved lightly back from her face and hung in a smooth coil, framing the slender neck and the small ears from which dangled gold hoop earrings. She had caught Mary's eye and was coming towards her, threading a way between all the tables and chairs, moving with that singleness of purpose she had displayed in the foyer of the ship, her expression the same half smiling, come-hither one that so intrigued Mr Willison.

'Who—' Freddy, whose view had become obstructed, took a pace sideways. 'Oh, that's Rendle's sister. Haven't you met her yet?'

'No, I thought I'd give her a couple of days to shake down.'

Miranda reached them. Because of the great oak cabinet and two or three people grouped in front of it, Freddy had been out of her line of vision; now she saw him and caught a dismayed breath. She hoped he realized that she hadn't been aware of him; the last thing she wanted was to give an impression of deliberately placing herself in his vicinity. The last thing she had expected, too, was that Freddy Clayton would be here at all. Mrs. Sangster and her Thursday at homes did not sound in the least his cup of tea. And to come at once—just three days after his arrival in Lisbon—Miranda could only conclude that he had been dragged here, against his inclination, by Mrs Willison.

She gave him a casual little nod and put out her hand to Mary.

'I'm Miranda,' she said. 'Ada Rendle's daughter.'

'You couldn't be anyone else,' Mary responded, 'with those eyes and that nose. You are exactly like your mother when she was your age. I am so glad to see you again.'

'Thank you. I am so glad, too. Charles tells me you have very kindly asked us to dine with you on Sunday. I am looking forward to it.'

Nice child, thought Mary.

'We are also looking forward to it,' she said. 'You know Sir Frederick Clayton, I believe?'

'I used to know him.' Miranda flickered a smile at the young man. 'But we hadn't seen each other for about two years until we found ourselves in the same ship.'

'We didn't see much of each other on board,' Freddy returned easily. 'Poor Miranda was confined to quarters.'

'A bad sailor? What a shame. Your brother is such a good one and adores the sea. Where *is* Charles, by the way, and Sybil? They didn't send you alone, did they?'

'Oh no.' Miranda's clear, composed little voice did not alter but Mary, watching her shrewdly, saw the quick flutter of her dark eyelashes and a momentary contraction of the pretty mouth. 'They are both here but Sybil wanted to fix her hair and a maid took her up to a bedroom. Charles is waiting for her in the hall; Mrs Sangster asked me to come right in.'

'I see.' Mary guessed that there had been a scene, trifling enough, but wearisome and, to Charles's sister, probably infuriating. Sybil delaying as usual, fussing about her appearance, Charles unwisely announcing that he and Miranda were ready to start, Sybil flying into one of her uncalled-for tempers. No doubt she had nagged at him all the way to Mrs Sangster's and had gone upstairs upon arrival, not because her hair needed attention but to continue venting her ill-humour upon her long-suffering husband.

'Here they come,' Miranda said, and lifted a hand to signal her brother. The two approached; Sybil, in the lead, rather noisily greeting this acquaintance and that. She wore a short, tight skirt and, despite the heat of the day, one of her fashionable high-collared jerseys. Her round face was flushed, as well it might be with her throat encased in wool, and she advanced with an air of aggressiveness characteristic of her. Freddy watched her coming, with speculative eyes and the hint of quizzical smile. Miranda cast him a glance; a faint blush touched her cheekbones, then her dark head was lifted higher.

'All set now, Sybil? It looks perfect.' She slid an arm about the small woman's shoulders. 'You haven't met Sir Frederick Clayton. This is my sister-in-law, Freddy.'

He shook hands with Sybil and gave Charles a friendly, 'Hallo, old man.'

Sybil appeared gratified.

'*The* Sir Frederick?' she inquired.

'I can't claim to being *The*. Just Frederick Clayton, at your service.'

56

'I don't imagine there's another one. I mean, I've often seen your name in the papers at home. But I didn't know——' she looked suspiciously at Charles and Miranda, 'that you were a friend of the family, or were in Lisbon. Have you been here long?'

'No, I travelled out on the ship with Miranda.'

'You did? They never told me a word about it.'

'I am deflated. I had supposed my arrival would create more impression.'

They all laughed, except Sybil who said shrilly:

'That's Charles all over. You'd think he'd have told me a friend had arrived. But oh, no. I have to find out for myself. I'm the last person to be informed.'

'I expect,' Freddy said cheerfully, 'he would have informed you in time. Charles is not a man to be hurried.'

'You're telling me. Well, now that I do know, you must come and dine with us. I'll arrange a day, next week.'

'Thank you very much. I shall be delighted.'

'How are you getting on?' Charles asked. 'Hotel comfortable?'

'Quite, thanks, but I am hoping to find a small place of my own, service flat if they run to them here. I'm doing a spot of writing——'

'So Miranda told me. Glad you are making a fairly long stay. I'm by way of being a rather good guide if you want local colour and so on.'

'Just what I do want,' Freddy rejoined with a warmth which was not all owing to his need for a guide. Poor devil, he was saying inwardly. The two men chatted on for a few minutes; Miranda said to Mary Willison:

'What a strange old house this is and in such a picturesque—but slummy quarter.'

Mary explained about the old houses in this section.

'Of course, there's the snag of the street being too narrow for cars, but the garage is only a few minutes' walk. This house has a walled garden, for one thing, which naturally appeals to an Englishwoman, and although the whole place is ridiculously large for anyone living alone, Mrs Sangster doesn't seem to find it so. After all, she needs plenty of room,' Mary said with a mischievous glance at the crammed apartment.

'She must be very popular. Are there always as many people at her at homes as there are today?'

'No. This is the first Thursday in the month, always a special occasion when she issues definite invitations to newcomers or visitors or perhaps some tourists she wants to entertain. On the other Thursdays she is merely at home if anyone cares to drop in. Usually half a dozen or more do drop in. It is an institution; she gives us China tea and scones and jam and Madeira cake; it never varies—and tastes like home—'

'English tea-room?' Miranda suggested.

'Exactly. Not that people come only for that, but it *is* a sort of homey oasis, unchanging, provincial—'

'You can't call Mrs Sangster provincial,' Sybil interposed truculently. 'I mean, a woman who has moved in Embassy circles and lived abroad for donkey's years.'

Mary's smooth forehead was momentarily creased by an impatient frown.

'I meant provincial in its broad and pleasanter sense. Miranda understands, I think.'

'Yes, I do.' But Miranda looked as if something were puzzling her none the less.

There was now a slight commotion near the doorway, more guests arriving, chattering with infectious verve, causing everyone to glance in their direction. They were the Radizlos, with Tamara and several other Hungarians. Bela and Olga were being introduced here and there by their established compatriots; Tamara, neglected, stood hesitantly in the background, her eyes searching the assembled company.

She caught sight of the group of friends standing at the far end of the room by the fireplace; her face lit up with its radiant smile and she rushed towards them.

Mrs Sangster's drawing-room was at no time a place in which it was safe to rush. Even empty of people it required negotiation and a watching of one's step. Tamara wasn't watching anything except Charles Rendle upon whom her gaze was fixed. By a miracle she cleared numerous obstacles but at the last instant she tripped over the outspread claw-foot of one of the overladen small tables; Charles sprang forward just in time to prevent a disastrous crash.

'Easy does it,' he said, smiling down at her, holding her steady.

'Oh—my—' Tamara looked conscience-stricken but her voice held an hilarious note. 'If I had fallen—so many little things to break—I could never again show my face. Thank you, Mr Rendle. You were so quick. And so strong. You catch me with one hand and that table with the other, and save us both.'

Sybil stared. *Mr Rendle?* She knew Charles, then, this dizzy blonde? Sybil disliked blondes. Who on earth —and why—and how——

Freddy, who had followed on Charles's heels, grinned and shook his head.

'At it again, Mara? You need a permanent rescue squad.'

'Please?' Her gay little face crinkled. 'Oh, I comprehend,' she went on in her engaging accent, 'you *ta-quine*—no—you tease me, Freddy, because on the ship I am also stumbling and nearly fall. But it is not hangover this time.'

So she knew Sir Frederick, too, this obnoxious chit, thought Sybil. Actually calling him Freddy. And still hanging on to Charles as if she owned him—Sybil's thin lips disappeared as the tiny mouth tightened.

'Charles,' she said in an ominous tone, 'if you have quite finished—'

Quickly he led the young girl to her.

'This is the Princess Tamara, from Hungary. She travelled out with Miranda and we met for a moment on the dock. My wife, Princess.'

A startled look widened Tamara's brown eyes. Politely she said:

'How do you do, Mrs Rendle. Such a pleasure—'

'How do you do. A princess? Am I supposed to curtsey?' Sybil spoke facetiously but the rude intent was there. Tamara, however, took the words at face value.

'Oh no,' she replied kindly, 'is not necessary to curtsey to me.'

Freddy emitted a sort of gasp, hurriedly succeeded by an unconvincing cough. Mary said hastily:

'May I introduce myself? I am Mrs Willison. My husband has told me about you.'

'Oh, that so kind Mr Willison. I am very happy to meet you, Madame. And I have not yet spoken to Mees Rendle. I did hope to see you here today, Mees Rendle.'

Mrs Sangster bustled along the room.

'Tea is ready; if you will all come in—'

There was a general move. Mary tucked Tamara's arm within her own.

'We must have a chat together.' Her eyes invited Miranda to join them and the three walked off, Freddy following.

'Coming, Sybil?' Charles said as she stood staring after them.

'Naturally I am coming. Did you expect me to stay here alone while everyone's having tea? I must say, Charles, you made a nice spectacle of yourself.'

'In what way?'

'You know very well. Dashing to that girl, letting her cling to you in front of the whole room—'

'If I hadn't dashed,' he retorted mildly, 'both she and the table would have come headlong and dear knows what priceless treasures might have been broken.'

'Serve her right if they had been.'

'But it wouldn't have served Mrs Sangster right.' Charles gave his wife the rallying, placating smile he so frequently did give her.

She was unappeased.

'Is the girl tight?'

'Tight! Good heavens, no. What on earth put such an idea into your head?'

'She behaved like it. Prancing up the room and tumbling over her own feet and rattling away nineteen to the dozen in that silly manner as if she thought herself the cat's whiskers—besides, you heard her say she'd had a hangover on the ship.'

'She's only eighteen,' Charles said sharply. 'I heard her, yes; just some shipboard nonsense between her and Clayton. Please, Sybil, don't get such ridiculous ideas.'

'You seem very concerned about her. What is it to you whether she drinks or not?'

'I should be concerned about any girl of her age if I thought she drank. In this case it is sheer absurdity, but if such a thing were hinted about her—you know how gossip spreads—'

'Are you accusing me of being a gossip? I can assure you, I'm not interested in the creature to talk about her one way or the other. Mary Willison may take her up—she's the world's worst snob and will love trotting a princess around, even a phoney Hungarian one. But if you think I am going to follow suit you're very much mistaken.'

'All I am thinking about,' Charles returned, 'is that the tea will be getting cold. Come along, Sybil, and don't let's worry our heads over what Mary chooses to do.'

Some time later when people were drifting back from the dining-room where tea had been served, Miranda came alone into the drawing-room and crossed to one of the long windows, curious to see whether it gave upon the walled garden. She drew the white lace curtain cautiously aside and peered out. The garden was there, a surprisingly large one, with flowers in profusion, some espaliered fruit trees and several astonishing geraniums, like trees themselves, topping the old grey walls. A man was working on a border; as if he had noted the slight movement at the window he straightened up and looked towards it. Miranda dropped the curtain at once, disagreeably impressed.

'How extraordinary.' She uttered the words aloud, and someone passing behind her said:

'What is extraordinary?'

She turned and saw Freddy Clayton.

'Mrs Sangster's gardener. And anybody less like one's idea of a gardener—'

'Let me see.' Freddy drew the lace aside but the man was again bending over his work and this time did not lift his head.

'What does he look like?'

'Creepy. Like a rat.'

'He may be all the better gardener for that. Rats are skilled diggers. Tell me,' Freddy continued, civilly making conversation, 'what do you think of our hostess's—collection?'

Miranda's gaze travelled slowly about the great room. She took her time in answering; he remembered that this had been one of her characteristics, by no means a common trait. She paid attention to your question and replied to it intelligently.

When she had sufficiently considered this one she said:

'It is all wrong.'

Freddy laughed.

'Aesthetically, it is indeed. But a delightfully disarming room, don't you think, once you get over the first shock.'

'I think it's a frightening room.'

'Frightening! This naïve clutter?'

Miranda nodded.

'Perhaps,' he said lightly, 'the house is haunted. It is old enough, in all conscience. Are you psychic, by any chance?'

'It isn't a ghost I feel. I simply—' she stopped. Sybil and Charles had joined them, saying they were ready to leave.

Freddy remained by the window for a minute or two

63

as the others went off to make their adieux to Mrs Sangster.

'I wonder,' he said to himself, 'just what she does feel?'

But he had no intention of pursuing the matter. Miranda's feelings could not concern him less.

CHAPTER FIVE

'IF THE Senhor will enter—' the Portuguese caretaker ushered Sir Frederick Clayton into the lift, the gate clanged and they began to ascend. Freddy made a little grimace and straightened his shoulders as if bracing himself for something he would gladly have forgone.

He was dining with the Rendles, in response to a third invitation. More than a fortnight had elapsed since that afternoon at Mrs Sangster's when Sybil had declared he must dine with them and he, in duty bound, expressed himself as delighted. When she rang up and invited him for a certain evening he had truthfully replied that he was already booked, and when the same thing happened a second time Charles suggested to his wife that they leave it for the present.

He had seen something of Freddy during this interval and learned that he was being extensively entertained; the popular young man had come armed with letters of introduction to members of the Diplomatic Corps and various other people and he was also occupied in trying to find a place of his own. Let him get his breath, settle down; they had made their hospitable overture and it was better not to appear insistent. Sybil, however, had taken offence at the suggestion and immediately tried again, and this time Sir Frederick was not engaged.

He accepted with considerable reluctance. From what Sybil had said about a family dinner he judged he was to be the only guest and he did not relish the thought of spending an evening with Miranda in the intimacy of the family circle. He had nothing to say to her and was impatient of the situation between them. Not that it was a matter of any great moment but it had its awkward side. Still less did he enjoy the prospect of an intimate evening with Charles's tiresome wife.

Poor devil; if Charles hadn't been such a thoroughly good chap Freddy would ruthlessly have cut the Rendles out, meeting them with civility if occasion demanded and making it clear that he did not care to further the acquaintanceship. But one couldn't do that to Charles.

The two men had always liked what little they knew of each other and now, having done some sightseeing and flat hunting together their mutual regard had ripened to genuine friendship. The differences in their characters made them all the better companions; Freddy found in Charles a stability and kindliness lacking in his own volatile circle, and Freddy's gay insouciance held its corresponding appeal for the more serious other.

'So there we are,' the unwilling guest said to himself as the lift grunted to a stop. 'I'm not cutting out Charles; I'll grin and bear with his womenfolk.'

A smiling maid admitted him to the flat and conducted him to the long, low attic drawing-room with its plaster walls and matting-covered floor and sparse, shining furniture. It was lit by four table lamps in spreading amber shades that diffused a soft but sufficient light, etching patterns on walls and ceiling, leaving the far recesses in dusky shadow. Freddy experienced a shock of agreeable surprise; what an unusual room. And what a setting he thought, involuntarily, for dark-haired Miranda, coming forward to welcome him in her shimmering, full-skirted, amber frock.

'Good evening Freddy,' Miranda said. 'Sybil and Charles will be here in a moment.'

'I expect I'm a bit early. I wasn't sure of the distance.'

'You are right on time. Did you have any difficulty in finding the way?"

'None at all. Your brother's directions were quite clear. This is a most delightful room.'

'I am glad you think so. Charles took over the furnishings, just as they were, from the former Portuguese tenants.'

So that was the answer. Freddy had been wondering, like Miranda before him, if this could be Sybil's taste.

Sybil herself now came in; he responded to her greeting by an appropriate expression of his pleasure, adding that he had just been admiring her charming room.

'You don't have to be polite about it to me,' Sybil retorted. 'I am not responsible. Well, you have found time for us at last, Sir Frederick. I was beginning to think we weren't grand enough for you; we hear you have been dining with His Excellency and all the other bigwigs.' It was facetiously spoken but one of those remarks so difficult to reply to.

Freddy, inwardly saying 'Hang the woman', grinned cheerfully and said aloud, 'On the contrary, Mrs Rendle, I was beginning to despair of your timing and about to invite myself. Hallo, Charles—' he turned with relief as his host appeared.

'Did Joao put your car away?' Charles asked, crossing to a table where a tray with bottles and glasses had been placed.

'Yes, thanks. Most convenient arrangement you have here.'

'The old stables. This was quite an imposing property at one time. Sherry or cocktail? I suppose you won't have white port, the correct apertif in Portugal.'

'Heaven forbid,' the other returned, with feeling. 'I feel that I ought to say sherry, the room calls for it, cocktails are quite out of character. But being a Philistine—'

'You'll have a Martini,' Charles smiled. 'The same for you, of course, Sybil. Miranda?'

'I'll keep in character and have sherry, Charles.'

'Dark an' sweet?'

Her dimple flickered; the phrase evidently held a double meaning, some family allusion coined or adopted by Charles in reference to his young sister.

'No,' she answered, 'the medium, goldy sherry to match my frock.'

Her brother cast her an amused, affectionate glance.

'And the frock matches the lamplight. A new one?'

She nodded.

'I have been shopping in Rua Serpa Pinto.'

'Very successfully, if one may say so,' Freddy contributed.

Sybil, whose blue taffeta dinner dress had what was then the new tight skirt and stiff, widely cuffed bodice, said:

'Miranda goes in for that sort of picture thing. Personally, I've always been the tailored type.'

Again, there seemed no adequate reply to this interesting piece of information but Freddy was spared the necessity as Sybil hurried to her husband's side.

'Charles, what *are* you doing? Putting toothpicks in those olives—'

'They are here, on this dish. Isn't that what they're meant for?'

'But I told Maria—yes, the stupid idiot has put out both. Why can't you use your eyes, Charles?'

'Sorry, Sybil. It's these little gadgets, is it?'

'Of course. You have seen them before.' She hastily impaled more olives on slender glass sticks topped by gaily coloured cocks. 'There's no use my trying to do anything decently—'

'Men are all the same,' Miranda's clear little flat voice interposed. 'If they can get hold of the wrong thing, trust them to do it.'

'You're telling me,' Sybil rejoined.

Charles laughed.

'Ganging up on me, are you?'

Freddy, swept by a devastating wave of boredom, dutifully played his part.

'You haven't a chance, old boy. Two women against one man.'

When they were presently seated at the dinner table he started the conversational ball rolling by asking Miranda if she had as yet explored Lisbon. She replied that she was in process of doing so.

'I want to prowl around by myself and not be a

nuisance. Charles is going to stake me to a little car if he can find one secondhand. We don't want anything expensive as it is just to run about in while I am here.'

'I believe I know the very thing for you, then. Mrs Willison told me last evening that she wants to sell that baby Citroën of hers. She's investing in a larger car and a chauffeur.'

'They've got a chauffeur,' Sybil said in the sharp, contradictory fashion which was one of her irritating characteristics. 'I mean, that Pedro of theirs drives Mr Willison's car.'

'Pedro is also butler and factotum generally. Not always available.'

'So Mary Willison is getting too grand to drive herself? What next?'

'It is a matter of neuritis, not an access of grandeur,' Freddy explained. 'She can't altogether trust one of her arms and hands and must not risk driving. For the time being, at any rate.'

'Poor Mrs Willison,' Miranda said. 'What a shame. I had no idea she suffered from neuritis.'

'Neither had I,' Sybil said, 'but I've always thought she looked unhealthy. So scrawny for her age and such a pasty complexion.'

This was hardly a correct description of Mary's slender figure and fine pale skin but no one disputed the point. Charles said:

'Is this official? May I quote you, Freddy, and get in touch with her?'

'Certainly. There is no secret about it.'

'Right. It would suit you, poppet?'

'I'd adore to have that baby car. I have driven in it; the tiny thing slips along like a water beetle—'

'Are you a good driver?' Freddy inquired abruptly. She gave him a cool little smile.

'Very good indeed.'

'And you don't mind saying so,' Sybil observed. 'Personally, I let other people blow my trumpet.'

Miranda was unabashed.

'I can't say anything else.'

The dinner was admirable, perfectly cooked and served, but Freddy found it an irksome meal. Conversation could not run smoothly because Sybil at once brought every topic around to her own exclusive angle, which had the effect of blighting and ending the subject. She also indulged in what appeared to be a fixed habit; finding fault with her husband. Charles took it in good part, amiable and indulgent; Freddy, a conscientious guest, continued to play up. But his boredom increased and, not for the first time, he thanked his stars for his escape, his thrice-blessed freedom. He might have been—he very nearly had been—tied by the heel as Charles was tied; not to a Sybil, true, but at any rate to an exigeante, stupid-tempered girl. What utter fools men could make of themselves.

When they were back again in the drawing-room and Freddy was silently calculating as to how soon he could make his departure, he reflected ruefully that he must return this hospitality. A dinner at one of the fashionable restaurants? Another foursome? No, he couldn't face it. He'd invite two or three other people to join them, but even so it would be a grim affair with this deadly bore of a woman, and what right had he to inflict her upon his friends?

Then he was seized by inspiration. Estoril was the answer. He would make up a dinner party; they could dance, have a flutter at the tables, there was bound to be a gay crowd at the resort and Sybil's shrill voice and wearisome tongue could not dominate the proceedings to any appreciable extent.

'Have you been to Estoril?' he asked Miranda.

She had not been there.

'Then I wonder, Mrs Rendle—' he turned to his hostess and suggested the party. The suggestion was well received and a date fixed for the following Saturday.

'I expect you've already been dining and dancing at Estoril, Sir Frederick,' Sybil said.

'I have driven out a couple of times, for a swim, and and stayed on to dine.'

'Have you bought a car, or did you bring one with you?'

'I brought it with me.'

'The same one?' Her tone was arch.

'The same?' he echoed.

'I mean the one you had the famous crash in.'

Miranda's eyes flashed to his, were instantly withdrawn.

Astonished, and more than a little annoyed by what he considered sheer impertinence on the part of a woman who had met him only once before in her life, Freddy replied briefly:

'Yes, it is the car that caused the crash.'

'The papers did make a song and dance about it,' Sybil pursued. 'They love to get something on a person who is well known, don't they?'

He shrugged.

'So far as that goes, their report was accurate enough.'

71

'So far as they knew,' Charles amended.

'What are you getting at?' his wife snapped. 'Must you be so mysterious, Charles?'

'The report was accurate,' he said, 'except for the fact that Freddy wasn't driving. He took the rap for a young cousin who had the grace, later on, to admit the truth to certain of Freddy's friends. I heard about it from Jack Billings,' Charles added as the other man cocked an inquiring eyebrow.

Miranda sat very still. Sybil cried loudly:

'You mean to say you said you were driving, when you weren't? What on earth for? Supposing someone had been killed—'

'There wasn't time to go into all that. I had to think fast and it seemed the only answer. The accident was a very bad show and my cousin's University would have taken an extremely dim view of it. He would almost certainly have been sent down.'

'Serve him right if he had been. Teach him a lesson.'

'Too drastic a one. His career depended upon his degree.'

'All the same,' Charles said, 'it was more than he deserved. Wild young scamp—you were in the country, weren't you, and got a message that he was in some sort of scrape and had come down to London to enlist your help—as usual?'

'I was at the farm, yes, when he—Peter—telephoned. I told him to meet me at my flat but he failed to turn up. Eventually I ran him to earth; I knew his likely haunts, of course.'

'What happened then? I've never understood why you allowed him to drive. He was tight, wasn't he?'

'Decidedly so. He had two girls in tow and wanted to continue making a night of it. The girls, decent kids,

72

had had enough of him and only wanted to get home to bed. I tipped them off that I'd drive them home and simply told the boy to come along and we'd go somewhere; he was in no state to be argued with and I didn't want a noisy scene. The girls got into the back of the car and Peter, before I could stop him, jumped in, took the wheel and started up, I just managed to scramble in after him—and hope for the best.'

'A hope that was not realized,' Charles commented. 'Well, it might have been worse. No one killed or crippled. It must have cost your insurance company a pretty penny. How is the youngster shaping now, by the way?'

'Excellently. He was badly shaken by the whole thing and from then on stopped playing the fool.'

A clock on the mantelshelf struck; Freddy stood up.

'I am overstaying my welcome.'

'It is still early,' Charles said. 'How about a whisky and soda?'

'Nothing, thanks. I must get along. It has been so nice, Mrs Rendle, thank you so much—' he took his polite leave of her and turned to the girl who had risen and stood with one hand tightly closed on the back of her chair. In spite of the soft and flattering lamplight he saw that her face was pale and pinched, and the grey eyes that met his held a look of desperate mortification.

Instinctively, he shrank; the last thing he wanted was anything in the nature of a post mortem. Confound the woman, Sybil, for bringing up the subject. Impertinent, fatuous—he suspected that there was more in it than mere fatuity. He was much mistaken if it had not been a deliberate dig at himself, a spiteful little thrust, although her motive remained obscure.

73

Probably she had no definite motive, was just naturally malicious.

'Goodnight, Freddy,' Miranda said in a somewhat breathless voice.

'Goodnight, Miranda. I hope you will get the baby car and find it a success.' His casual glance and light tone rejected the appeal in those mortified eyes. He left her with that, joining Charles who said, 'I'll bring the lift up for you,' and the two men went out side by side.

Sybil embarked on a complacent monologue; she thought it had all gone off very well. A simple family party, nothing overdone, a lot of people seemed to be making a great fuss of Frederick Clayton but she had shown that she did not consider him anyone special . . . Miranda listened with half an ear, her own thoughts in turmoil.

So this was the true story; the story Freddy had meant to confide in her and to which she had refused a hearing. He had done this, taken the onus upon himself in order to protect his graceless young kinsman. A mad thing to do; an unfair thing, if you came to that, towards the girl he had asked to marry him. But Miranda would have forgiven him; she understood exactly how it occurred. An impulsive, generous action, taken on the spur of the instant.

How could she have been so unreasonable, so cruel, jumping to the worst conclusion, bitterly accusing him, refusing to listen to any explanation. Hot colour stung her cheeks as she recalled what she had said to him. Small wonder that he had cut her short, called it a day and walked out of her life.

She writhed inwardly as she thought of her behaviour towards him since they had met so unex-

74

pectedly on their way to Lisbon. Airy, self-satisfied, sweetly inimical. And all the time he had known her for the silly, arrogant, wrong-headed girl she was— or had been.

'How can I ever face him again?'

But she was going to face him, and at the first opportunity. There was something that had to be done. She owed Frederick Clayton an apology, the humblest of apologies, and she would know no peace until she had offered it to him.

Mrs Willison was delighted to let Miranda have her car and a day or so later, having complied with the regulations and received her licence—a process speeded up through the good offices of a Portuguese friend of Charles's—Miranda found herself in proud possession of the little Citroën.

'I notice *I* am not given a car of my own,' Sybil observed.

'You can't drive,' her husband reminded her.

'What has that to do with it? If Mary can have a car and a chauffeur—

'There is a car and chauffeur at your disposal whenever you wish,' he said patiently. 'You have only to ring the hire people.'

'Hiring's not the same thing.'

'Well, there's a private car and chauffeur at Madame's service now,' Miranda said gaily. 'The Citroën, and me.'

It was Miranda's constant endeavour to placate her sister-in-law, ranging herself on Sybil's side, treating her with cheerful camaraderie. It went sorely against the grain and was not worth the effort as far as Sybil was concerned. There was no response; the elder woman seemed encased in a scaly armour which neither affection, kindness nor sympathy could penetrate. One got no further; one got, indeed, nowhere with her. But she was Charles's wife and for her brother's sake Miranda persisted in her thankless task.

Her relief was extreme, now, when Sybil retorted acidly that she wasn't going to risk her life in that idiotic pint-sized thing with a girl driver of Miranda's age. Nothing would induce her to set foot in it. Miranda was well aware that this decision arose solely from Sybil's jealous resentment, but for once she blessed the other's ill nature.

Thanks to several sightseeing expeditions and the careful study of a map, Miranda by this time was fairly conversant with the general outlay of Lisbon and her first independent drive was to the old quarter in which Mrs Sangster was established. She had been fascinated by her former glimpse of it and was eager to explore further. It was quite safe to do so; one could go where one pleased in this gentlest of cities with perfect confidence.

Leaving her car in the park belonging to the garage which was so conveniently situated, she made her way along the colourful street, pausing for a moment as she came to the blank, impressive façade of Mrs Sangster's mansion. She would have liked to explore this, too; penetrate to the unknown upper floors, prowl through the many rooms that must be there.

Not for nothing had Miranda that inquiring, tip-tilted little nose, she possessed a lively curiosity and the house had made a strong impression upon her. An impression repellent, slightly sinister and, for that very reason, alluring. But curiosity in this instance must remain unsatisfied; with a final glance at the tantalizing

76

exterior she walked on, charmed with all she saw; the rough-walled old houses, the balconies, the huge iron lanterns suspended here and there, the incredibly tiny gardens, the sudden glimpse through some narrow by-way of the river, and a ship with a red sail.

Presently she came to a garden much larger than any she had passed; backed by a church and flanked by crumbling grey walls. It was overrun with sprawling, neglected flowering bushes and vines and, at this hour, lay in deep shadow. Miranda, who had been walking for some time in the heat to which she was still not wholly acclimatized, thought it looked very cool and inviting; she noticed that there were some stone benches beneath the bushes and decided to go in and rest for a little.

She found a bench at the far end, hidden behind a great tangle of fragrant shrub and creeper; the growth was not so thick as to prevent her from seeing out but no one could have discerned a figure seated there until within the space of a few yards. She chose this corner, not from any wish to hide, but because its bowerlike appearance attracted her.

There was no one else in the garden but she had not been long in her flowery retreat before two people, evidently seized by the same impulse as herself, came in and sat down in the shade. She recognized both; Mrs Sangster and Count Radizlo.

'How funny,' she thought, then recollected what she had been told about Mrs Sangster's efforts on behalf of the refugees. No doubt the excellent soul had taken the count to meet someone whom she hoped to interest in the unfortunate exile, someone whose business premises lay in the vicinity.

Miranda debated as to whether or not she should

reveal herself. She didn't particularly want to and there seemed no point in doing so. Moreover, the other two were absorbed in conversation, probably discussing the interview that had just taken place, and they would hardly welcome interruption.

'I'll stay where I am,' she concluded. 'They won't discover me and it isn't as if I could hear what they are saying. I'm not eavesdropping.'

When they had rested for a short space, the count and his benevolent companion departed; a few minutes later someone else arrived, a young man in a hurry who came swiftly between the tall bushes straight to Miranda's bower. He did not see her, standing with his back towards her.

Miranda caught an astounded breath. With the next breath she was on her feet.

'Freddy!'

He started violently and wheeled about.

'Miranda——what on earth——what are you doing here?"

'Sightseeing. I left my car at the garage——I have got the baby Citroën, thanks to you.'

'Good.'

'And I came into this garden to sit down and get cool,' Miranda continued. 'It's an extraordinary thing; Mrs Sangster and Count Radizlo where here about five minutes ago, and now you. I wonder who will turn up next?' She spoke more quickly than usual, nervously thinking of what she had to say to him, waiting for the right moment.

Freddy grinned.

'I dashed in because I caught sight of the count and Mrs Sangster and I didn't want to be corralled. I took it they were on their way to the good lady's house for a cup of tea. Did she ask you to join them?'

'She didn't see me. I did not want to be corralled, either, and sat like a mouse until they had gone. I felt a little guilty about meeting the count because I haven't yet got in touch with the Princess Tamara. It's rather difficult, not as if I were in my own home. But now that I've got the car—'

He nodded.

'Mara will be very glad if you look her up. You will meet her on Saturday, by the way, at Estoril. I've asked her and the Radizlos and one or two others.'

'I'll fix up something with her.' Miranda paused, swallowed, was about to speak again when he said, forestalling her:

'I must be getting on. I've been collecting a bit of local colour.' He paused in his turn, and added as a polite afterthought, 'Are you going back now? There's a short cut from here to the garage; my car is there too.'

'I'm not quite ready to go home yet. But—I—'

'Well,' he interposed, 'when you are ready, take the first turn to the left and go straight on. It will bring you to the garage, believe it or not.' He smiled. 'Till Saturday, then.'

'Freddy—wait a minute. There is something I want to say to you. An apology—'

He made a quick movement of distaste.

'It is quite unnecessary. I had no intention of ever bringing up that ancient story again but, as things went the other evening I couldn't help myself. Forget it, Miranda.'

'I can't—and I *must* say it. I'm so dreadfully

ashamed—I have no excuse to offer for the way I behaved, the things I said to you, except that I had had a shock and—and—'

'Please,' he said, 'don't let us rake it up again. I understand; you were only a kid then, years younger than your age. It is all over and forgotten.'

'Yes—but—'

'Well, if you feel you must apologize at this late date—apology accepted. All right now?'

'Thank you,' she faltered, mortified again, feeling as if she had been doused with cool water. 'I—I gather you don't bear any—any malice—'

'Good heavens, no!' Freddy spoke forcibly, from strong conviction, his customary tact deserting him. He might just as well have said, 'On the contrary I owe you a debt of gratitude.'

For a breathing space Miranda stood silent, gazing fixedly down at the ground. Then she said, in a voice that had regained its composure:

'That's all, Freddy. It had to be said, and now we'll—'

'Let it rest,' he finished for her. 'Sure you don't want to come along home?' He felt a twinge of compunction at leaving her alone.

'Quite sure. I want to go into this old church first.'

'Right you are. Don't stay too long.' He lifted his hat and strode away.

CHAPTER SIX

CHARLES HANDED his sister into the back of the car and took his place at the wheel beside Sybil.

'We're in luck tonight,' he said. 'If it had been an evening like yesterday—'

They were setting out for Estoril. Yesterday there had been heavy rain and wind, lasting into the small hours, but it had cleared later in the morning and this evening was warm and still with a full moon mounting the sky.

'I wonder who Sir Frederick has asked to meet us,' Sybil said as they drove away. 'Did he tell you, Charles?'

'No. I understand it is to be quite a party, a dozen or so, but I don't know whom he has invited.'

Miranda could have enlightened them as to three of the other guests but she held her peace. She suspected that her sister-in-law would be far from pleased to learn that the Radizlos and Tamara were included, and she had no desire to hear Sybil's views on the subject.

Freddy was entertaining his friends at a very fashionable and expensive hotel, a favourite resort of various members of ex-Royal houses. 'Doing us well,' Sybil had commented and Miranda, for her part, was eagerly looking forward to it all. It would be the first time she had danced since her arrival in Lisbon.

She had regained her normal cheerful spirits. The encounter with Freddy two days ago in the old church-yard had been a chilling experience, a blow to her youthful ego if nothing more, and her first reaction had been a passionate, 'I wish I had bitten my tongue out before I said a word to him.' But Miranda was quick to revive; she had a resilient nature, plenty of pride and a fund of common sense.

She had done the right, the only thing; admitting her fault, offering her apology. And if his reassurance might have been less emphatically expressed, at least it proved that he cherished no active animosity against her. The affair, so far as Freddy was concerned, had obviously taken on the aspect of an unpleasant but remote and negligible episode.

Negligible or not, however, she had been perfectly aware of his suppressed annoyance at finding himself faced with her again, his impatience with the absurd situation. Now, there was nothing unspoken between them, no more need for an elaborate pretence, treating each other with false and barbed cordiality. They could meet, if not on an exactly friendly footing, at any rate upon a candid one, without embarrassment. For the rest, there was no use dwelling on what might have been if she, two years ago, had behaved differently. What was done, was done.

'So that's that,' Miranda said to herself, resting an elbow on the arm of the car seat and gazing out into the night.

They had left the city behind them and were driving along the coastal road. On one side was the moonlit sea; on the other a dark immensity pricked by the light of occasional villages. Miranda could only guess at the grandeur of the scenery and promised herself an early drive out here in daylight. At length they came to Estoril and drew up at their rendezvous.

The hotel foyer, large, luxurious and crowded, presented a brilliant scene. It was a gala occasion; men in full dress, their women companions glamorous in soft-hued summer evening frocks of organdie, chiffon and delicate lace, strolled to and fro; recognizing and hailing friends, gathering in animated groups to exchange gossip and smoke a cigarette before going in to dine, chattering in a variety of tongues. Miranda wondered which, if any, among them might be the Royalties of whom she had been promised a glimpse.

She caught sight of Freddy and felt a tingle of pride, the impersonal pride of a compatriot. He was no Royalty but he stood out, a distinguished figure; taller than the majority of the other men, with his easy bearing and laughing dark eyes, his thick, smooth, russet brown hair and the face Mary Willison called nice-ugly which was so singularly an attractive one.

He saw the Rendles at the same moment and hastened forward to conduct them to where his own group was gathered. These were Henry Ashwin, a brother ex-officer of Freddy's on holiday with his vivacious American wife, Major and Mrs Morland who owned an estate in the wine-growing province of Douro, and a young man, Fergus Seton, an under-secretary at the British Embassy who was doing his first tour of foreign duty. Sybil, who had not before met any of them, was gratified; the very type of people she would have chosen to meet.

'Are we all here, Sir Frederick?' she asked when the preliminaries had been completed. 'Shall we go in?'

Whatever these other friends of his might imagine,

she was the principal guest, the party was being given in return for her hospitality and she intended that no one should be under any misapprehension on this point.

'There are three more to come. Here they are—' Freddy hurried away to collect the last of his guests. Sybil's face changed; she stared with astonished displeasure as the Hungarian trio approached.

Count Radizlo looked handsome and debonair in his white tie and tails, a gardenia in his buttonhole; Olga was classically elegant in a clinging, strapless dress with a double row of pearls, pearl earrings, and one or two glittering rings on her slender hands. Tamara wore an ankle length, flared skirt of fine black poplin and a top with a scooped out neckline of white organdie. Her fair, shoulder-length hair with its shallow natural wave was held by a black velvet ribbon, drawn up behind her small ears and tied on the top of her head.

Apparently lacking jewellery, she had fastened a length of the same velvet about her throat and had stitched some sequins to the centre of this necklet in the shape of a star; the ends of the ribbon hung from a tiny bow at the back down to her waist. And clasping each of her wrists was a band of wider velvet also tied into little bows and sprinkled with sequins.

Miranda had seen the simple outfit before, although not with its present embellishments. Tamara had been wearing it at the shipboard dance on the eve of their arrival in Lisbon, and she had worn it again, the sheer top discreetly covered by a small jersey bolero, on the afternoon of Mrs Sangster's at-home. Her only dress-up costume? Bless her, Miranda thought, touched by the necklet and bracelets.

She smiled at the younger girl who gave her a faint, diffident smile in return, very unlike her usual radiance. And as Freddy introduced the Radizlos and the princess to the strangers, adding, 'You know Mr and Mrs Rendle, of course, and Miss Rendle,' Tamara only bowed nervously and made no attempt to come forward.

Remembering the joyous face and eager rush towards herself and Charles in Mrs Sangster's drawing-room, Miranda felt a pang of remorse. She had promised to get in touch with the girl, exchanged addresses and telephone numbers, yet she had done nothing about it. Tamara was evidently feeling snubbed, ill at ease. Miranda went quickly to her.

'I am so glad to see you—I have been meaning to get hold of you but what with one thing and another—'

'Please,' the other protested, 'you have so many friends and engagements, naturally there is no time—'

'Well, I did have to meet a good many of Charles' and Sybil's friends, and when you are a visitor you aren't quite your own mistress. But I have a car of my own now and will be more independent. I want to explore the countryside and would love it if you would come with me. May I ring you up?"

Tamara's rather strained face brightened.

'I shall be most happy. I had feared—but I see it is not so. You are looking lovely, Mees Rendle. Your white dress and the sandals that match your stole—so clear a red—are beautiful and very chic. Everyone here is beautifully dressed; I am sorry I have nothing better to wear—'

'You look sweet,' Miranda declared, 'and exactly right for a girl of your age. Charles,' as her brother joined them, 'doesn't the princess look charming? I'd like a picture of her, just as she is tonight.'

'So should I. Alice in Wonderland, grown up. Which is probably Greek to her,' Charles said with his pleasant smile.

'No, it is not. I have seen that book with its English drawings—so funny—I liked it very much.' She put out her hand and he took it in his warm, friendly grasp.

'And how is the princess? Now that Miranda has settled in, you and she must see something of each other.'

Two pink patches of colour stained Tamara's cheeks.

'I think I am not so well five minutes ago, but now I recover. I have said to myself that you and your sister had forgotten me. But you have not?'

'No, we hadn't forgotten.'

Charles's sister experienced then a disconcerting sensation as if a ghostly finger had lightly tapped her breast. A premonitory tap?

Nonsense.

'Don't be idiotic,' Miranda admonished herself.

All the same, she was conscious of satisfaction a moment later when the young under-secretary approached, saying that the others were making a move into the restaurant. He looked directly at Tamara and she, with every appearance of willingness, went gaily off with him.

As the party of twelve, in twos and threes, threaded their way through the crowd the American Louise Ashwin said in an undertone to her host:

'What fascinating people your Hungarians are,

Freddy. Say nothing to Henry, but I've fallen heavily for the count. As for that adorable princess child with her velvet bows—'

Sybil, beside them, laughed and said without troubling to lower her voice:

'Princess! These people really are priceless. I mean, the way an umpteenth cousin of an umpteenth cousin hangs on to some silly title. Too ridiculous. Oh—' she cast a glance over her shoulder; Tamara was just behind. 'I'm *sorry*. I had no idea—'

You knew dam' well she was there, Freddy commented silently. Fergus Seton looked astounded; Tamara replied lightly:

'Do not be sorry, Mrs Rendle. It makes nothing, what you say,' and went on chattering to her companion.

Freddy suppressed a grin. The girl, no doubt, was simply brushing away, politely, a remark unwittingly overheard, but the rejoiner was capable of a double meaning.

The restaurant, with its vine-trellised walls, small tinkling fountains and banks of flowers was like a glassed-in garden. On a broad dais a Cuban band in white and silver uniforms played a beguiling tango. The table reserved for Sir Frederick Clayton was on the edge of the dancing floor; with the ease of long practice Freddy indicated their places to his guests.

'No dithering,' Miranda approved. 'He's a man who knows his own mind.'

As was customary on such gala evenings, there were favours at each lady's place and tonight, as an innovation, they had been wrapped in coloured paper tied with tinsel ribbon. The idea proved a success so far as

Freddy's table was concerned; amused, and as eagerly as if they expected to find treasures within, the ladies unwrapped their packages.

The contents were varied and showed considerable imagination; minute plastic boxes in the form of flowers, holding face powder; filigree gilt scent bottles; shoulder sprays of spun glass. There was a cry from Tamara as she discovered a little fan made of stiffened black lace.

'Show me—' Miranda bent forward. 'Oh, what a pet of a thing.'

'Is lovely.' Tamara looked across at Charles. 'The fan of the White Rabbit—so very small—but I think his fan was white.'

'I rather think it was,' Charles smiled.

'Why the White Rabbit?' inquired young Seton who sat between the two girls. 'What's it all about?'

'Just a foolishness. Mr Rendle said I looked like Alice in Wonderland.'

'You? Not a bit of it.'

'No? You do not agree?'

He shook his head.

'As I remember, Alice was a plain child.'

'And that is a pretty compliment. Thank you, Mr Seton.'

Louise Ashwin murmured to her neighbour, Charles:

'Cute kid. You certainly have to hand it to these Europeans. Imagine an American or English girl of sixteen, seventeen, whatever she is—'

'The princess is eighteen.'

She gave him a swift glance, struck by something in his tone.

'A girl of eighteen, then, taking a compliment the way she did. The poise of the infant.'

'She is not always poised,' he said, smilingly, and again with that lingering undertone. 'She can behave, at times, like—well, like the impulsive child she is.'

Miranda was dancing with Freddy. Her feet in the small red sandals were light as thistledown; the music was an exaggerated slow blues and she drifted like a leaf in her partner's arms.

'So easy to lead,' he said.

She responded by an upward glance and smile, thinking how wise she had been to clear the air between them. Tonight was the first time since their meeting on board ship that he had spoken to her in that careless, light fashion; the studied civility, masking a reluctance to speak to her at all, was gone. 'He simply takes me in his stride now,' she told herself, 'as he would any other girl.'

'Have you enjoyed it, Miranda?'

'Every minute. A perfect dinner, Freddy, and this marvellous band—it isn't ending, is it? I could go on for hours.'

'The band will go on but I fancy the others have had about enough dancing and would like to look in at the Casino. It was the original plan to wind up there.'

'Of course,' she agreed amenably. 'I had forgotten for the moment.' She waved a hand as Olga and Fergus Seton passed them. 'What a nice boy that is.'

'Yes, he's a good youngster. Going places, too, all set for a jolly fine career.'

Miranda's lashes flickered. A fine career. Freddy

ought to be set for the same thing. Or, since he had no inclination in any such direction, he should at least be attending to his land, making a success of the farm by his own personal effort, doing something to justify his existence. Nature had endowed him well; good looks, superb health, a strong personality and a first class brain. Yet he frittered it all away, bent only upon amusement. Look at him now, neglecting his property, coming out here on the absurd pretence of writing articles, to idle in the sun. Playboy, indeed.

'Anything wrong?' he asked, glancing down at the sober young face.

'No—I was only thinking—'

'Thinking what?'

'Something that is no business of mine.'

'*My* business, then?'

'Your farm,' she said. 'I was wondering why you don't look after it yourself.'

He gave her his graceless grin.

'Why should I, when I can get someone to look after it for me?'

'Yes, but—'

'I'm no advocate of work for work's sake, Miranda, if that's what you are driving at. A dreary code—'

She laughed; he was incorrigible, impervious to the opinion of anyone else and she did not want to appear a tedious bore. If he liked to waste his life, it was his affair.

'I guess you've got something there,' she said and let it go at that.

'Steady,' said Charles, tensing his arm about his partner's waist.

'Oh, my—' Tamara's tone was rueful. 'Is the third

time I do that. I cannot balance; I think this music is too slow for me, I take my step too soon.'

'I don't think much of this music, myself. Creeping around isn't my idea of dancing. Suppose we sit it out.'

'I think we shall have to—' she looked doubtfully across at their table where the Morlands and Sybil and Henry Ashwin were sitting the slow blues out.

'We needn't go back,' he said. 'We'll find some chairs—'

They made their way to a trellised alcove and found two empty basket chairs, half hidden behind the massed flowers. One of the little fountains was close at hand, set in a pool of water-lilies.

'This is better.' Charles drew out his cigarette case. 'You don't smoke; mind if I do?'

'Please smoke, Mr Rendle, then we shall both be comfortable.' With a restful sigh she leaned back against the striped linen cushion.

'Tired, Princess?'

'Not tired. Only so happy. Such a wonderful evening; I have not before been to a party like this.'

'It is your first dance?'

'In Geneva last summer I attended tea dances, but at night, no.'

'Geneva?'

'Where I lived for so many years, with Mama.'

'Would it distress you to tell me something of your life?'

'I am glad to tell you. You know nothing about me, do you?'

Briefly, she told him her story, from the time she had discovered Mama superintending the packing of trunks, to Mama's death and her subsequent wanderings with Bela and Olga.

'And so we come to Lisbon,' she finished, 'and I hope we shall remain.'

It was clear that she and her mother had lived very simply but in comfort during their years in Switzerland; he wondered whether Tamara possessed anything of her own now or was dependent upon the kindness of her mother's old friends, the Radizlos. He knew something of the generosity that obtained among these exiled aristocrats, their loyalty to each other, sharing and sharing alike.

'Are you—have you—' he began, then checked himself, fearing to sound intrusive. She guessed what he meant and was not affronted.

'I am very lucky,' she said. 'There is a sum of money that Mama gave in trust for me to Bela. Enough to pay for my food and where I sleep and to buy the clothes I must have. I cannot buy much; only what is necessary. That is why,' she smiled, disclosing the little milk white teeth, 'I appear tonight as Alice in Wonderland. At first I am sorry, but I think you and your sister like me this way, Mr Rendle.'

'We do.'

'And that also has made me happy.'

He saw that the losses she has sustained and her present hazardous state—for who knew how long the sum of money might last—left her untouched. True, he had seen those big tears that morning on the dock as she watched the meeting between himself and Miranda, but it had obviously been a passing emotion, gone as swiftly as it had arisen. She lived for the day alone; 'so happy' tonight because Freddy had included her in his party and the dress of which she had not been proud was approved.

Innocent, unimaginative child. Sublimely unaware

of the perils which surely surrounded her. His troubled eyes rested upon her as she leant serenely back again, her hands idly playing with the black lace fan. He felt an intense desire to take those small hands in his, never let them go, hold her fast and safely. But all he could do, as the band ceased to play, was escort her back to the table where Sybil eyed them unfavourably and demanded:

'Where have you been? You suddenly vanished—'

'I had to give up trying to cope with that so-called dance,' Charles said.

'But no,' Tamara protested. 'Mr. Rendle is being gallant. I could not balance to such slow music and he had pity for me.'

'Couldn't balance,' Sybil echoed. 'That sounds like too much champagne.'

'Perhaps,' the princess agreed, sweetly indifferent.

'Oh—' Miranda uttered a startled, amused cry. The blues had ended and with her partner she was crossing the floor. 'Freddy—look—at our table—'

'Mrs Sangster, as I live.'

'Then you do see what I see. I didn't believe my eyes. *Mrs Sangster* at a gala dinner dance—'

'She hasn't been dancing,' he grinned, 'or we could never have missed her. I expect she is with some tourist friends who are doing Estoril. What an imposing figure.'

'She certainly is.'

Mrs Sangster was wearing a voluminous dress with modest décolletage and elbow sleeves, of plum-coloured net over satin, and a majestic set—necklace, earrings, wide bracelets and formidable brooch—of garnets surrounded by heavy, beaded gold. Just so, might a mid-Victorian vicar's wife—a well-to-do vicar's wife—have dressed for an evening soirée.

It appeared that Freddy's conjecture was correct. The good lady was acting as courier to some acquaintances from England; they had greatly enjoyed the fessive dinner, had been fortunate enough to catch sight of several ex-Royalties and were going on to have a look at the Casino. She had left them for a few minutes in order to say good evening to her friends over here.

'We're winding up at the Casino too,' Freddy said. 'How about it, everyone? Had enough dancing?'

'I'm all for going,' Louise Ashwin declared.

'And I,' Count Radizlo smiled, 'if it is agreeable to the rest. I have a feeling that this is my lucky night.'

Mrs Sangster regarded him with auntlike severity.

'You would do better to leave the gambling alone, Count, and put your—' she coughed slightly, 'your resources to a wiser use. But I might as well save my breath; you young people won't listen to the advice of an elderly woman.'

'One may not take such advice, Madame,' he answered charmingly, "but I assure you one fully appreciates the kindness of heart that prompts it.'

Mrs Sangster, saying that if no one had any objection they would join forces, signalled to his friends, a pleasant middle-aged husband and wife, and presently they all walked over to the Casino. The Radizlos, and the two Ashwins sought the baccarat room; the others made for one of the roulette tables. As they stood on the fringe of the crowd, awaiting their chance to get in, Miranda said to Tamara:

'Are you going to have a flutter?'

'I should like very much, but I must be content to watch.'

'Good girl,' Mrs Sangster applauded. 'You have the sense not to risk your money.'

Tamara laughed.

'It is not sense, Mrs Sangster. I have no money to risk. Not even a jewel to sell.'

'No jewellery? I should have thought—but I suppose your mother had to dispose of it.'

'Yes, I think so. Mama had very many and such beautiful jewels—they were in the bank in Geneva— but now they are all gone.' She spoke cheerfully, as if this were one of those things that happen and which it is a waste of time to regret.

The crowd about the table shifted and the newcomers pressed in to secure places.

'Come along, Mara,' Freddy called, 'you must try your luck; I'll stake you.'

'I do not know what that is, Freddy.'

'I'll place the bet and you can pay me back and keep the winnings.'

'Oh, how kind—but what if I lose?'

'Then we'll go on until you do win.'

'There's no guarantee of that,' Sybil said. 'People can go on losing all night. Personally, I'd never let anyone stake me. I mean, it is simply—'

Tamara stepped forward.

'Thank you, Freddy. I choose for myself, yes? Please do not move, Mr Rendle,' as Charles made way for her. 'There is plenty of room and I think you may bring me good luck.'

Sybil's mouth tightened. Miranda said hastily:

'That was nice of Freddy. He's the only one of us who knows the princess intimately enough to do it.'

'All I hope,' Sybil retorted acidly, 'is that he won't find himself let in for something. I mean, what does he know of the girl? Personally, between ourselves, I was rather surprised at his asking those three people to-night. I mean, if they turn out impostors—'

Mrs Morland crisply interposed.

'I am sure Frederick would never dream of introducing anyone of whose credentials he was not entirely satisfied.' She turned to Miranda. 'Miss Rendle, there is such a crowd here, shall we see if we can find more room at one of the other tables?'

Miranda, faintly flushing, assented. She understood. Poor Sybil; why must she always antagonize people? She had been so elated at meeting the Morlands and had informed Miranda, during an interval in the powder-room, as to their standing, their fine estate and the famous house parties they gave.

'Now that they've met us as Sir Frederick's guests and know that he and Charles are old friends, we'll be right in with them. They are sure to ask us up to their place.'

Not they, Miranda thought grimly. They have had enough of Sybil already.

She had seen for herself the way in which Charles's friends regarded his wife. Sybil had been welcomed by all of them in the beginning and was still invited to the majority of the parties but there were distinct signs of restiveness among the other women. And what a chance she had had. It wasn't every bride who came out to a foreign city under such auspices. Her husband well established and popular; his greatest friends, the Willisons, leaders of the British set. Sybil's place had been ready and waiting; she had only to make the grade—

'What's the matter with her?' Miranda pondered as she walked off beside the elder woman.

They found a less crowded table, had a number of flutters, and decided it was not their lucky night. As they strolled about, stopping now and then to watch the play, Miranda for the second time uttered a startled exclamation. A man in a neat blue suit was coming towards them; a stock figure with a sharp-featured face.

'What is it?' her companion inquired.

'That man—I thought I had seen him before, digging in Mrs Sangster's garden. But it can't be—'

'It can be, and is,' Mrs. Morland smiled. 'Good evening, Jenks.'

'Good evening, Madame.' He touched the sleek hair at his temple and passed on.

'That is Mrs Sangster's devoted factotum,' Mrs Morland explained. 'Does everything; drives the car, gardens—she has had him for years and he's a privileged servant. Evidently she told him he could come in and have a look round instead of waiting in the car.'

'I see,' Miranda said. He still made her feel creepy, but if Mrs Sangster, sensible and shrewd, had had him in her employ for years he must be a worthy character. Like his mistress, he was not responsible for his looks.

'It is getting late,' Mrs Morland continued. 'I think I must find my husband—'

As she spoke, the baccarat players came in and the others at the roulette table joined them.

'How did you make out?' Charles asked the count.

'Excellently. Tonight I could not do wrong.'

'Nor I,' Tamara cried joyously. 'Bela, Olga, this so kind Freddy staked me and I have won what he says makes fifteen English pounds.'

'Well done, Mara,' the countess said. 'Now you can buy yourself an evening frock and other things that you need.'

'Yes. Is wonderful.'

CHAPTER SEVEN

ON A MORNING some week or so later Miranda, her soft dark hair loose on her shoulders, a little shirred jacket of peach coloured nylon tied with ribbons at the base of her throat, sat propped against pillows enjoying her coffee and rolls.

She had seen a good deal of the princess during this week. On the day after Freddy's party Mary Willison had called up, saying she wanted them to come in that evening for cocktails and asking whether they would mind calling for Tamara and bringing her with them; it was not very far out of their way. Miranda, who answered the telephone, pleased to find that Mary was taking the princess up and knowing that the proposal would not appeal to Sybil, replied that she would call for Tamara in her own car. She had done so, and driven her home again, and after this had taken the younger girl for several drives. She was becoming very fond of her; they were Miranda and Mara to each other now.

On one auspicious afternoon they had chanced to encounter Charles who was walking along the pavement in Rossio Square. He saw them, signalled his sister to stop and, taking the wheel, had driven them up into the hills where, on a pine-scented terrace overlooking the great river the girls drank iced chocolate and consumed quantities of cream-filled meringues.

'What a happy day,' Tamara had said when they left her at her door. 'I cannot find words to thank you for all the pleasure you give me.'

'Poor kitten,' Miranda was thinking as she sipped her coffee, 'it only shows how lonely she must have been before I got round to making friends with her.'

There was a tap on the bedroom door and Charles, as he did each morning, came in with the post. They liked to open their letters from home together and indulge in a brother and sisterly chat free from the interruptions of Sybil. There were several letters for Miranda this morning and also a very large parchment envelope.

'What in the world is this?'

'I can't imagine. I seem to have one, too.'

Miranda looked at the envelope and saw upon it the name of an exclusive and extremely expensive photographer whose studio was in the Rua Garrett.

'Good heavens!'

Instinct informing her, she swiftly slit the stiff paper with the penknife her brother produced. As she expected, the enclosure was a portrait of a young girl, wearing a black skirt and sheer white blouse and velvet necklet, her hair held by a ribbon tied in a bow across the top of her head, velvet bows on her wrists. Across the ivory mount at the bottom, in large, dashing, almost challenging handwriting was the signature: *Tamara*.

'Charles! That child. Spending her money like this—

99

Mary says his prices are fantastic—but isn't it the *most* adorable thing?'

'It is.' He had extracted his own copy and sat gazing down at it.

'There's a note with mine,' Miranda said, and read it aloud.

Dear Miranda,

Your brother and you have said that you wished for a picture of me in the dress I wore that evening at Estoril. I am happy to send them, as small return for your so kind friendship. I hope they will please you.

'Can you beat it?' Miranda demanded colloquially. 'We did say so; do you remember? *She* remembered, and took it seriously. Oh, dear, they must have cost a couple of pounds, if not more, and she needs every penny of those winnings of hers. Mad child—but sweet—'

'It is typical,' Charles said with his slow smile. 'They are like that, these impulsive, irresponsible people. They can't change—'

'I know. Charles—' she stretched out a hand and took his copy from him. 'I'll take care of this. It's sweet and impulsive and a lovely gesture but Sybil might not see it that way. And you could hardly blame her.'

When her brother had left her Miranda sprang out of bed and crossed to the small oak desk, black with age, which she and Charles had discovered during a prowl through an antique shop. Miranda had fallen in love with it, and as she had no sort of writing table in her bedroom Charles had bought it for her. One of its charms was a secret drawer whose mechanisms had been demonstrated to her by the old proprietor; she opened it now, slipped in the second copy of Tamara's photograph and snapped the spring shut.

'*That's* safe,' she said aloud.

She picked up her own copy, smiling and shaking her head at the girl portrayed. Tamara shouldn't have sent one to Sybil's husband but the ethics of the case had evidently escaped her. Affectionate impetuous little creature—not that she was in reality little. One thought and spoke of her as being so but she was nearly as tall as Miranda, a slim and upright young figure with the unmistakable stamp of her ancestry. In general she behaved with the spontaneity of a child but there were occasions when she assumed what Louise Ashwin called poise and Miranda called grownupness. Certainly, there was nothing childlike about that bold signature, the signature of an imperious adult—or a princess. Miranda studied it for a moment with speculative eyes as she placed the portrait on her mantelpiece.

The bedroom door opened without ceremony and Sybil, in dressing-gown and slippers, came in.

'What's that?' she demanded.

'You may well ask,' Miranda laughed. 'I happened to say I'd like a picture of Mara dressed as she was at Freddy's party, and this is the result. She's so grateful because I have taken her for a few drives. Sweet of her —but I hate to think of what it must have cost.'

'Ridiculous get-up. Tying ribbons all over herself. I could hardly keep my face straight when I saw her. And that idiot Charles saying she looked like Alice in Wonderland. I expect that was the idea in sending it to you; so Charles could see it.'

Miranda's lips parted on a suspended breath.

'She's the complete vamp,' Sybil continued. Anything in trousers. Even a dull married man like Charles, even old Mr Willison. I watched her making up to him at Mary's the other evening, talking in that silly way. So hap*pee* to be there, such a love*lee* house—'

Miranda breathed again.

'She can't help her accent, Sybil.'

'She doesn't want to. Knows it attracts the men. She's after Sir Frederick, of course, with the unfortunate Fergus Seton as second string.'

'Young Seton seems very much smitten.'

'More fool he. I mean, the Foreign Office isn't likely to welcome a phoney Hungarian. It would probably finish his career. But that's up to him. I hear that the Morlands have gone back to their country place and took those Ashwin friends of Sir Frederick's with them.'

'Did they? How nice for the Ashwins to visit a Portuguese estate and see the real life.'

'I daresay. It would have been nice for me, too. They could just as well have asked us.'

'Why should they? They only met us that night.'

'They only met the Ashwins that night. Charles has no gumption: I mean, he was simply polite to the Morlands, didn't make the slightest effort—I told him he might sometimes consider my side of things and all he says is, what more could he do? That's Charles all over, never puts his best foot forward, perfectly content to grub along—' she was off on her favourite tack; Charles always let her down, she got no sympathy or support—

'Well,' she finished at length, 'there it is. I must go and have my bath. I suppose Charles has finished shaving by this time.'

One of these days, Miranda silently informed her, I

shall take you by the heels when you are in your bath, and drown you.

Sybil departed, Miranda dressed, wrote a note to Tamara, and went out to her balcony. It was a beautiful day, the hot sun tempered by a breeze. She stood gazing down across the descending rooftops; she had explored the city very thoroughly since obtaining her car, and found every aspect of it pleasing.

It was not, so some of the visitors returning after a lapse of years complained, what once it had been. Its size had doubled during and since the war. The beloved Lisbon of the thirties, soft coloured, a little faded, just a little shabby, peaceful and withdrawn, had blossomed into a modern metropolis. But the Lisbonese had not spoiled their city; old and new were delightfully blended. Houses were still built with traditional pointed gables and lacelike iron balconies, still washed pink and green and blue or covered with tiny glazed tiles.

Along the busy thoroughfares in the centre of the town with their endless procession of handsome cars, up-to-date buses, and pavements crowded with well-dressed men, elegantly clad women and befurbelowed children, the *varinas*, the fisher girls, walked their unconcerned way, wearing their shawls and aprons, their hoop earrings and gold necklaces, baskets of fish nonchalantly balanced on their heads. In the quieter sections unexpected squares had been preserved, pastel-tinted oases of enchanting façades, with sometimes a small church tucked into a corner. And everywhere one came upon the *miradouros*, resting places and lookouts, with a bench or two in the shade of a vine, a bed of flowers and always a cool little fountain. Miranda loved it all; best of all she loved the labyrinths of the old quarters with their shadowy lanes and the gentle, dignified inhabitants among whom it was so safe to wander.

As she stood now on the balcony, the sun warm on her shoulders, she heard Sybil's shrill tones and Charles, who was leaving for his office, replying. A sudden impatience with them both seized Miranda, a sudden desire to get away, out into a fresher air. There was an expedition she had lately had in mind; she would make it today, and alone. Fond though she was of Tamara, she was not in the mood for a chattering young companion.

There was never any difficulty in pursuing her own plans; in this respect, her sister-in-law was the least exacting of hostesses. Sybil was far from adverse to Miranda's being there—in many ways Charles's sister was a social asset—but she had no affection for the girl and no desire for her constant company. Sybil herself filled in her time with housekeeping—she was a very good housekeeper—visits to the hairdresser, manicurist and, five afternoons a week, playing bridge. She belonged to a bridge club; Miranda in a confidential moment had said to Mrs Willison that she wondered how the other members put up with her.

'Well, she's an expert player, and they elected her before they knew what they were in for. I doubt very much, though, that she'll be asked to join again; they re-form each year.'

'Poor Sybil. What a *fool* she is, Mary.'

Mary shrugged.

'It's the way she's made.'

Sybil, today, having a morning appointment for a permanent wave, was lunching in town; Miranda ate her lunch in peace and, a short time later, was driving out of the city.

It happened that on this same afternoon Frederick Clayton was seized by an urge identical with Miranda's; to get out into a fresher air and enjoy his own exclusive company. Having spent some time absorbing local colour in a somewhat peculiar quarter, he was driving down the Avenida da Liberdade, approaching the Rossio, when he saw Charles Rendle coming out of one of the dark, close-aired cafés so dear to the Portuguese heart. Charles waved a hand and Freddy drew up at the kerb.

'Can I give you a lift?'

'No, thanks. I want to walk a bit—been having a chat with Pierera. Funny, the way they prefer to sit indoors in an atmosphere you could cut.'

'Don't they ever sit out at these tables?'

'Very seldom. The tables are for the benefit of other nationals, and the tourists.'

'Curious people, Hallo—here's Mara."

Charles turned quickly about; Tamara was coming towards them.

'And what have you been doing?' Freddy inquired as she stopped beside them.

'Shopping,' she answered buoyantly, 'with the winnings from your stake.'

'Is there any of it left?' Charles asked, smilingly.

'A little.'

'If you have done all your shopping,' Freddy said, 'shall I drive you home?'

'That would be kind—' she glanced sideways at Charles who said, to the other man's considerable surprise:

'Perhaps the princess will come with me and have an ice. I'll see her safely home.'

'I should like—but do you not wish to return now to your office, Mr Rendle?'

'No, I have finished for the day.'

'Then thank you, I should enjoy to have an ice-cream.'

'Right you are.' Freddy let in his clutch, nodded goodbye and drove on, his eyes a trifle thoughtful.

Leaving the city and heading west he eschewed the highway and took the route that follows the river; past Alges with its rose-pink villas, past the vineyards of Carcavelos that sweep down the slope, Estoril descending to the sea and Monte Estoril with its aloes and eucalyptus whose heady perfume enveloped the road. At Cascais, the ancient fortified town, he stopped to have a look at the fortress and the harbour where shawled women and men in big woollen caps were drying their nets, then he went on again.

Now the country changed; the lush growth ended, the breeze had a sharper tang of the sea, mingled with the hot scent of pines. Presently there were no more pines, only a low yellow scrub, and heather and a tumble of sand dunes. There were few people about; apparently no tourists had arrived today, or perhaps they had come and gone for it was nearing sunset. Freddy parked his car and made for the shore.

As he tramped along, rejoicing in the wild and solitary scent after the crowds and bustle of Lisbon, he saw the figure of a girl silhouetted against the sky. She stood with her back to the declining sun and he could not distinguish her face, only that she was wearing big hoop earrings and that her dark hair hung in a loose coil half way to her shoulders. A *varina*—but there was no shawl, no apron—'Well, I'll be—' he ejaculated and instinctively looked for cover. But there was no cover and she must have seen and recognized him.

She stood quite still as he approached; a characteristic of hers, he remembered. As he drew closer he saw that she was smiling, a smile just marked enough to deepen her absurd dimple.

'Hallo, Freddy,' she said. 'You seem to have had the same idea that I had.'

'Really, Miranda.' His tone was crisp. He had wanted no intruder on his refreshing solitude, least of all this girl to whom, although the situation between them was no longer strained, he still had nothing to say. 'Do you mean to tell me you came out here by yourself? What on earth for?'

'What did you come for?'

'A breather. I felt a bit jaded.'

'That's why I came.'

'Are you going back now? You know how quickly it gets dark after sunset.'

'I can't go yet; something's wrong with my car. They are fixing it for me at the petrol station down the road.'

'What went wrong?'

'I don't know. The man said it was nothing much and they'd be able to do it.'

'Don't know? I thought you were such a good driver.'

'I am a very good driver but I'm no mechanic, Freddy. The insides of a car are one of life's great mysteries to me.'

He was not amused.

'You should make it your business to solve that mystery. All drivers should understand the workings of their cars.'

'I expect you are right. Perhaps I had better make

a start at once. I'll go down and see how they are getting on and let you continue your walk. There's a rather marvellous bit of coast farther on; black and savage. It's worth seeing.'

She spoke in her customary unhurried tones, without a trace of umbrage, but he was suddenly ashamed of his ungraciousness.

'Did they tell you at the petrol station how long the repair would take?'

'I don't think it will be ready for another half hour.'

'Then come and show me your piece of coast.'

She gave him a swift, inquiring look from under lashes. He grinned.

'Grumpy, wasn't I? Sorry, Miranda. Will you come?'

She was sure he would prefer going on by himself but to say so, make an issue of it, would be childish and tiresome on her part.

'I'd like to come,' she said.

'Why were you feeling jaded?' he said as they made their way over the barren ground. 'Too many late nights?'

'No, I haven't had any really late nights since your party. I just wanted to shake off everything and everybody for a while.'

'Too much sister-in-law,' he thought.

'I hear you have been taking Tamara out,' he said. 'I looked in at Mrs Sangster's yesterday and she and the Radizlos were there. Mara was full of her drives with you.'

'I've loved having her. I felt rather mean not bringing her with me today.'

'There's no necessity for taking her every time you go out. I saw her today, as well; she was quite happy, spending her winnings she told me.' He did not add that Charles had taken her to have an ice; that was Charles's business.

'How was Mrs Sangster?' Miranda asked. 'Oh—by the way—you remember that man we saw in her garden, the one I said looked like a rat?'

A close observer might have noted a tautening in Sir Frederick's tall figure as he replied:

'Yes, I remember the chap.'

'Did you see him that night at the Casino?'

'At the Casino? No.'

'He was there. It was while you were playing and Mrs Morland and I were rambling around. His name is Jenks and Mrs Morland told me that he has been with Mrs Sangster for years—does everything, acts as her chauffeur—'

'What was he doing in the Casino?'

'Mrs Sangster must have told him he could come in, instead of waiting in the car. Apparently, she thinks the world of him.'

'So much for first impressions,' Freddy said lightly.

'He still gives me the creeps,' Miranda returned. 'I don't like to think of his being her confidential man-servant. It *may* be all right but—'

'If Mrs Sangster has had him for years I don't think we need be alarmed. She's a very capable woman and no fool.'

'I know, but lots of capable women have been taken in by a clever man. He plays up to her and she relies more and more on him and then finds he's been embezzling or something—'

'I shouldn't think he has any facility for embezzling. And he's probably the soul of honesty; why shouldn't he be?'

'It's just a feeling I have. I'd like to find out—I'd like to ransack the whole house, as a matter of fact.'

'What do you expect to find in the house? Jenks running a secret establishment on the top floor?'

She laughed.

'I don't suppose I'd find a thing. But the place does fascinate me.'

'Then keep your illusions. You aren't likely to discover anything more lurid than Mrs Sangster's drawing-room. Isn't that enough for you?'

They trudged on, coming to the place Miranda wanted him to see.

'Grim spot,' Freddy commented.

'I'd love to see it in stormy weather; wouldn't it be terrifying? They say unhappy lovers used to come out here and commit suicide.'

'Did they indeed. And I suppose that fascinates you, too. Come along, Miranda, let's make tracks back again.'

'But you do like it, don't you? It was worth seeing?' The black-lashed eyes were raised to his with the expression of one who displays a treasure and hopes it is appreciated.

'It is well worth seeing but we must go back. Time's getting on; your car ought to be ready by now.'

She assented cheerfully but he felt another twinge of compunction at the thought of her driving home alone. It was her own doing, she had chosen to come out alone; but it seemed a forlorn sort of thing.

'Are you hungry?' he asked abruptly. 'Did you stop anywhere for some tea?'

'No. I stopped to explore but I didn't bother about tea.'

'Neither did I. How about going to have a look at

your car and then sampling one of these taverns? I'm told the food is excellent.'

She looked startled.

'That would be fun—but you don't want to dine at this hour—'

'I want to eat,' he smiled. 'I only had a sandwich for lunch and this air has given me a craving for lobster. Do you like lobster?'

'Adore it.'

'That's settled then. Except—will your brother be worried? I'm not sure that one can telephone in from here.'

'It doesn't matter. Charles and Sybil are going to a dinner the firm is giving for the Staff. I told Charles I might join Mary and some of the others on the beach and we'd probably stay on to dine. So they won't worry.'

They found the car adjusted, said they would call for it later and strolled back towards the lighthouse where a number of *bistros* were dotted among the dunes. As she walked sedately beside him, Miranda marvelled at the changes and chances of life. Incredible, that she and Frederick Clayton who, two years ago had bitterly quarrelled and hoped never to set eyes on each other again and, little more than a week ago had been eyeing each other with mutual disfavour, should be on their way to dinner, alone together, in this highly improbable spot.

Not that she flattered herself. She knew he had asked her on a kindly impulse and would still have preferred his own company. But, again, to refuse would have been childish, an ill-mannered rebuff.

'So here we are,' she thought. 'The last two people—'

'How about this one?' Freddy said. 'Look all right to you?'

She said it did and they entered a dim, low raftered room and were shown by a smiling proprietor to a corner table. Yes, there was lobster, already prepared —the Senhor and Senhora would prefer it grilled? Certainly it should be done for them. And chicken to follow and a bottle of wine of the country.

The lobster, freshly caught, was delicious; so was the peppery chicken. The wine was light and dry.

'Just one glass for me,' Miranda said, 'I mustn't forget I have to drive.'

'If you think you are driving yourself to Lisbon you are mistaken.'

'But I must. I can't leave my car here.'

'You can drive to Cascais and we'll leave it in a garage there. I'll get hold of Seton or someone and run out first thing in the morning to collect it for you.'

'All that trouble? Nonsense. I can perfectly well go back alone tonight. I like driving—and such a short run—'

'Don't argue, Miranda. You may be an expert and all the rest of it but you are coming in my car. We aren't going to form a procession of two—'

'We wouldn't need to do that.'

'*I* would. I'd feel bound to keep an eye on you and I don't propose to put any such strain on myself.'

Her dimple flickered.

'In that case—all right, Freddy. As for collecting the car, Charles will bring me. It's Saturday and we're coming out anyway to Estoril for a swim.'

She left it there, making no more comment one way or the other.

He said to himself that one had to credit her with

being a very easy companion; amenable, and with a composure beyond her years. She had matured astonishingly.

They talked of this and that, presently of Tamara again and the fact that Fergus Seton appeared greatly taken with her.

'It would be a happy solution for Mara if it comes off,' he said.

'It would, indeed. Of course he is very young—'

'They are exactly the right age for each other. It's a great mistake on both sides when a girl falls for a man years older than herself. They don't see alike, think alike—' Freddy was merely voicing an opinion, momentarily forgetting that the girl who faced him across the table had fallen for a man nine years her elder and that it proved a mistake in very truth. He realized what he was saying, and checked himself; the last thing he wanted was to reopen that closed subject. Miranda smiled.

'I couldn't agree more. May I have another half glass of wine, Freddy, as I'm only driving to Cascais?'

'You may.' He filled her glass; he had an obscure feeling that she well deserved it.

'Oh, that's too much.'

'It won't hurt you. And we'll have a big pot of coffee to counteract it.'

They had had to wait for their specially grilled lobster and had not hurried over their meal. It was growing dark; a lantern was lit in the doorway and one or two more in the low room. Only a few people were there besides themselves; Portuguese couples who discussed their own affairs and did not stare at the strangers. The strong hot coffee was brought; Freddy produced cigarettes. Miranda leant an elbow on the table top, her gaze idly following the curling blue smoke. In spite of her conviction that she had entirely disorganized his afternoon, she was enjoying this fortuitous interlude. She liked the bistro that now, with the lanterns casting shadows on the whitewashed walls, took on a romantic aspect; Freddy, whether or not a reluctant host, was, as always, a delightful one.

'He was exasperated when he met me,' she thought, 'it was plain enough. What he wanted was probably a strenuous five-mile tramp and then I sort of gate-crashed—but how beautifully he resigned himself.' A faint, mischievous smile flitted across her face. 'We're both behaving beautifully, playing our parts—two well brought-up people—'

'Dreaming?' Freddy inquired.

'I believe I was, very nearly. The effects of such a good meal.'

'Have some more coffee.'

'Well, if you are going to—'

As he poured the coffee, from somewhere close at hand came the thrumming of a guitar and then a voice raised in song; a long-drawn note, high and clear and indescribably tragic. A hush fell upon the room; the Portuguese people sat intent.

'A *fado*,' Freddy murmured with a rueful grin. Miranda nodded. She knew that this was the music so passionately loved in this country but had not before heard it. The song continued, sweet and anguished, it seemed to be crying all the sorrows of the world. Freddy, who disliked fados, sighed and lit another cigarette; the Portuguese faces were enraptured; Miranda gave a slight shiver. It was getting under her skin, it wailed of things for ever lost, of dead lovers—it was too much—

114

At length it ended. Freddy drew a breath of relief.

'That's over. Shall we make a move before it starts again?'

'Yes. I don't think I could stand any more of it.' She spoke gaily but he saw the glitter on her dark lashes.

'Tears, Miranda?'

'Repressed hysterics.' She brushed a hand across her eyes. 'Of all the *nerve-racking* music. And that is what these people enjoy. Talk about the English taking their pleasures sadly—'

He laughed, signalled the waiter and paid the bill. The guitar throbbed again, high and insistent.

'Quick,' he said, 'or we'll be caught.'

They hurried out and down the road to where Freddy had parked his car, then collected Miranda's.

'You go ahead,' he directed and the procession of two set out for Cascais. They found a garage, left the Citroën and he drove her back to Lisbon.

They did not talk much on the way; Freddy was a fast driver, there was a good deal of traffic and his attention was fully occupied. Miranda, seated beside him, reflected again on the queer twists of life. Here she was, in the very car in which, two years ago, she had so frequently been driven, the car that had been the initial cause of the broken engagement between them. She wondered whether the same thought had occurred to Freddy.

When they reached the old converted mansion she asked him politely if he would come up and have a drink.

'No, thanks very much. I must get on.'

'Then thank *you* very much for a delicious dinner, and for bringing me home.'

'Not at all. Nice of you to stay and try out the tavern with me. Goodnight, Miranda.'

'Goodnight.'

He got into his car again and drove off, with something of the briskness of a man who has done his good deed.

Miranda went up to the flat; Charles and Sybil had not as yet returned from the Staff entertainment. In her bedroom she stood by the window opening upon the balcony, looking down at the lights of the city, wondering what gay friends Freddy was joining. For him, who kept late hours, the evening was doubtless just beginning; for her, it was over. She stirred restlessly; I wish——but she didn't know what she wished.

Not for Frederick Clayton; not for the man she knew him now to be. A charming idler, and unconscionable egoist——for what else was a man whose object in life was his own amusement? No staying power, incapable even of sustained affection.

'For he couldn't really have loved me,' she told herself, 'No one who really loved a girl would have let her go, as he did, without so much as a second attempt.' If he had given her time to recover——after all she was only nineteen——and then once more approached——but he had not done so.

No, it wasn't the unstable Freddy she wanted, a man one could not resist liking but could never respect. Then what was it? Why this sudden restlessness?

'I don't know what's got *into* me,' she said. 'I expect it is just a hankering to go on somewhere, make a night of it as he is doing.'

Meantime, Freddy had driven to a certain bar frequented by members of the British community. As usual, it was well filled; he stood for a moment surveying the cheerful assemblage, then strolled to the bar counter where several men whom he knew were standing.

'Hallo, Clayton.' A lean, grey-haired man made room for him.

'Good evening, sir.'

'How are the articles coming on? Still collecting local colour?'

'Him and his articles,' a voice farther down the line jeered. 'I'll believe in them, Freddy, when I see them in print.'

'Wait for it, then, Bill.'

'I'm not likely to live long enough.'

'You misjudge me.' Freddy ordered a beer.

'So you have something to work on, have you?' the elderly man pursued under cover of the general medley of voices.

'I believe so. Of course, I'm working on a hunch—'

The other nodded, rather dubiously.

'You may be right, although I can't for the life of me see what put the idea into your head.'

'I could be wrong,' Freddy countered, 'and I'm not as yet prepared to say how and where the idea come to me.'

'Quite. I'm not pressing you. I only hope it's the right track, although you can understand one's concern for a very innocent party.'

'I understand perfectly, sir. I'm concerned, myself.'

'Well—' the elderly man set down his empty glass. 'Get on with it—no, I won't have another, thanks, I'm due at home—' he said goodnight and departed. Freddy chatted for a time with various acquaintances, then made his own departure.

CHAPTER EIGHT

'GIVE ME your parcels,' Charles said to Tamara as
Freddy drove away. 'There's a café a little farther on
where they serve superlative ices, according to my
sister.'

She handed him her two flat packages and they
made their way along the beautiful avenue lined with
palms and acacias and jewelled with glowing beds of
flowers.

'I like so much this Avenida da Liberdade,' Tamara
said.

'It is very fine. The Champs Elysées of Lisbon.'

'Is better than the Champs Elysées, I think. Not so
magnifique but more *sympathique*.' She used French
words when their English equivalents, although she
knew them, came less readily to her eager tongue;
Tamara spoke as quickly as Miranda spoke deliberately. 'But as for that, she continued, 'I find it so with
all this city.'

'It seems to you a sympathetic city?'

'Yes. Perhaps because I have found so many good
friends. You and your sister, and kind Mrs Sangster
and the Willisons, and Freddy who asked me to his
party where I meet more nice people—'

He thought: we Rendles haven't been very good
friends to her. A few drives in Miranda's car—and
not so much as a cup of tea in our own house. He won-

dered what Tamara herself though of this lack of hospitality; perhaps Sybil could be persuaded to include the Radizlos and the princess in the cocktail party she was shortly giving. She had declared she wasn't going to take up Sir Frederick Clayton's Hungarian protégées, but now that Mary and some of the others in Mary's set were doing so, she might reconsider.

'In Paris,' Tamara was saying, 'we knew only exiles like ourselves, and in London no one. Lisbon is best.'

'Well,' he smiled above his uncomfortable reflections, 'British people are generally more forthcoming in a foreign country. Here we are—' they had reached the café and sat down at one of the table on the terrace. 'What will you have? Chocolate, strawberry, vanilla—'

'Chocolate, please.'

'And cakes? Miranda tells me they make some special concoctions of almond paste—'

'They sound wonderful.'

He ordered the ice-cream and cakes and, since he had to have something, a sherbet for himself.

'How pleasant it is here,' Tamara said, leaning back in her small chair. She was wearing a flax blue cotton skirt, full and not short, and a sleeveless white top with a Peter Pan collar. The rounded bare arms were already dusted with tawny gold from the Portuguese sun; she wore no hat, her hair was tied back by a narrow blue ribbon. She looked very young and very fresh in her simple dress that, doubtless made by herself, could have cost no more than a few shillings.

Charles felt a tug at his heart. Nothing could have become her better or been more suitable for a bright summer day but the implication was there, as it had been on the night of Freddy's party. She had so little, this Cinderella princess, and so cheerfully made the best of what she did have.

'And now,' he said, when their order had been placed before them, 'I have to thank you for a most delightful surprise this morning.'

'It pleased you, Mr Rendle?'

'Very much indeed. A charming photograph and a perfect likeness. Miranda has written you, on behalf of us both; it was extraordinarily sweet of you to send them to us.'

'You said you wished for them and I was so happy to do it.'

'I'm afraid it made a large hole in those winnings of yours, Princess.'

'Not so large. Please, do not continue to call me Princess. Miranda and all my new friends have stopped doing so.'

'Shall I say Mara, as the others do?'

'Not Mara. Not my *petit nom* that is used by everyone and means nothing.'

He felt an obscure sense of warning, of something that ought to be stopped here and now. But he told himself not to be ridiculous and said, lightly:

'Tamara, then. I don't care for nicknames myself. I refuse to answer to Charlie.'

'Charlie! Oh, my, how could anyone call you that?'

'They don't after the first time.'

'I am glad you are firm, Mr Rendle.'

'Mr Rendle? If I am to call you Tamara—'

The brown eyes with their short, thick, darker brown lashes, so piquant a feature in contrast with the fair hair, gave him a quick look, half laughing, half serious.

'I shall still say Mr Rendle. It is not yet time, I think, for me to say Charles. It would be incorrect.'

He was conscious of relief. It might not be incorrect but it would certainly astonish and annoy Sybil to hear him addressed by this girl as Charles.

'Just as you like,' he said. 'I see you treat your elders with proper respect.' The obscure something that had troubled him made him glad to emphasize the difference in their ages.

She remained unimpressed.

'You are not so much my elder. You are only a few years older than Fergus Seton, and younger than Freddy, and she took a spoonful of ice-cream, savouring it with relish.

Charles gave it up.

'Have some more of these things.' He pushed the plate of cakes towards her.

'But I am eating them all."

'That's what you're supposed to do. I'm not a great sweet-eater.'

'And what you want now is to smoke, yes?'

'No hurry.'

'Please do. Then I shall not feel I must hurry, and can eat all these so good sweets.'

He lit a cigarette and watched her as she disposed of the rich concoctions with youthful appetite.

'How about another ice?' he suggested.

'No, thank you. Even my greediness has an end.' She looked regretfully at her empty plate. 'Pleasant things end too soon; I wish it were just beginning. It has been so enjoyable; my first visit to a café on this beautiful Avenida.'

He felt a glow invading him; her pleasure and appreciation were heartwarming. Charles, since his marriage, had become accustomed to rebuff rather than appreciation, his every effort a dismal failure. Darling child; a few cakes and a chocolate ice on a café pavement, and she was radiant. He thought of how happy a thing it would be to give her greater and less fleeting pleasures; to give her, above all, the security she so woefully lacked.

He lit a second cigarette, guessing that this was what she hoped he would do, prolonging her enjoyable hour. In the centre of the avenue people strolled under the trees or rested on the benches; Portuguese women, who allowed no concession to summer heat, dressed in Paris gowns of silk and lace, many with glittering jewels, their faces heavily made up, their coiffures immaculate under flowered Paris hats; sallow, black-eyed children in starched white walking sedately beside them; plump nurses, their abundant, satin-smooth hair drawn back into huge buns, carrying bundles of lacy frills from which peeped baby faces; a sprinkling of tourists, coolly but, in deference to Portuguese prejudice, adequately clad. Tamara, leaning back again, her hands restfully crossed in her lap, watched it all with serene eyes; he wondered what sort of life she lived in the crowded dwelling among her compatriots, and asked a discreet question or two.

She answered readily as she always did, telling him that everyone there was nice to her and that she had a room of her own. She did not know very much about the others; sometimes they were in, sometimes out. The men procured odd jobs from time to time; several of the women were employed in the showrooms of dressmaking or millinery establishments. Some still had jewellery to dispose of; they all hoped eventually to obtain visas for North or South America where they confidently expected to find El Dorado.

A happy-go-lucky lot, and kind in their careless fashion to Tamara. But he gathered that, as the only young creature in the house—the others being at least in their thirties—she was in general left to her own devices. She must have many lonely days and lonelier evenings. He saw, too, that although she lived for the moment, ardently and touchingly giving herself to any small diversion that came her way, she lived also in the shadow of apprehension, fearing that Bela would once again decide to move on. It was all wrong—'And I can't do a thing about it,' he thought with a miserable sense of frustration. Then he sharply called himself to order. Tamara was not his responsibility, not in any way his business.

He stubbed out the cigarette.

'I think perhaps we had better—'

'Yes,' she agreed, 'it is time to go.'

'I'll call a taxi; my car is out of commission today.'

'I could go back the way I came, Mr Rendle, by bus.'

'You could, but you aren't being allowed to.'

Tamara wasn't his responsibility but he was seeing her safely home. He hailed a passing taxicab and they got in and were whirled away. She sat relaxed in her corner, the full skirt spreading about her slim young legs, her bare arms with their patina of dusky gold again lightly crossed. She did not chatter; Charles, for his part, was ill at ease. He was taking her home, yes, rounding off the episode in the correct manner, but it seemed to him a poor performance to leave it at that. Nothing further suggested, none of the usual 'We'll be seeing you' sort of thing, no hospitality offered. A flat goodbye, and no more. She had sent him, and Miranda, her photographs, she innocently believed them to be her friends. Miranda *was* her friend but the Rendle doors remained closed to her. What did she—what could she think of it?

They arrived at the steep little street and drew up at the house.

'Thank you so much,' she said as they stood together on the pavement, holding out her hand to him in her cordial, un-English fashion, 'for a lovely afternoon.'

'I am so glad—I enjoyed it, too,' he said, jerkily.

If she thought this insufficient, if she expected something more, she gave no sign. The brown eyes raised to his were unclouded, the distracting little teeth showed in the gayest of smiles.

'I think you did not very much enjoy the sherbet; you ate it only to be polite. Oh—my parcels—' they had been left on the seat of the cab. Charles extracted them.

'How I am careless.' She took them from him.

'My fault,' he said. 'I was carrying them.'

'So. We will not make an argument while the meter of your taxi ticks on. Goodbye, Mr Rendle.'

'Goodbye, Tamara.'

He stood watching her as she ran up the shallow steps and opened the unlocked door. She turned to wave, he waved back, the door closed behind her.

Sybil was at home when he reached the flat, having arrived a few minutes earlier.

'Is that you, Charles?' She came into the hallway. 'Have you got the car back?'

'No, they are giving it a thorough cleaning. It won't be ready until tomorrow.'

'You should have taken it in before it got into such

a state. That's you all over, Charles; always putting things off—'

She was wearing a suit of beige canvas-weave linen, the skirt tight and short, the jacket basqued, and an immense cravat wound about her throat and tied in a knot with long ends. The outfit was undeniably *dernier cri* and had been imported, or very skilfully copied, but it did not suit the stocky, short-necked figure. Her hair, newly cut, was tortured into a myriad stiff, ridged curls; her round face, flushed from the heat, looked froglike as it always did above her fashionable choking collars.

Charles had an instant's vision of a flowing blue skirt, a little sleeveless bodice, fair hair tied back and falling in soft, shallow waves. A vision cool, sweet, refreshing—

'Well, don't stand there like an owl,' his wife said impatiently. 'We have to change and there isn't too much time. You know how long it always takes you.'

'Right.' He gave her his quiet smile and went on to his dressing-room.

Sybil looked after him with a dissatisfied face. You never got any change out of Charles, he refused to argue, far less to quarrel, it was like beating your head against a wooden post. '*Superior*,' she said to herself with a tightening mouth.

The theory advanced by Mary Willison to Frederick Clayton in regard to this marriage was substantially correct. Charles, in brief, had one day discovered himself engaged to a young woman of whom he knew nothing save that she had a pair of big, round kitten's eyes in a small round pussy-cat face, played a good hand at bridge—with Mr Willison and another passenger they had played bridge on the trip from Barce-

125

lona—and that life had given her a raw deal. He was not the first man to find himself thus entangled, with barely a clue as to how it had come about. Some men would have set about extricating themselves but to Charles Rendle, chivalrous and quixotic to a fault, such an idea did not present itself. He had misled Sybil, he owed her a debt and must fulfil it.

He was less dismayed than might have been expected. He wasn't in love with her but he was not and never had been in love with anyone else. He liked girls, as any normal young man does, but they had played a very minor part in his life; two years of war, a return to his interrupted studies, the obtaining of his engineering degrees and subsequent making good in his job had absorbed all his energies and interest; the emotional side of his nature was unawakened.

Sybil's pretty face and plump little figure—she hadn't thickened and grown stocky until some time afterwards—definitely attracted him; he saw nothing of her temper; her unhappy experience roused his instant sympathy; as Mary put it to Freddy, she was someone small and hurt. If, in the end, she had misinterpreted him, jumped to a conclusion for which there was little or no justification, the fault was not hers. He alone was to blame; and to let her down, trusting and believing in him as she did, was out of the question.

When she arrived in Lisbon and he took her to the Willisons who had offered to put her up, he hardly recognized her. There was now no trace of pathos; she exuded complacency, even arrogance. In vulgar parlance she had got her man; a young man with money into the bargain; there was no more need to restrain her natural proclivities and the essential Sybil could have full play.

She swelled with importance, and made a point of aggressively disagreeing with Mary to whom she had taken a dislike at sight. 'She thinks she is a little tin god because her husband is wealthy; doesn't she know that Charles has a lot of private means? I'll show her ladyship, put her in her place—'

This spirited intention suffered a check when she saw the flat Charles had taken and Mary herself had helped him to find. The charm of the lovely old place was lost upon her; her taste was for all that the word plush implies and she was outraged. So this was what Mrs Willison, who had a grand house in a grand quarter, thought good enough for Mrs Charles Rendle.

She declared that she would not live in it, Charles must find something better but Charles, whose gentleness did not stem from weakness, stood firm. Flats were hard to come by, they were lucky to have one at all. When she pointed out that they could well afford a house in one of the fashionable sections he replied, as she had told Miranda, that for a young junior in the firm to branch out in so blatant a fashion would be bad taste.

She was forced to give way, bitterly observing that Charles might as well be a mere salaried employee for all the show he made; people would never guess that he had money. She made it her business to inform her new acquaintances on this subject whenever opportunity arose, but it wasn't the same thing as *showing* them. It was a bad start to their life together and Sybil's temper, a naturally malignant one, was not improved because Charles refused to play. He met her nagging with imperturbable good humour; when she flew into a rage, as she not infrequently did, he merely looked at her, saying nothing, of all attitudes the most frustrat-

127

ing. She saw how highly his friends valued him and grew jealous, barely conscious of what ailed her but with a blind instinct to assert herself and strike at something that threatened her ego. These manifestations developed by degrees, in the months that followed.

Meantime, during the interim period before the marriage arrangements were completed, the two Willisons eyed the situation with increasing misgivings.

'Of all the wretched women,' Mary said to her husband. 'She's far worse than I expected from what you told me about her. Can't we stop it, John? Bring Charles to his senses?'

'We can't interfere. It is Charles's business. After all, he's twenty-seven, old enough to form his own judgments.'

'What's twenty-seven? He's nothing but an idealistic boy, and that woman will never see thirty again; she's probably more than that. She will spoil his life; a nagging shrew if ever I saw one.'

'But we cannot live his life for him, my dear. And perhaps,' said Mr Willison without much conviction, 'we are taking too serious a view. Young women are often nervous and touchy immediately before their weddings. When she is married and settled down, matters may improve. You'll give her a chance, Mary, for the boy's sake? You won't prejudice anyone in advance?' He knew his wife's lively and indiscreet tongue.

'I'll give her a chance. I'll launch her, introduce her —I only hope my friends will forgive me—and keep the peace with her myself.'

So Charles and Sybil were married, and Sybil was duly launched, and Charles gave no sign that he found his marriage other than a happy one, exposing to the world that steady, kindly, impenetrable front, exciting the admiration or, conversely, the exasperation of all who cared for him.

Miranda, standing restlessly in her balcony, heard the asthmatic whine of the ancient lift and its grunt of relief as it achieved the top floor. She brushed her hands back across her hair as if brushing away something that must not be seen, and ran to the drawing-room, snapping on the lights.

'Hallo, you two,' she said as her brother and sister-in-law appeared. 'I was beginning to think you were never coming home.'

'Been alone long, poppet?' Charles poured a tonic water for his wife and one for himself.

'Only about half an hour. How did the party go?' Charles looked tired, Miranda thought; his eyes, grey and black-lashed like her own, a little strained. Something must have upset Sybil again and she had been taking it out on him.

This, however, did not appear to be the case; Sybil was in a highly complacent humour.

'It went off very well,' she said. 'The Staff were so pleased; we all stayed on for a while after the dinner and I danced with several of them and went into the Paul Jones. It didn't hurt me; I mean, as I said to Lady Brewster—' Sir Robert Brewster was the head of Charles's firm—'it meant so much to them, they were simply thrilled.'

'They must have been,' thought Miranda sardonically.

'Charles did his duty, too,' Sybil continued, 'and then we went home with the Brewsters and played bridge. Major and Mrs Morland were there.'

'The Morlands? Back in Lisbon again?'

'They are always coming to and fro, it seems,' Charles said. 'Mrs Morland asked about you, poppet; apparently she's taken a fancy to you.'

'She entertains a lot,' Sybil explained, 'and Miranda's a girl fresh from home, a new face. People are always trying to get hold of someone new. I told her I was giving a cocktail party for you, Miranda, and we'd be pleased to see her and the Major if they were still in town. She said they'd still be here and would be glad to come. Mary Willison *will* be surprised; she never introduced me to the Morlands; looks on them as her own preserve, I suppose.'

'We'll put one over Mary, then,' Miranda smiled. So this was the reason for Sybil's good humour.

'The only thing is,' Sybil continued, 'I happened to mention I had asked Sir Frederick and his friends the Ashwins and we got on to Sir Frederick's party that night and Mrs Morland said how attractive those Hungarian people were, she wants to meet them again. I had no intention of taking them up—I know you run the girl around in your car, Miranda, but that's nothing to do with me—'

Charles made as if to speak; his sister flashed him a glance.

'Why should you take them up, Sybil? There's no necessity; they are being invited to all sorts of houses now. If Mrs Morland wants to meet them, she has only to ask Mary or Freddy or some of her other friends.'

It worked, as Miranda had hoped. Sybil wasn't going to be left behind. If the Radizlos and the girl who called herself a princess were becoming the fashion—

'Personally,' she said, 'I don't bow and scrape to foreigners just because they have titles; I'm not that kind. But as I'll probably keep meeting them, it may be a bit awkward. I'll ask them to come, on Friday; it will please Mrs Sangster, too.' Sybil always professed extreme regard for Mrs Sangster; chiefly, Miranda uncharitably suspected, because the elder lady was plain, dowdy, and could in no way be considered a rival.

CHAPTER NINE

MIRANDA PAUSED for a moment to take stock of the party. She had been a trifle nervous about it, fearing that certain people invited might refuse, those restive ones who were betraying that they had had about as much of Charles Rendle's wife as they could stand. But nearly everyone had accepted and the room was gratifyingly filled.

Sybil, flushed with success, was explaining to Mrs Morland that this flat was a temporary makeshift, she was looking for a house in the Park section; Mrs Sangster had buttonholded the Major, no doubt urging upon him the claims of some of her refugees. Charles was introducing various people to Louise and Henry Ashwin; Tamara and the Radizlos had not yet appeared, nor had Freddy Clayton—yes, here was Freddy, coming in through the doorway now. Sybil advanced to greet him and Miranda joined her.

'How is the Citroën behaving?' he asked. 'I heard from Charles that you retrieved it safely on Saturday.'

'We did, and it is behaving very well.'

Miranda was wearing a cocktail frock of grey lace,

and pinned to the lace below her left shoulder was a brooch in the form of a large, flat star, a fine diamond embedded in its centre, and each point tipped with a smaller diamond. Something in her attitude, in the way she wore it, caught Freddy's attention; he guessed that it was a new acquisition and she, immensely proud of it. A word of appreciation was clearly called for. 'What a charming brooch,' he said. 'Antique, isn't it?'

'Yes.' Her slim fingers went up to touch it. 'Second-hand, at any rate. The stones are real,' she said naïvely.

'So I see. And who has been giving you diamonds?'

'It's from Charles and Sybil. A birthday present. This is my birthday party.'

As she spoke, she remembered that it was on a former birthday that she and Freddy Clayton had first met. Her lashes flickered and she cast him an involuntary self-conscious glance. But the fact held no significance for Freddy; he had forgotten, if indeed he had ever known. She could not recall whether or not she had told him on that bewitched evening.

He said, pleasantly:

'Why didn't Charles let me know? I should have come armed with a floral tribute.'

'That's just why we didn't let anyone know.'

'It's a very good piece,' Sybil said of the brooch, 'but it doesn't show up properly on that dress. I can't imagine why Miranda chose a grey one; only blondes can wear grey, it is all wrong for brunettes. I mean, even I wouldn't dream of wearing it, although there are a lot of gold highlights in my hair.'

Instantly bored, which was the unfortunate effect Sybil had upon him every time she opened her mouth, Freddy replied:

'That rather depends on the colour of the bru-

132

nette's eyes, doesn't it? Well, many congratulations, Miranda—' he moved on in his easy way, to speak to someone else.

Charles, circulating among his guests, seeing that empty glasses were refilled, stopped at the far end of the room for a chat with Mrs Sangster who now sat in state in one of the few armchairs.

'Sybil tells me she has invited the Radizlos,' Mrs Sangster was saying.

'Yes. They haven't turned up yet.'

'These people have no idea of time. I must say, that is something you must learn in Diplomatic circles; absolute punctuality. Not one minute after the hour, not one minute beforehand, as my husband used to say.'

In actual fact, although Charles and the majority of the British community were unaware of it, the late Mr Sangster could hardly have been called a Diplomat; he had been engaged in the export and import business and had represented some South American Republic as pro-consul. But this was all past history, and if his widow had increased his stature with the passing years, no one was any the worse. It was a harmless little fable, to which the one or two old friends who knew the true version were very willing to subscribe.

'Must have taken some doing,' Charles commented, 'to cut it as fine as that.'

'Only a matter of training. It is just as easy to form a good habit as a bad one. Ah, here are our dilatory pair—' He turned to see that the Radizlos had arrived and were talking with the Ashwins and Mrs Morland. He shook hands with them, signalled the maid Maria with her tray, and looking towards the doorway caught sight of Tamara speaking to Sybil and Miranda. He threaded his way to them; she looked up, saw him and, not rushing as once before she had rushed, but was an indescribable air of content, stepped forward and gave him her hand. Miranda blinked; she had experienced a momentary illusion that Tamara had walked straight into Charles's arms.

'So you got here at last,' he said in his friendly fashion. 'We had almost given you up.'

'Is Olga,' she laughed. 'Bela and I were ready, but always one must wait for her. What a lovely room this is, Mr Rendle.'

'You like it?'

'Who would not like it? So beautiful but with air of home and—' she used the word she had used a day or so earlier '*sympathique*. It must be great happiness to live in such a place.'

'That's a matter of opinion,' Sybil said.

'Please?'

'I'm afraid my wife doesn't altogether agree with you,' Charles explained, with a smile at Sybil.

'Personally,' she returned, 'I think it quite frightful. But my tastes don't run to this converted farmhouse kind of thing.'

'Is it so?' Tamara's tone was polite but expressed unmistakable indifference to Mrs Rendle's tastes; indifference, in fact, to the very existence of Charles's wife. Miranda was irresistibly reminded of that challenging signature at the foot of the princess's photograph. Hastily, she said:

'I love your frock, Mara. It looks like Paris, to me.'

'Is a copy of one from Paris.'

The frock was organdie, pale pink dotted with deeper pink; it had short, puffed sleeves and a bouffant skirt.

'I am glad you approve,' Tamara continued. 'I wished for one truly good dress.'

'You couldn't have done better. You can wear it any time, anywhere; afternoon or evening.'

'Is also *pratique*. It will wash.' She looked at Charles. 'This was in the big flat box.'

'What box?' Sybil demanded.

'One I caried one day when I meet Mr Rendle and Freddy. They ask what I am doing and I tell them, spending my winnings from Freddy's stake.'

'Come and show it to Freddy, then. He has a proprietary interest.' Miranda linked an arm, a somewhat firm arm, in Tamara's and drew her away.

Freddy, who could be counted upon to play up, admired the frock in most satisfactory terms; Fergus Seton joined them; Miranda said:

'Fergus, will you look after the princess? Get her a drink and some doodahs; if you go into the dining-room you'll find a whole tableful.'

The two went off together. Freddy grinned.

'Matchmaking, Miranda?'

She answered, rather soberly: 'Doing my best.'

'I'm glad you are taking an interest in her,' he said. 'She needs a friend, poor forlorn child.'

Child? Miranda echoed inwardly. I wonder. I'm not so sure.

The cocktail party had passed its peak; dusk was pressing at the windows and amber lamps bloomed softly in the long, low room. Most of the guests, including young Fergus Seton, were gone, but Major and Mrs Morland, the Willisons, Mrs Sangster and the Radizlos and one or two others still lingered. There were sufficient chairs now for all who cared to sit down;

Charles had refilled such glasses as wanted filling; fresh cigarettes were lit. It was no longer necessary to shout against a barrier of voices, and scraps of conversation floated on the air above the general murmur.

''Yes, to Switzerland for a week or so—the Children's Village—such a wonderful organization, I'm hoping to—'

'So you are convent bred, Miranda—I'm going to call you Miranda—'

'Personally, Major, I've always been used—my husband simply doesn't appreciate—Charles! I asked you to draw the curtains—'

'On my way, Sybil.'

'Please do not pull this one, Mr Rendle. Is so lovely to look down at the lights of the city. Will you point out to me what we see from here? I cannot tell which way we are facing.'

Charles pulled the other curtains and joined Tamara by the window at the far end of the room. Mrs Morland continued to interrogate Miranda, patently approving of Miranda's replies. Mary Willison watched them with amused eyes; Adelaide Morland, as Sybil had said, entertained a great deal and was always on the lookout for a fresh face, but there was more to it than that in the present case, or Mary was much mistaken.

Freddy Clayton strolled over and took the empty chair beside her; she was seated a little apart, and momentarily alone.

'What are you smiling to yourself about?'

With a flicker of her eyes she indicated the elder woman and the girl. At the same moment Mrs Morland's voice, assured, rather loud, the typical voice of

136

an English châtelaine, rose again above the chatter of the rest.

'So you are content to help your aunt run her house instead of rushing out to model frocks or some such nonsense. How refreshing.'

'Adelaide is putting Miranda through a cross examination,' Mary said.

'So I hear. But they both look pleased enough. Rather nice for Miranda if the good lady has taken to her; she may ask her up for one of the famous weekends.'

Mary's eyes twinkled.

'I am sure she will.'

'Why does it amuse you?'

'Adelaide has a son, remember?'

'A son?' Freddy echoed, rather sharply.

'Didn't you know?'

'As a matter of fact, yes, but it barely registered. Morland and his wife are old friends of my people, but I hadn't met them until I came to Lisbon; brought a letter to them. They very kindly stood me a dinner at the Aviz last time they were down and I asked them out to Estoril.'

'Didn't the Ashwins mention young Morland? They spent a couple of days up there.'

'I haven't seen Louise and Henry since they got back, until this evening. What's the son like?'

'A very fine boy and extremely capable. He runs the whole place and seldom if ever comes to Lisbon. Works as hard as his labourers; they do, you know, these big Portuguese landowners.'

'He isn't Portuguese and his father is rolling in money; all sorts of interests outside this country. What's the idea, slaving away like that?'

'Love of the land. He's heart and soul bound up in the old family estate.' The Morlands, in addition to a large tract in the arid vine-growing province of Douro, owned another property in beautiful fertile country which Mrs Morland, whose family had long been established in Portugal, had inherited from her father.

'How old is this paragon?'

'Twenty-six or seven. Adelaide is anxious to see him married; Jim is the only child and she wants grandchildren; a grandson in particular.'

'And you think Miranda is being vetted for the part of daughter-in-law?'

'I do think so. Adelaide wants her son to marry, but she has definite ideas as to the type of girl he chooses; someone who will be content to live up country and devote herself to the life there. It would be an excellent match for Miranda and it is time she was settled. She's getting on—'

'Good heavens, Mary! She is only twenty-one, today.'

'I know. But girls are marrying at eighteen these days. I can't imagine why she hasn't been snapped up long ago. She's unusually attractive.'

Quite, thought Freddy. And no doubt plenty of men had found her so, but had sheered off when they discovered how exigeante and unreasonable she could be.

'Anyhow,' Mary concluded, 'let us hope she and Jim will fall for each other. He's a thoroughly nice person and I'm sure Miranda would prove a worthy successor to Adelaide. Those old homesteads are really feudal and the wife of the owner has an important role. Besides—' Mary's eyes softened as her glance strayed to the far window, 'it would mean everything to Charles to have his sister established out here. He adores her, and he needs every bit of comfort he can get.'

'How true. Well, if Miranda sees fit to bury herself on a Portuguese farm in order to comfort her brother—' Freddy dismissed the subject with an indifferent shrug. But he felt decidedly ruffled. While Miranda and her affairs could hardly concern him less, this high-handed 'vetting' of her went against his grain. He disliked the thought of the girl's beng invited to the Morlands', accepting in all innocence, unaware of her hostess's ulterior motive. Thrown at the son's head— He didn't much care for the sound of Jim Morland, either. He might be a very decent chap in his way, but a man whose sole apparent interest in life was slaving on his land seemed to Freddy a pretty grim proposition as a husband for any girl.

'Yes, those are the riding lights of ships,' Charles was saying. 'We get a sight of the Tagus from here.'

'Is wonderful view. Down and down—' she gave a little shiver.

Charles's hand closed on her arm.

'Come back. Do heights affect you that way?'

'Le vertige? Oh no. But if I were in grief and stood at this window, at night, I think perhaps—' she looked up at him and he saw her young face sombre as he had never before seen it, the brown eyes darkened until they appeared black. He caught a glimpse of the Slavic propensity for sudden, irrational tragedy, as characteristic as the irresponsible gaiety. There was nothing childlike about her at this moment and he was troubled by the aspect of an unsuspected Tamara. The possibilities, the unplumbed depths—he had thought of her as wholly on the surface, a shallow, sunshiny little stream rippling unconcernedly along—He said, hurriedly:

'But you are not unhappy—'

'What have I to make me happy?'

Charles drew a breath.

'Little enough, God knows. But I supposed—you have always seemed—'

'You would care, if I were grieving?'

'I should care very much.' The words spoke themselves.

'And if I threw myself down there?'

'Don't talk like that,' he said on a note of harshness.

'You cannot bear to hear it?' as suddenly as it had been assumed the tragic mask lifted, the brown eyes filled with light. 'So, I am happy then. And I shall not throw myself from your window.'

'On second thoughts,' a voice behind them put in, 'it's not a very sound idea.' Freddy Clayton had approached, unobserved, as they stood looking out into the night. They turned to face him, Tamara flashing, Charles with a strained expression. Freddy's gay eyes, a little quizzical, went from one to the other. 'Mara, Mrs Willison would like a word with you; she's thinking of getting up a picnic—'

'I will go to her—' She ran off in a whirl of pink skirts. Charles, with an abrupt gesture drew out his cigarette case, offered it to his friend.

'Thanks. Has Mara been treating you to dramatics? They are rather given to it, these charming people.'

'No, no. Nothing of the sort. She had a touch of vertigo, though she won't admit it.'

'I see. Dangerous thing, that. I knew a chap once who was subject to it—' Freddy reflected that the touch of vertigo had been oddly delayed; Tamara had stood

140

alone at the open casement, gazing out and downward for several minutes before Charles came to interpret the view to her. He wondered what actually had occurred.

'Charles—' Miranda came swiftly towards them, 'Sybil says will you please come—Mrs Morland has suggested our going up to her place next week for a long weekend. Can you manage Friday till Tuesday? It would be such fun, I'm dying to see Santa Joana—'

'How very kind of her.' Charles smiled at his sister's eager face. 'I expect I shall be able to wangle it, poppet.' He went off; Freddy said to himself that the potential mother-in-law hadn't wasted any time.

'Is this to be a large house party or just yourselves?' he inquired.

'Just ourselves, I believe. But from something Mrs Morland said I have an idea that she may be going to invite you, too, Freddy. Will you be able to come?'

'I think not.' Freddy spoke with a curtness unusual in him. 'I'm more or less booked up for next weekend.'

'Oh.' Miranda blinked, her expression changed. 'What a pity,' she said in a cool little voice. 'It would have been more local colour for you.' Her tone clearly indicated a scornful disbelief in the seriousness of Freddy's articles. Unmoved, he returned:

'That is a consideration. I shall hope to be invited again later on. I think you are wanted, Miranda, people are beginning to leave—'

Mrs Morland was saying to Charles, 'We'll expect you, then.' Sybil looked triumphant. Mrs Sangster, flying to Switzerland next day, was explaining—to the considerable apprehension of her much-badgered friends—that she had an adoption scheme in mind. Miranda was congratulated on her birthday, now an open secret; Charles conducted his guests in twos and threes to the lift and at length the Rendles were left alone.

'Thank you for my party, Sybil,' Miranda said. 'I enjoyed it so much and it was a great success.'

'You're telling me,' Sybil rejoined in her gracious fashion. 'It couldn't have been more successful. The way they stayed on, and Mrs Morland asking us up— I mean, it shows she was impressed—the only wonder is that Charles didn't say he couldn't ask for the couple of extra days. Putting in a spanner, spoiling everything —it would have been just like you, Charles.'

'Now don't reproach me for something I might have done, and didn't,' he said smilingly.

Miranda looked at her sister-in-law from under veiled lashes. One of these days—yes, definitely.

'I'll go and take off my new frock,' she said. Not least of the amenities of life in Lisbon was that after a party you did not wearily have to start clearing away glasses, disposing of uneaten snacks, emptying ashtrays; there were maids to attend to all that. Miranda went to her room and with a rather set expression began to unfasten the lace dress.

'So he won't come. Not that it matters to me whether he does or not—' but Freddy's instant and curt rejection of the possible invitation had been something like a slap in the face. He must surely want, as everyone who had heard of it wanted, to visit the interesting old homestead, but he wasn't going to make a fourth in a house party consisting of the three Rendles.

Suddenly Miranda blushed.

She had been the only girl, save Tamara, at Freddy's Estoril party and Mrs Morland probably assumed that he and she enjoyed each other's company and was asking him—if she did ask him—on that account.

'He saw it at once, of course. It would be an uncomfortable situation for us both. Thank goodness he isn't coming.'

But for all that, a little of the edge had been rubbed off her pleasure in the anticipated visit.

In the drawing-room Sybil was still harping upon the theme of what Charles might have done and might still do.

'If you spoil this, Charles, I'll never forgive you. I mean, the Morlands won't ask us a second time if we back out at the last minute.'

'Why should we back out at the last minute?'

'Because someone in that office of yours may go sick or something and I know you so well, you'll offer to stay. You let people walk over you—I suppose you think it makes you popular—'

'No one is likely to go sick, and in any case I promise I won't do you out of your weekend, Sybil.'

'That's really noble of you.'

'Not at all. I want very much to see Santa Joana myself.'

He was not looking forward with any joy to the visit; there was no joy in anything, anywhere, with Sybil. Charles, although many people censured him for what seemed a blind complacency, asking themselves why he couldn't *see* through the wretched woman, was under no illusions in regard to his wife. He foresaw now that she would succeed in boring his hostess to distraction, if not irrevocably antagonizing her. In all likelihood she would accomplish both; four days was a perilously long time where Sybil was concerned.

Nevertheless, he spoke the truth in saying he wished to go. He was the least conceited of men, he had scouted the possibility of any such thing, but after what had occurred this evening he could no longer shut his eyes to the fact that Tamara had conceived a youthful infatuation for him. He insisted that it was no more than this, a passing adolescent fancy, not to be taken seriously. Yet to let it go on, allow her to believe herself encouraged, was not to be thought of. And how, short of harsh rebuff, was he to stop it?

Mrs Morland's invitation, therefore, came at an opportune moment. To get right away for a few days, safe from any encounter with her during the various weekend diversions; away, if one came to that, from the city which had taken on a new and poignant quality because it held the enchanting, troubling girl, would give him a breathing space, a time to marshal his forces and decide what must be done.

Perhaps his going would prove a salutary check: cause her to realize—dear, blessed, impetuous child—that she had taken too much for granted. He recalled bidding goodnight to her a short half hour ago; the upraised face, the small fingers curling around his; the supremely confident—'If not before, we shall meet on Saturday; Mrs Willison is going to give a bathing picnic.'

Well, they would not meet. There had been no chance to tell her so as she turned away and other people crowded around to say goodbye. Nor had he any intention of presently informing her, making it appear that he considered their seeing or not seeing each other, a matter of any significance. Miranda, if Miranda saw her meantime, would tell her, or Tamara could discover it for herself when he failed to turn up at Mary's picnic.

She would be disappointed. She would be shocked and chagrined, this little princess who so arrogantly had signed her photograph, who serenely brushed aside the very existence of Sybil. Charles felt a familiar tug at his heart as he pictured her incredulous dismay, but something of the sort was needed.

It was Charles, however, who was dismayed a day or so later. The proposed picnic did not develop. Miranda, having been asked to come in for a glass of sherry at the Willisons' and say au revoir to Mrs Morland who was leaving next day, came home with the news that the house party was not to consist of themselves alone.

'Mary and Mr Willison are going—Mrs Morland wants some older people to play bridge—and the rest of the party is for her son. It seems he is only about twenty-six; I had got the impression of a man in his middle thirties. Mara has been invited, and Fergus Seton and one or two others.

'Freddy is going, too. Mary says he will take Mara and Fergus in his car. There'll be a lot of us; it must be a big house—'

'I'm told Mrs Morland often gives these large house parties,' Sybil said. 'It's no trouble for her, she has umpteen servants. The young ones are obviously being asked for you, Miranda, and the bridge players as a compliment to me. What are you staring at, Charles? Charles! Wake up. Do you hear what Miranda is saying? That the Morlands are giving a really grand do in our honour?'

'I heard,' he said.

CHAPTER TEN

SANTA JOANA, as the house was called after the patron saint of the original owner, was a long, rambling building whose white walls enclosed numerous courtyards. It stood in the midst of gardens where hollyhocks and orange blossom, giant geraniums and roses, petunias and marigolds, clambering nasturtiums and an occasional strayed olive tree mingled their colours and their perfumes in delightful disregard for conformity. Behind the house, some distance away, was a back-drop of green forest.

'What a heavenly place,' Miranda said as their host and hostess welcomed them at the main entrance under an arched doorway with a coat of arms cut in the lintel above.

'Not always heaven,' Major Morland smiled. 'Summer can be sizzling up here, but this is an exceptionally mild season.'

When they had been shown to their rooms and had freshened themselves after the long dusty drive, they made their way as directed to the central courtyard; a cool and shaded space giving upon the garden, with vine-clad walls, stone flags and a tinkling fountain. The Rendles were the last to arrive; they found their fellow guests clustered in little groups, some reclining in basket chairs, sipping iced drinks.

'I think you know everyone,' Mrs Morland said.

'Come and sit down, Mrs Rendle.' She led Sybil to where Mary and Lady Brewster were seated. Charles, with a comprehensive nod and smile to the assembled company crossed the patio and joined the elder men. Tamara stood with the young people by the wide entrance; she was wearing, as Charles had not failed to note, her freshly laundered blue skirt and white top; the other girls, including Miranda, had changed into flowery summer frocks.

'The *darling*,' thought Charles with another pang in the region of his heart.

Miranda, in pale green linen and green linen sandals walked towards the young group, her eyes taking quick stock of them. Freddy Clayton leaning negligently against a pillar; Fergus Seton and another young man from the Embassy; two sisters whom she had several times met and the Cinderella princess. There was no sign of Mrs Morland's son.

'Hello, everybody,' Miranda said. 'Isn't this the most perfect place? And such a lovely big party.'

'It's your first visit, I expect,' one of the sisters said. 'Have you brought tennis things?'

'Yes. Mrs Morland said to bring them. Do you play, Mara?'

'A little. And I have a pair of shoes. But I think no one will want to play with me when they see how I do.'

'I'll take you on,' Fergus said, 'and we'll have a spot of practice first thing in the morning.'

'That will be kind of you.' She looked appreciative if not elated.

Freddy came forward.

'Let me get you a drink, Miranda.' From a table set with huge jug and glasses he brought her an iced orange juice.

'Thank you. *Ummm*—delicious.' She drank part of it and stepped out into the garden. 'I must see more—'

Freddy leisurely followed.

'Nice old place, isn't it?'

'Fascinating. I adore the way the flowers and orange trees are all mixed up. As if it had just *grown*, never been planned. It is beautifully kept, though.' She gave him a sideways glance. 'So you came after all, Freddy. I thought you were booked up.'

'I was able to get out of my tentative engagements.'

When you knew it was to be a large party, Miranda thought. But she didn't hold it against him.

'I'm so glad Mara was asked,' she said. 'And Fergus —Do you think Mrs Morland is doing a little match-making?'

'I shouldn't be surprised.' If Mary Willison were right, Mrs Morland was attempting to do exactly this, in another direction.

'I wonder,' Miranda continued, as if following her companion's train of thought, 'what the son is like? Has he put in an appearance yet?'

'No. He seems to be detained somewhere on the estate. He acts as manager, runs the whole place. A most estimable young man by all accounts.'

With a touch of asperity, she countered.

'So I have heard. I suppose *you* would think better of him if he idled on his father's money, played around Lisbon, drove a high-powered car—'

Freddy grinned.

'That is an unjustifiable attack. I yield to no one in my admiration for the earnest worker.' His tone conjured an irresistible vision of a dull plodder. She was provoked, and was casting about in her mind for a scathing retort when they caught the sound of hooves and a rider cantered into view at the end of an avenue of acacias. He came on, in the dapple of sun and shadow, riding as if he and his mount were one, a dashing figure in his white shirt and fawn breeches and hard, wide-brimmed hat.

'The earnest worker,' Miranda muttered with a sly glance and a satisfied feeling that Freddy had been worsted.

The rider was about to turn towards the stables, then appearing to reconsider, he rode forward and drew up, swinging himself from the saddle.

'How do you do. I'm Jim Morland. Sorry to be so late.'

Freddy introduced himself and Miranda and the three walked back to the patio, Jim with his hat in his hand and the bridle over an arm. He was a man of Freddy's height with a cool, erect bearing, fair hair bleached by the sun and a deeply tanned face. Attractive, Miranda decided. She liked the way he smiled, the sun-wrinkles deepening around the narrowed blue eyes.

A groom materialized to take the horse; Mrs Morland presented her son to the four people he had not as yet met; the Rendles and the princess and Fergus Seton. He greeted them pleasantly and said to the company in general as he moved to welcome the other guests:

'I'm not very presentable—I was held up—'

'That's quite all right,' Sybil assured him. 'Your mother explained to me why you weren't here when I arrived. I mean, I perfectly understood.'

Jim's thick eyelashes, bleached like his hair, blinked a little. Miranda said to herself, 'She *would*.'

Some time later they were all assembled in the great drawing-room, a typical white-walled apartment furnished with dark oak, mellowed old rugs and some beautiful ancient tapestries. An immense stone fireplace had the same coat of arms as was cut above the main entrance, emblazoned above it. Aperitifs were served; the guests and their hosts stood chattering together; Charles strolled across the floor to examine a tapestry and found Tamara at his side. She was now wearing her black and white Alice in Wonderland dress.

'What a lovely room,' she said.

'It is. A perfect specimen, I imagine, of an old Portuguese manor.'

'Yes, I think so. Is all most lovely and there are to be three more days here. Such a happiness.'

'I am so glad for you,' he smiled, 'that for once you are in a party of young people.' He glanced at the youthful members who had foregathered at the end of the room.

'Young people? One of them, Freddy, is older than you are.'

'That is true. But Freddy is a gay bachelor and I'm a sober married man. It makes a world of difference.'

'To me it makes none,' she returned calmly. 'I see you only as—Charles.'

You do, indeed, he thought, wanting to gather her to his heart and at the same time wanting to shake her. Extraordinary girl; had she no sense of right and wrong, no moral code? But why should she have? Only eighteen, homeless, stateless, living on the edge of disaster in a community that lived precariously on its wits —poor little Tamara, adorable, loving child—At this moment, to Charles's infinite relief, Jim Morland approached them.

'How are the glasses going? Let me fill yours, Rendle.' He took the glass and refilled it from a silver shaker. 'If you are interested in tapestries, princess, we have a rather fine Gobelin over here—'

Tamara did not know what a Gobelin was and had no desire to find out but she answered with her bewitching smile.

'I should like very much to see it, Mr Morland. And the other treasures in this beautiful room.' She went off beside him; Charles, who did not follow, said to himself that Tamara might have no moral code but at least—thank heaven—she possessed good manners. However reluctantly, she could be trusted to accede to everything required of her during the weekend, and this, he devoutly hoped, would save a situation that threatened to get out of hand. The young group would claim her at all times; as for him, he would strictly adhere to the elder contingent.

Putting this resolve at once into practice, he joined his wife who was holding forth to some of the others by the fireplace.

CHAPTER ELEVEN

MIRANDA CAME into the garden where the rest of the house party were congregated. Breakfast trays, with a continental breakfast, had been carried to the bedrooms at eight o'clock; 'And you'll find elevenses,'

Mrs Morland had told her guests overnight, 'in the patio at half past eleven. So just come down when you feel like it.'

No one, however, was inclined to linger in bed; the country air, the morning scents and morning colours, not yet drained by the sun, lured them out of doors when the coffee and rolls were disposed of.

Major Morland was escorting Mrs Rendle along the orange alleys, looking slightly distracted as she volubly discoursed to him. Sybil was in a good humour; she had excelled herself at bridge last evening and, what was more, had made her position entirely clear to these wealthy Morlands. She knew, as everyone knew, that they and the Brewsters belonged to a small circle who played for very high stakes; Mary Willison had said something about this as they sat down to play and Mrs Morland replied that Mary and her husband and Mrs Rendle were not going to be let in for anything of the sort. Sybil, eagerly seizing the chance, at once asserted that, for her part, she didn't care how high the stakes were, she could afford it, and went on to inform her hostess that Charles had private means. Mrs Morland had looked very much surprised; as well she might, thought Charles's triumphant wife.

Mary and Lady Brewster were now sauntering among the beds of flowers; Charles stood chatting with his chief, Sir Robert. The sisters, Pamela and Jill, fresh-faced, games-loving English girls were already in tennis shorts, as were Fergus Seton and the other Embassy secretary; Tamara wore again her cotton skirt and sleeveless top, and a pair of canvas shoes. Freddy Clayton and Jim Morland leant side by side against a broken bit of old stone wall; Jim, practical in navy blue slacks and shirt, Freddy immaculate in white flannels and a shirt of white silk. Miranda regarded the two men for a thoughtful moment, gave her head a barely perceptible shake and with her light, unhurried step crossed the grass.

A few minutes later Mrs Morland appeared.

'So here you all are. A lovely morning, isn't it. I see these young people are ready for tennis. You'll play, of course, Frederick?'

'Yes. I'm hoping to take Charles down a peg or two; he rather fancies himself at tennis.'

So much for Charles's resolve to adhere strictly to the elder contingent. Everyone knew he was a keen player; there was no getting out of it.

Mrs Morland turned to Miranda.

'You were saying last evening, my dear, that you would like to see something of the estate. How about making a little tour now? It's a good chance—if it would suit you—'

'I'd love to go, Mrs Morland. I'm longing to explore—'

'Miranda's an inveterate explorer,' her brother smiled.

'Then I think the best thing will be for Jim to take her, in his roadster. They had better start at once, to get the best of the cool hours. Have you a shady hat, Miranda?'

'Yes, I brought one.'

'Run and get it, then, and a scarf to tie it down.'

'I'll bring the car out to the drive,' Jim said. 'Come along when you are ready, Miss Rendle.'

Miranda ran off; Freddy Clayton said to himself:

'Round one to the matchmaking mamma.'

'It's a marvellous place,' Miranda said when the tour had ended and the powerful small car was headed for home. 'Thank you very much indeed for showing it all to me.'

They had driven along leafy tracks, laced on either side with wild grape vines; through an acacia forest; past cornfields where, because of the slaty ground, men were reaping with scythes, and grazing land with their scattered herds among whom the herders rode in wide-brimmed hats and sheepskins. They had stopped in a grove of cork oak, where small black pigs rooted in the sparse undergrowth for acorns; no woodcutters were in sight but they caught the rhythmic sound of hatchets and Miranda saw great piles of bark lining the glades. They had also inspected the olive groves, and presses, the dairy where maids were busy making cheeses, the cluster of workers' cottages, low, white-washed, embowered in orange trees and hollyhocks.

'It is very nice to find someone who enjoys being shown,' Jim responded. 'Most people couldn't care less.'

'And you care a great deal, don't you?'

From under discreet eyelashes she studied the firm, blunt profile below the ruffled sun-bleached hair. He had been an attentive if impersonal host; it was clear that his interest lay in exhibiting the property, rather than in the fact that he was conducting a pretty girl. A cool and somewhat hardbitten young man; estimable, Freddy had called him in his supercilious fashion. And estimable he undoubtedly was; a resolute character, supremely sure of himself, proud of this fine estate and the beautiful old house that would one day be his own. But his pride of possession took an admirable form; he worked for his own, ceaselessly striving to make what was good, still better.

'Well—' he negotiated a difficult turning, 'I was

born and brought up at Santa Joana. My mother came into the property shortly after she married and my father sent in his papers and became a very good cultivator. He was called back, of course, for the duration of the war, and my mother managed alone. As for me, I didn't even get to school in England; the war stopped that. So all my roots are here.'

'Has the place been in your mother's family a long time?'

'Since my great-grandfather's day. He bought the property from the widow of the owner, and married her daughter into the bargain.'

'So you had a Portuguese great-grandmother, whose family, I suppose, had owned Santa Joana for generations. No wonder your roots are here. And does it all go on in the same way? Mary Willison says it is absolutely patriarchal.'

'Things haven't changed very much.' He gave her a brief sketch of the life on these estates where the owners are less employers than heads of a great family. They assumed responsibility for all who were sick, lent a willing and wise ear to anyone in difficulties, provided trousseaux for brides and frequently stood as godparents to children. It was a full and by no means easy life; the master riding or driving daily about his vast domain, supervising every activity, constantly concerned with the welfare of each member of the self-contained community. The workers themselves, in addition to wages, received a percentage of all sales of crops and cattle, having thus a strong incentive and a definite stake in the property.'

'It sounds medieval,' Miranda declared, 'and perfectly idyllic. Do the peasants stay on here from father to son?'

'For the most part they do. Occasionally some of the youngsters get restless and go away.'

'I happen to know one who did,' she said.

'You?' He gave her a surprised glance.

'Mrs Sangster's little maid, Elita.'

'Oh, Elita. You have seen her? Yes, she became obsessed with finding a job in Lisbon. Her family wouldn't hear of it and she was fretting herself ill when Mrs Sangster came to the rescue.'

'Mrs Sangster for ever,' Miranda murmured.

Jim smiled.

'She wanted a maid who could speak some English. Elita had been with us as housemaid for a time and picked up quite a working knowledge of the language; she was very anxious to learn. And knowing Mrs Sangster, my mother explained to the parents that the girl would be in a good, safe home and advised them to let her go. How did you discover that she came from Santa Joana?'

'We have made friends,' Miranda replied. 'The first time I went to one of Mrs Sangster's at-homes I spilt some tea on my frock and Elita sponged it off. I thought her such a sweet, pretty child. And once or twice since then when I have been prowling along those old streets—it's a fascinating quarter—I have met her, doing some errand or other, and stopped for a word or two.'

There was more to it than this but Miranda, for reasons of her own, had never mentioned the incident nor, indeed, ever spoken of meeting Elita at all. She had done so now without thinking, but it didn't matter having casually told Jim Morland.

It was shortly after her first visit to Mrs Sangster's house that she had encountered the girl who, on her way to market, had lost the purse with the money entrusted to her and was in floods of tears. An unsuspected hole in her pocket was the cause; she had retraced her steps, hunted in vain, it was gone.

Miranda had inquired as to what was the matter, and endeavoured to console her, saying that if she couldn't make good the loss immediately—which it appeared she could not—Mrs Sangster would simply deduct it from her wages.

That, Elita wept, was not the point. The cook, whose duty it was to do the marketing was unwell and Elita had begged to be allowed to go in her stead. Her mistress demurred, considering her still too inexperienced, but finally consented. And now this inexcusable thing had happened. Mrs Sangster would be displeased; she might even decide that so careless a girl was of no further use, and send her home.

Miranda thought this an unlikely contingency but, moved by the other's distress, she impulsively offered to lend the required sum, and Elita, with equal impulsiveness and passionate gratitude accepted. Mrs Sangster remained in blissful ignorance of the transaction and in due course the girl repaid her benefactor, declaring that Mees Rendle had only to ask, and anything Elita could do for her would be done on the instant.

'She's a dear little thing,' Miranda concluded now, 'and seems to be doing very well.'

Jim nodded.

'My mother saw her when she was in Lisbon and brought back a reassuring report to Teresa and Jorge.'

They reached the house a little before lunch time and found the others in the patio, again sipping ice-cold drinks. Miranda waved as she came towards them, her eyes seeking and finding first a tall, white clad figure with a smooth, russet-brown head. She felt an odd sense of homecoming after a long absence as Freddy Clayton strolled nonchalantly forward and filled a glass for her.

'Spot of gin in it?'

'No, thanks.'

'Did you enjoy your expedition, Miranda?'

'Immensely. It's a beautiful place and so different from anything at home. I felt I had gone back a hundred years, or more. But it's all so perfectly organized—' she smiled at Jim. 'Mr Morland has the whole thing at his fingertips, knows about every single detail—'

'It's my job to know.' Jim poured a drink for himself. 'How did the tennis go, Clayton?'

'Charles gave me a drubbing.'

'Good for Charles,' his sister said. 'How did Mara get on?'

'Not too badly. She enlivened the proceedings and thoroughly enjoyed herself.'

'She's having a wonderful time. I'm so glad.' Miranda glanced at Tamara who was gaily chattering, then went over to thank her hostess for having suggested the expedition and repeat how much she had enjoyed it.

Mrs. Morland looked pleased and inquired as to just where Jim had taken her; the Major, chuckling, remarked that the boy had not let her off anything, except the apiary. Miranda said she would like to see the beehives, too, and he rejoined that they would spare her that but promised her a fresh comb to take back to Lisbon; Santa Joana prided itself on its honey.

'And one for this little honey-haired princess, too,'

he smiled as Tamara, to whom he had taken a great fancy, came to slide an arm around her favourite Miranda's waist.

Sybil, who had not been invited to view the estate nor offered a comb from the hive, grew restive. After all, she was the principal guest and her hosts appeared to have forgotten it. Making this fuss about the two girls, while she sat unheeded—

Charles had joined Freddy and Jim and the three stood talking together.

'Your son speaks with a Portuguese accent,' Sybil observed. And then, with an apologetic smile belied by the bright, malicious cat's eyes, 'I'm *sorry*—'

Miranda's lips parted; the Major stared; Tamara uttered an irrepressible 'Oh my,' half appalled, half hilarious, and cast Charles's wife a look of amused contempt.

Mrs Morland said:

'Miranda, my dear, if you want to wash—lunch will be ready in a few minutes—'

'Yes, I'm dusty and my hands are covered with cork bark—'

Miranda departed, saying to herself;

'What possesses Sybil? Is it simply plain, half-witted *dumbness*, or was she trying to be offensive? But why?'

CHAPTER TWELVE

MIRANDA PUSHED back the slatted shutters from the bedroom window; they had been closed against the sun but this end of the house was now in shadow. From below came a soft medley of voices; they were some distance away but she recognized Freddy Clayton's voice among them. It was Monday afternoon, the hour of siesta; the elder people had retired to their rooms, the young ones were lazily disposed in the shade out of doors.

'I wish,' Miranda thought, 'that the weekend were just beginning. It has been so perfect—'

It had, in truth, been a most delightful interlude. Plenty of good tennis which she greatly enjoyed, that fascinating tour of the estate with Jim, the cheerful gatherings in the patio for drinks and elevenses, dancing after dinner to the big radio-gramophone. And yesterday, in their several cars—Freddy had taken her and Tamara and Fergus in his Jaguar—they had all made an excusion to an entrancing old town, a place of roses and rushing streams and steep, tumbling streets of Gothic houses; going on for a picnic tea in a eucalyptus grove and returning home along the tree-lined roads in the brief, scented twilight. Now it was nearly all over—

'But there is still tonight.'

The house party was ending, tonight, with a dance

to which a number of people from the surrounding countryside had been invited, and the music would be provided by a rhumba band. Miranda's face brightened; she caught up her straw hat and ran down to join the others.

In a nearby bedroom, Charles, at his wife's command, also pushed back the shutters and caught, as his sister had done, the distant murmur of voices. He did not distinguish Freddy Clayton's but he heard, with remarkable distinctness, Tamara's quick gay tones. His hand tightened on the window frame as he pictured the chattering, laughing group, scattered on the warm grass under the deep-branched trees; the men stretched flat, the girls in their sun frocks, bare armed, with slim bare legs below the brief spreading skirts. He wanted badly to be with them; he wanted to escape from this room, heavy with the odours of face cream and nail varnish and setting lotions; away from the woman who sat, her face greased, her hair tied in a net, repainting her crimson claws.

But he made no move to go. When the after-luncheon coffee had been served in the patio and those others had sallied out into the garden he remained behind, accompanying his wife upstairs; the sober married man he had declared himself to be.

His early resolve, consistently to demonstrate this fact had not proved feasible. He was obliged to join in the tennis and, being no card player, take part in the impromptu dancing. Impossible to do otherwise, he couldn't sit and watch the bridge or read a book, he had to behave like a rational being. But the situation proved less difficult than he had feared. He and Tamara were always surrounded; the little exiled princess was exceedingly popular with the entire company and, as Charles had foreseen, sweetly amenable to one and all. Fergus Seton, obviously in love with her, was constantly at her side; his brother secretary and Jim Morland appeared to find her a refreshingly charming and amusing young girl. She herself was in radiant spirits; Charles wondered whether, in the pleasure and excitement of the house party, enjoying the attentions of these younger, gayer, unattached men, she might be getting over her fixed idea concerning himself. With an irrational pang at the thought—for he wanted above all things that she should get over it—he turned from the window, picked up a magazine and settled himself to endure the ensuing hour as best he could. Sybil, seated at the dressing-table, observed complacently;

'They've really done us well, haven't they? I mean, nothing spared. And now this dance tonight with a band—wherever they're fetching it from—as I said to Sir Robert, I'm being quite spoiled. I've had quite a lot of talk with him, Charles, and put him straight about ourselves. I mean, I don't think there's a doubt your getting the new job, and you can thank me for it.'

Charles sat abruptly upright.

'How did you know there was any new job in question?'

'I found a letter in your desk. Since you didn't choose to tell me, I had a perfect right to find out for myself. You're so secretive; you'd think it didn't concern me as much as it does you.'

'Did you speak of this to Sir Robert?'

'No. Not directly. But he realizes—I mean, I've explained a lot of thing to him—he has quite a proper impression of us now.'

Mary Willison and her hostess were enjoying a gossip together in the latter's sitting-room.

'I shouldn't criticize a guest in my house,' Adelaide Morland was saying, 'but that woman would drive me to anything. Of all the appalling creatures—Cedric declares she must be a bit mental but in my opinion it is just aggressive temper. I've never been so sorry for anyone in my life as I am for her unfortunate husband.'

'I'm desperately sorry for him, myself, but I have no patience with Charles. He ought to get rid of her—or beat her.'

'How can he get rid of her? And he isn't the wife-beating kind. Poor boy, she going to handicap his career. I've had a talk with Helen Brewster; this is in confidence, Mary. Young Rendle was earmarked for something very good indeed but Robert says it can't be done, with a wife like that. They had seen nothing of her until this weekend; now they have had an eye-opener. So have I!' Mrs Morland finished trenchantly. 'Never again.'

'I'm afraid everyone is going to drop her.' Mary said. 'Miranda's arrival starved things off for the time being; no one wanted to snub Charles's sister. It is a bleak prospect for Charles; inevitably he'll have to drop out too.'

'An uncomfortable situation for his friends. Helen things Robert may presently offer him a post in one of their big construction schemes abroad somewhere. Well—' Adelaide dismissed Charles and his problems. 'I wonder, Mary, if you have noticed something interesting?'

'Jim? Yes, I really believe he is attracted at last, that unimpressionable son of yours. We had begun to think him girlproof.'

'He has never before met one like Miranda. Pamela and Jill and all the others he knows are nice children but set to a pattern. Mad on games, given to what they call leg-pulling—nothing mysterious about them—'

'Do you call Miranda mysterious?'

'She's not all on the surface, at any rate. That composed little air—one feels there is something underneath—'

'And Jim wants to find out what it is,' Mary smiled. 'You'd be glad, Adelaide, if it comes off?'

'Very glad.'

'In spite of the sister-in-law?'

'I'd deal with the sister-in-law,' the other replied.

The great drawing-room had been cleared, the oaken floor waxed, the band seated on an improvised dais and the dance well under way. The friends from neighbouring estates had arrived; several girls with their chaperones and a corresponding number of men. One or two spoke a little English, most of them knew French, but the language question was of small moment; they and the English young people were linked by a common delight in dancing.

Miranda was executing a rhumba with Jim Morland to the inspiring rhythm of guitars and small drums and bean bags.

'You are a beautiful dancer,' he said.

'You are very good yourself, Jim.'

'But not in your class. I don't get much practice up here.'

'You never go down to Lisbon, do you?'

'I do, occasionally. I rather think I may come oftener now. You are staying for some time, aren't you?'

'All summer, I think.'

'Have you danced at the Aviz?'

'No.'

'Then perhaps you will let me take you there some evening.'

She replied demurely that she would, and felt a thrill—a very natural, feminine thrill—at having broken through the defences of this hard-bitten man. Pamela had informed her that, while always pleasant enough to them, he really never looked at a girl; well, he had obviously begun to look at Miranda and was liking what he saw.

When the rhumba ended they went out through the patio where numerous small tables and chairs had been placed for people to sit smoking and sipping wine cup in the dance intervals. She replied to her partner's inquiry that she didn't want anything to drink at the moment and they went on into the warm, still night. Strolling along the grass, Jim suggested a date for dining and dancing at the Aviz; she assented very happily to this invitation which was the first of its kind she had received since coming to Lisbon, and thought with amusement of the surprise of her friends when they learned of her conquest. As they returned to the house they met Charles coming out.

'Just going to have a breather,' he said, smilingly.

The other two went in; Charles lit a cigarette and walked swiftly along a path that led to a far end of the garden. A late moon was rising behind a thinly overcast sky; there was sufficient light to discern the flower beds and orange trees and denser growth beyond. He had been seized by a desire to get away for a few solitary minutes; from the festive scene for which he was not in the mood, from the sight of Sybil, flushed and complacent, shrilly holding forth to this one and that.

Sybil. He winced as he recalled what she had told him this afternoon. Here was end of the proposed new job; Charles was in no doubt on this score. It was a post of considerable importance, involving a certain amount of travel, making contacts, entertaining prospective customers in various countries; Sir Robert Brewster was a director of a big engineering combine of which the Lisbon firm was a minor organization. For a man of Charles's age to be considered for the post was a great tribute to his abilities and Charles had been astonished and immensely gratified.

None the less, he felt dubious about adopting, if and when a definite offer was made. Sybil was the stumbling block. She would never consent to remain at home while he travelled abroad and he knew, moreover, that there would be occasions when his wife *should* accompany a man in such a position to assist him on the social side. Could he risk Sybil? He wanted very much to accept the post for its own sake, and he wanted, for another reason, to leave Lisbon. Now, the matter was decided for him. Sir Robert, he was convinced, having been talked to and put straight by Mrs Rendle, would withdraw his proposal.

As he walked on, reaching the denser growth, Charles was suddenly enveloped in a wave of perfume and saw before him an arbour smothered in jasmine. The starry flowers were deeply scented; too deeply and poignantly to be borne, tonight. He turned to go back to the house, then stood still. Someone in floating skirts that showed pale in the faint light was running towards him.

'Oh, my.' Tamara stopped short. 'Charles—*you*—'

'What is the matter?' He drew her into the shelter of the arbour.

'Is nothing very bad. I am *agitée*—I did not wish to go in just yet. Poor Fergus could not believe—and he insist—and then we are both quarrelling and I run away and leave him—'

'Fergus,' Charles echoed sharply. 'You mean—'

'Yes. He has asked me to marry him.'

'And you refused?'

'Naturally I refused.'

'Not naturally at all.' He forced himself to smile, to speak in the indulgent, elder brother tone he had always employed towards her. 'No,' as she was about to protest, 'listen to me, Tamara. Don't act impulsively; give Fergus a chance. He spoke too soon; he should have waited, given *you* a chance. Fergus is a very fine boy, in every respect; your life would be secure with him. He's utterly devoted to you—we've all seen that—'

'Do you plead his cause, Charles? With *me*?'

'I'm asking you to listen, and take my advice. It's good advice, believe me. Make up your quarrel with Fergus, tell him not to rush you off your feet, give you time to think it over—'

'What talk is this? What am I to think over? You know why I refused Fergus Seton.'

He saw there was no use beating about the bush; she would have none of it.

'You refused him—because of me?'

'Because of you. Is it necessary to ask?'

'I know,' he said steadily, 'that you are fond of me and, I'm afraid, see me in a romatic light. I'm far from

167

that, Tamara. I'm a sober, settled, married man; your friend Miranda's brother and your own good friend who wishes you well and wants to see you safe and happy.'

'There is only one way in which I can be happy. And for you, also. From the very first day, when we looked at each other on the dock—it happened then. You cannot deny it.'

He saw again that pretence, playing the elder brother, was useless.

'I am not going either to deny or admit it,' he said. 'That's beside the point. You aren't a child—you know that I cannot—'

'You are married, yes. Is pity, but—'

'It is the simple, final answer,' he retorted.

'She, the answer,' Tamara cried scornfully. 'A stupid, underbred, scolding woman who makes your life a hell—'

'You mustn't speak of her like that.'

'I must not? I shall speak of her as I choose.'

'Not to me, Tamara.'

'Oh—' Tamara caught her breath. 'Then she—this Sybil—comes first?'

'There is no question of first and second. Sybil's my wife.'

'And I?'

'You are a darling girl with a foolish bee in your romatic little bonnet. Come, Tamara, be sensible. Go back to the house, now, and be nice to Fergus. Forget —we'll both forget this—wash it out—'

'You are sending me away?'

In the pallid light she seemed to shrink; he saw her face, ghost-white, the brown eyes like dark pools. Quickly, nervously, he said:

'I *must* send you away. People will be wondering what has become of you.'

'So,' she said in a broken, beaten tone. 'I am to go. You tell me to go. I have nothing; all I have ever had has been taken from me.'

'Oh—child—' he made a movement towards her, checked himself. He would not make a bad matter worse.

'We say goodbye, Charles? To—what has been between you and me?'

'It is all we can say, Tamara.'

'Goodbye, then.'

She turned and went slowly away; he knew that she hoped he would still call her back. He stood silent, watching the slender figure in the frilled pink dress, the dress she had so joyously and proudly displayed at Miranda's birthday party, its colour drained now as the colour was drained from Tamara's stricken face. She looked back as she reached the turning in the path; Charles made no sign.

For a short time longer he remained there, trying to pull himself together, orientate his thoughts. Blessed, mad girl; what had she expected of him? That he should ruthlessly cast aside his wife and place her, Tamara, in that wife's place? It seemed that she did expect it, had taken it for granted in her sublime fashion. She was Tamara; Sybil less than nothing in her arrogant young eyes. She had learned better now, learned a much needed lesson.

But Charles's face was drawn and his eyes heavy with pain as he stood there, drenched in the nostalgic perfume of the jasmine he would always henceforth connect with her. Poor child; poor, rejected little figure, no longer arrogant, creeping away. . . . A line from a poem, long forgotten, came back to him.

> *A little hand is knocking at my heart,*
> *And I have closed the door.*

CHAPTER THIRTEEN

THE GUESTS were taking their leave of Santa Joana, the cars drawn up for the early morning start on the long drive back to Lisbon. Tamara was already seated in the front of Freddy's Jaguar, the two young secretaries behind Fergus Seton looking somewhat grim; Tamara was very pale, with a hint of shadow below the big brown eyes. Freddy, crossing the grass to take his place at the wheel, cast a speculative glance at one or two of the others.

Charles stood at the open door of his car, waiting for his wife and sister. He, too, was oddly pale this morning; he looked as if he had not slept. Miranda was talking to Jim Morland, standing beside him in that way of hers, not figeting, her hands lightly clasped on the handle of her white bag. Jim, in riding kit, his wide-brimmed hat in his hand—for he was going off directly to his fields—looked just what he was; hard, virile, assured.

'They make a perfect pair, don't they,' Mary Willison smiled, passing Freddy on her way to join her husband.

They made, at any rate, a very good-looking pair and, on the face of it, eminently complementary. The fair, upstanding young man; the dark-haired girl with her delicately cut face and black-lashed grey eyes. But Freddy's original and unfounded prejudice was unchanged. Jim Morland was a good sort, a likeable chap enough, but he wasn't the type for Miranda. She was too finely wrought, too complicated, too fragile; a man of Jim's calibre would neither understand nor try to understand a girl of hers. He would ride roughshod—Freddy suddenly grinned at his own absurdity.

'I'm as bad as Mary. Taking for granted—they've only known each other four days. Why should Miranda fall for him, in any case? As for Morland, he's the least susceptible of fellows, or I'm much mistaken.'

He got into his car and moved off; the Brewsters with Pamela and Jill followed, the Willisons behind. Sybil was still condescendingly assuring her hosts that everything had been very well done indeed and they must all meet again shortly. At length she said her final goodbyes and the Rendle car followed the others. Mrs Morland drew a sigh of relief.

'Thank goodness, that is the last of her.'

'Incredible woman.' The major shook his head. From first to last he had been stunned and mystified by Mrs Charles Rendle.

A day or two later, Miranda was prowling through her favourite old quarter. She had chanced to meet Mrs Sangster's little maid, Elita, who was thrilled to hear that Mees Rendle had been to Santa Joana. They had talked together for a few minutes, then Miranda went on, walking slowly and soberly. She was perplexed and troubled; she wanted to confide in someone, talk it over, but there was no one to whom she could betray her secret.

Suddenly, with a quickening of her pulses she saw a familiar figure approaching. Freddy. She could tell Freddy. Curious, this feeling she had concerning him. They were not in reality friends, their relationship was in the nature of an armed truce, yet there was a queer sort of intimacy between them. She could say to him what she would say to no one else.

'It's an obsession,' he announced, stopping before her now.

'What is an obsession?'

'Your incessant haunting of this place.'

'You are here again, yourself.'

'But I have my definite motive.'

Miranda could have told him that she, too, had a definite motive these days, but only smiled her unbelieving smile. Freddy and his quest for local colour. . . .

'Have you a moment to spare?' she asked.

'Any number. Is something wrong, Miranda?'

'I'm afraid so. Shall we walk along?' They fell into step together. 'It's Tamara,' Miranda continued. 'I saw Fergus last evening and he told me he had asked her to marry him and she turned him down.'

Freddy nodded.

'Fergus isn't making any secret of it. He's a conscientious Scot; informed the Radizlos of his—intentions—before going to Santa Joana, and asked their permission. Not that they have any authority over Mara; she's not their ward, only a protégée.'

'I expect they are very much upset about it; such a chance for her—'

'I ran into Bela,' Freddy said, 'and found that they

172

are not in the least upset. They say Mara is too young to be thinking of marriage and in any case must please herself. I gather they didn't favour the idea at all.'

'They must be crazy. And I should never have thought they'd take that sort of attitude. Charming, of course, but they always struck me as hard as nails.'

'They are quite incalculable, these people. I agree, Bela and Olga should be exerting every bit of influence they possess to persuade that foolish girl to accept young Seton. They are all living with one foot on a landslide—Mara in particular—but there you have them. Crazy is the word.'

'That's only the half of it, Freddy. I am certain that Mara turned down Fergus because she—she is in love with Charles.'

'You've discovered that, have you?'

She gave him a startled look.

'Did *you* know?'

'I've had my suspicions; Santa Joana confirmed them. And Charles is in love with her, Miranda. Might as well face it.'

'Oh, Freddy, he is. He doesn't know I've guessed, and thank heaven Sybil hasn't tumbled to it. I don't think she will; she's too self-centred and conceited.'

'I gather there is no hope, for Charles?'

'Hope! You aren't suggesting that he should go off with Mara, desert his wife—'

'I suppose he wouldn't. Pity.' Freddy commented, judicially.

'What a thing to say.' Miranda was half laughing, half scandalized. 'What would you or anyone think of him if he did such a thing to Sybil? Or to Mara, come to that?'

'I can't vouch for anyone else. Speaking for myself,

I'd say it was the most sensible thing to do. Scandal wouldn't worry Mara, and Charles would be rid of his millstone.'

'You have no morals, Freddy.'

'So far as this particular case is concerned, none,' he agreed.

'To tell you the truth—I'm not sure that I have, either. Sybil has asked for it and only her pride would be hurt. She doesn't love Charles; sometimes I think she hates him. Don't ask me why—'

'Jealousy,' Freddy offered. 'Inferiority complex.'

'It could be. She's out of her element, whether she realizes it or not. If you ask me, she'd have done better and been happier if she had stayed at home among her own nice ordinary people in that industrial suburb.'

'Charles might put it to her, then, make it worth her while to go back—'

'Sybil would never consent. She may hate Charles but she loves being Mrs Charles Rendle. Besides, he will never ask her to set him free. He isn't a—a prig—but he has his own standards. He's taken on Sybil and he will stand by his bargain.'

'And continue to make a complete mess of his life.'

'I know. When I think of all the years to come—tied to that woman—I can't bear it. And yet—!' Miranda hesitated.

'You think he is right?'

'Not that, exactly. Only—if he deserted Sybil for Mara he—he just wouldn't be Charles.'

'I see.' Freddy spoke with unexpected gentleness.

'But don't think I am forgetting poor little Mara's side,' Miranda pursued. 'I'm terribly sorry for her—and so worried about the whole thing—'

'You'll have to leave it to them, Miranda. There's nothing you can do. If Mara has any sense—!'

'She hasn't.' Miranda laughed, blinking her lashes as if she could as easily have cried. 'Not one grain, Freddy.'

'She may develop a few grains when she grasps that Charles, as the Victorians would have put it, is not for her. And Fergus isn't a Scot for nothing. He's genuinely in love with her and he'll never let go. Don't fret any more about it; they've got to work things out for themselves.'

'I can't stop worrying but I feel better now. Thank you for letting me inflict all this on you, Freddy. I felt I just had to tell someone and the only possible, safe person was you.'

'Nice of you to feel like that. I'm afraid I haven't been much help—'

'It's been a comfort,' she said simply.

He looked down at her, touched in spite of himself. Bless her, he thought. Then, hastily shying away from personalities or sentiment—the last thing he desired —he said lightly:

'In any future problem, count me yours to command. I shall have to leave you now, I'm meeting a chap—'

'Oh—and I have kept you—'

'There was no hurry. Goodbye, Miranda. Don't get lost.' He hurried off in the direction of the river.

She watched him as he threaded his quick course along the cluttered street. He wasn't really interested in the troubles of those others, but he had listened patiently as she had known he would. Unstable in many matters, one could always rely on Freddy's cordial response. Purely impersonal, it was none the less a heartening and warming sort of thing.

'But I mustn't make a habit of relying on him,' she warned herself. 'I'll probably never set eyes on him again, once he's gone back to England.'

Circumstances had forced them upon each other out here, but he was not likely to continue the friendship, such as it was, when there was no longer any necessity. Their paths would not cross at any point and he would go on his own way, giving her no further thought.

'I wish . . .' she said, as she had said on the evening he had driven her home from Cascais and left her in the same brisk manner, his polite duty done. Now, as then, she didn't know what she wished, but as she slowly made her way to the car park she was conscious of that same restless unease.

CHAPTER FOURTEEN

'WELL—I'LL be damned,' Freddy Clayton ejaculated silently.

With the elderly, distinguished-looking friend he had met in the English bar some time ago he was seated in the glittering restaurant of the Aviz, Lisbon's most beautiful and expensive hotel. A dance orchestra was playing a tango and among the dancers he recognized a certain fair young man with a dark-haired girl in a white organza frock. The young man executed the steps with precision if some stiffness; the girl was equally precise but pliant as a willow wand, light as a leaf. Freddy, taken aback, stared; his friend, following his gaze, said in a tone of surprise:

'Hallo, that's the Morland boy. Stepping out—and time he did. Who is the pretty creature who's enticed him down from the wilds? Do you know?'

'Miranda Rendle. Charles Rendle's sister. He's in the Brewster concern.'

'Don't think I know him. There was a Mrs Rendle at Mrs Sangster's one afternoon when Dora and I were there. Woman with a voice like a pea-hen.'

Freddy grinned.

'That's Charles's wife.'

Miranda and Jim were now in line with Freddy's table; she saw him over her partner's shoulder, the grey eyes widened and her dimple—her silly dimple as Freddy termed it—flickered in a smile of pleased surprise. Freddy bowed, and resumed his interrupted conversation with his companion.

'I'm convinced he's our man, although there isn't sufficient evidence so far. I've got a fairly good dossier—real name Janco—origins obscure. At one time employed as ship's steward—' he went on to give a detailed list of his suspect's activities.

'I still can't see it,' the elder man said presently. 'Everything seemed to point—which was, of course, why I asked for you, a man with an entrée everywhere—'

'I'm not eliminating any possibility. Nevertheless—' the two men, disposing of an excellent dinner and enjoying the music and the gay assemblage, continued their discussion.

Miranda, in spite of her anxieties on her brother's

177

account and the obscure unease which had dogged her since the encounter with Freddy, was also enjoying her evening. A party is a party in whatever circumstances, and a dinner dance at the Aviz with a good-looking partner, among the very cream of the local and international set, provided something out of the ordinary run of parties. The band was the most alluring she had ever heard; she was wearing her prettiest frock; she saw the admiration in Jim Morland's eyes reflected in those of more than one man.

Then she caught sight of Freddy and felt a glow of increased pleasure. Not that she would be able to dance with him, nor, in all probability, exchange a word with him. But he was there; it seemed the final happy touch to a delightful occasion.

She made no further attempt to catch his eye; nothing is less gratifying to a man than to have his dancing partner continually looking towards and smiling at some other man, and Miranda was never guilty of such a breach. But she cast an occasional veiled glance in his direction, satisfied with a glimpse of the immaculately brushed hair, the bent profile as he talked with his elderly friend. When at length one such discreet glance was rewarded only by the sight of an empty table being reset for later guests she felt acute disappointment. Freddy was gone; the evening continued enjoyable but had lost some of its tang.

She did not see him again until the following Thursday when they met in Mrs Sangster's drawing-room. The good lady had returned from Switzerland, acquainting her friends of the fact, and the usual at-home was in progress. Miranda, to whom the drawing-room still presented its intriguing and slightly macabre aspect, was standing in the embrasure of one of the deep windows, gazing at the astonishing collection on the opposite wall, when Freddy appeared and stopped to have a word with her.

'How nice of you to come,' she said. Dropping in at Mrs Sangster's was, to be sure, like dropping in at a club, but it always surprised her that the casual and sophisticated Freddy should do so.

'Everyone appears to have come,' he rejoined. 'And how is Miranda? Did you enjoy your dance on Saturday?'

'Very much. Jim gave me a wonderful evening. And then on Sunday he drove me to Cintra—you've been there, I expect—'

'I have. Was it your first visit?'

'Yes. What a place! I've never dreamed of anything so wild and beautiful and romantic. The groves and the flowers and the springs—Jim showed me everything, the Palace and castles and the old monastery—and we had dinner on a balcony with a great rock wall behind—'

'Didn't miss a thing? The inveterate explorer. I wonder Charles hasn't taken you long ago.'

'We were going, but something always prevented it. I'm glad, now. Sybil would have ruined Cintra.'

'She undoubtedly would have destroyed the romance.' Freddy drew out his long, thin, platinum case, and elegant trifle very different from Jim's thick square silver one. She took the offered cigarette and he lit it and his own. 'Morland's gone back, of course?'

'Yes, but he is coming down again in a week or two.'

'Is he, indeed? This looks serious.'

'Don't be ridiculous, Freddy. He has taken me to one dance and for one sightseeing expedition—'

'But he's coming again, and Morland would never

desert his beloved fastness, drive all that distance, spend two nights in Lisbon—which he detests—merely to entertain a pretty girl and leave it there. Are you going to marry him, Miranda?'

She felt an irrational pang at the lightly spoken question which showed so clearly that, if she did marry him, it couldn't affect Freddy less. But she answered in the same vein:

'He hasn't asked me yet.'

'Give him time. Do you want to bury yourself at Santa Joana?'

'I shouldn't allow myself to be *buried*.'

Freddy smiled. 'That's what *you* think.'

'It's only a matter of starting off on the right foot,' she assured him airily. 'Making it plain from the beginning—'

'You fancy you can manage a man of that stamp? It's you who'll be managed. You'll meet your match; tantrums won't avail you—'

She thought, I met my match once before. In you.

'I don't go in for tantrums now,' she said on the same gay note. 'I have grown up. As for Jim—do you dislike him, Freddy?'

'Dislike him? Certainly not. We got on very well but we haven't much in common. He's a serious, rather single-minded chap—'

'He doesn't fritter his life away.'

'Meaning that I do?' Freddy suggested, amusedly.

'If you do,' she returned quickly, 'it is your own life and no business of anyone else. I wasn't being catty; I meant—just what I said. Jim *is* single-minded, perhaps too much so, but running and making a success of a place like Santa Joana—' she broke off. 'Freddy, we

180

are being nonsensical. Discussing it as if—he probably hasn't the slightest intention of asking me and I haven't the faintest idea of what I'd say if he did. We really mustn't take Jim's name in vain like this—'

'You are quite right. Well, whatever happens and however you decide—good luck, Miranda.' He gave her a friendly nod and went on; she turned and gazed abstractedly out of the window, engrossed by the new problem that had arisen.

For all her disclaimer, she was perfectly aware that Jim Morland's interest in her was serious. It was early days, nothing definite had been said, but Miranda was not deceived.

He would ask her to marry him and she must gravely consider, make up her mind—

She wasn't in love with him but he had attracted her at sight as he came riding through the sun and shadow along the acacia avenue. His hard-bitten air and the legend of his imperviousness to girls had naturally piqued her; his subsequent capitulation had been a feather in her pretty cap. In addition, she liked him, found him a stimulating companion and admired very much the way in which the rich man's son devoted himself to his exacting duties. He was very different from and, in her opinion, stood head and shoulders above the young men she was accustomed to meet in London. They were all shaped in the same mould; pleasant, sometimes charming, but shadowy figures in comparison with this forceful personality.

Besides—there was Santa Joana. To be the châtelaine of that vast estate—head, with her husband, of the feudal community—what a proud position and absorbing, worthwhile existence.

'Shall I do it? Marry Jim and make him happy and at last begin to live? I could be very happy myself—with him—at Santa Joana—'

From the end of the room came a burst of laughter and someone said:

'How long are you staying, Freddy?'

'I'm not sure. Possibly another month—'

Miranda had her answer. It was as simple as that. Simple and swift and clarifying as a light snapped on in a dark room. Freddy. She couldn't marry Jim Morland because Freddy Clayton stood between them.

'Oh, no—' Miranda's lips parted on a sharp breath, she put up a hand as if to shield her face from an impending blow. 'I can't be— I *will not*—' but there was no use denying it.

Here was the solution of that unease which had lately troubled her, the glow of warmth when she caught sight of him, the restlessness when he was no longer there. She was in love—for a second time she had fallen in love—with Freddy.

She stood rigid, staring blindly out, then with a quick, nervous gesture brushed her hand across her eyes, back over the dark hair.

'I can take it—I've *got* to take it.'

'Miranda?' Someone touched her arm; she turned to see Tamara. The two girls had not met since their return from the house party.

'Mara dear, I'm so glad—are you all right again?' Telephoning to suggest a meeting, she had been informed that the princess was suffering from migraine and confined to her room. Suspecting that the princess was also suffering from an emotional crisis, Miranda had sent a message of condolence and did not offer to visit the invalid.

182

'Oh yes, thank you, I am quite well. Was nothing
—a *coup d'air*—'

Tamara spoke in her usual gay fashion, pink colour
in her cheeks, the brown eyes very bright. Too bright,
perhaps, and there was a brittle quality in her gaiety
as if at a touch it might shatter. She was wearing the
black and white dress that had so appealed to
Charles—

Miranda cast a glance towards the end of the room
where Charles himself stood in a group of their espe-
cial friends, Freddy among them. Mrs Sangster was
also there, in the act of welcoming Count and Countess Radizlo.

'I must pay my respects to my hostess,' Tamara said.
'Will you come, Miranda?'

The girls edged their way along the crowded room.

'So here is our little princess.' Mrs Sangster shook
hands with her. 'I had you in mind, my dear, when I
was in the country that was your home for so many
years.'

'How kind, Madame. You have enjoyed your trip?'

'It was all most interesting and instructive.'

'Did you visit Geneva?'

'I flew to Geneva and spent several days there.'

'You had good weather, I hope,' the princess continued politely.

'Not very good, but I was far too much occupied to
pay attention to the weather.'

Miranda was conscious of something electric in the
atmosphere. It could hardly have been otherwise of
course, with Tamara, slender and very erect, standing
there within a few feet of Charles who stood with his
stocky, overdressed wife beside him; Tamara turning
to say how do you do to them both in a high, sweet,

careless voice; Charles, his handsome grey eyes looking as if they had been pulled back at the corners by string, steadily smiling. But there was something else, a second undercurrent, unless Miranda was imagining it. She wondered if Freddy had also sensed it.

Later, when they were all circulating about the long table in the dining-room, collecting cups of tea from Elita, helping themselves to scones and honey, she found him at her side.

'Mary wants some of this cake,' he said. 'Will you cut it for me? Cutting cake is one of the few things that defeat me.'

She cut two slices, laid them on the plate he held.

'Freddy—'

'Yes?'

'I was wondering whether you felt something rather queer—'

'Where and when?'

'When Mrs Sangster was saying how busy she had been in Geneva. It seemed to me there was a—a sort of vibration—'

'Vibrations are more in your line than mine, Miranda. But you may be right; Mrs Sangster's business, one can only assume, had to do with her new adoption scheme and her friends know what it means when the good lady is on the charitable warpath. If you felt something in the air, it was probably a general apprehensive shudder.'

'Well, perhaps—' she laughed, and left it at that, not wanting to bore him with her fancies or appear whimsical. He gave her a smile and went off with his plate of cake.

She turned from the table and saw Sybil standing alone as so frequently, at intervals, she did stand on

184

occasions such as this. No one willingly sought or remained in the company of the aggressive-tempered and
devastatingly boring Mrs Rendle.

'Does she *see* it, herself?' Miranda pondered. With a
sigh, she went over to her sister-in-law.

'More tea, Sybil?'

'Yes, I think I will. And make sure that stupid girl
doesn't put in too much milk. I mean, she simply
drowns it if you don't water her.'

'Oh—my—' Tamara, on the other side of the room,
vivaciously chattering with Freddy and Mary Willison,
tipped her saucer and the cup slid to the floor. 'Always
I am doing that, I start to talk and forget what I am
holding—thank you, Mr Rendle—' Charles, approaching with Mary's husband, had retrieved the cup from the
thick carpet.

'No harm done,' he said. 'Luckily it was empty.'

'Yes. How terrible if I had stained this so beautiful
rug.'

'May I get you some more?'

'No, I think I am not safe with filled teacups. But if
you offer me a scone—'

The scones were small, crisp, and had been split and
buttered. She took one and, with her eyes fixed upon
him, sank her little milk-white teeth into it. A trick,
thought the observant Freddy, as old as Eve.

Whether or not it was a trick, Charles felt an intol-
erable urge to kiss the provocative red mouth. She
finished the scone, refused another.

'Already I have had more than one, and cake also.
How are you, Mr Rendle? We have not met since Santa
Joana. Was so lovely to see Miranda here today.'

A trifle jerkily he said:

185

'We were sorry to hear you were not well, Tamara.'

'I was not very ill. I think I catch a small chill in Freddy's so fast car, the windows open and I had no hat or scarf. Such foolishness; I deserved my migraine.'

'I feel decidedly guilty,' Freddy said, 'and shall have to make amends. How about another session at the Casino?'

'Oh, I should like very much. Soon?'

'Tomorrow, if that suits Olga. I'll have a word with her.' He strolled away in search of the countess. Mary said, with an indulgent look at the sparkling young face:

'I hope you'll be as lucky as you were last time.'

'Was Mr Rendle, I think, who brought me that luck,' Tamara declared buoyantly. 'He stood beside me and I said to myself this is my mascot.'

Charles, beginning to feel frayed, forced a smile. She was 'needling' him, in Miranda's jargon.

A number of people now surged about their end of the table; Charles stepped aside to make way for them and Tamara, with a swift movement followed. He felt her small fingers brush against his hand.

'Charles?' It was the merest whisper. He looked down at her; she was smiling, she still hoped, she was not yet convinced— Then, as if she read her answer in his steady, unhappy gaze, like shattered glass the febrile gaiety vanished, the bright colour died and he saw, as once before he had seen, the brown eyes widen and fill with tears. The tears did not fall; she had sufficient control this time to hold them in check. She just stood there, for a breathing space, looking at him with those desolate drowned eyes.

Freddy came back.

'I've fixed it up—' he broke off. 'Mara, you look rather washed out. Has the headache started again?'

'I feel suddenly some pain—is better now—'

'Would you like me to drive you home? I'm leaving, and it will save you that walk and the long bus ride. Olga and Bela are going on somewhere.'

'Thank you, Freddy. I think it would be well to go home and rest. I must not have any migraine tomorrow.'

'Come along, then, and say goodbye to Mrs Sangster.'

They walked off together; Charles, feeling like a murderer, stood looking after them. Home. To that casual, indifferent household, that forlorn little room —she would cry when she got there, lock herself in and cry—

From across the room Miranda also saw them depart. Still dutifully attending to her sister-in-law, she had been covertly watching those others from the moment Tamara dropped her teacup. And although the final brief scene between Tamara and Charles had been unnoticed by anyone else it had not escaped Charles's sister. Nor had Freddy's obvious, instant grasp of the situation.

Freddy. Her heart rose on a bitter wave. 'If I could only go back, put the clock back two years—have my chance again—' but there was no going back. She had had her chance and thrown it away and there would be no second one.

CHAPTER FIFTEEN

'MIRANDA? FREDDY HERE.'

Miranda's heart jumped, the hand holding the telephone receiver tightened.

'Hallo, Freddy.'

'Are you free this evening?'

'Yes.'

'Would you like to come out to Estoril? I've got the Radizlos and Mara coming, and the Ashwins and another chap. Going out about nine-thirty or so to have a flutter at the Casino and then on to the Wonder Bar.'

'I'd love to come.'

'Right. I'll pick you up.'

Miranda replaced the receiver and felt her hands shaking.

'This won't do,' she admonished herself. 'If you are going to start panicking every time you hear his voice—.' But of course she wouldn't, she wasn't so weak and silly. She had simply been taken off guard. Freddy's was the last voice she expected to hear; it was the first time he had telephoned her since that dreadful day two years ago.

When at half past nine she heard his ring at the door of the flat her heart quivered again but she controlled the tremor and met him, as he was ushered into the drawing-room with her customary composure.

'This is nice, Freddy. I do like a party on the spur of the moment.'

'Personally,' Sybil said—'good evening, Sir Frederick—personally, I prefer being given more notice. I mean, I hate things being sprung on me. Charles can't seem to grasp it, I can't get it into his head—'

Charles, unable to recall a single instance when he had sprung anything upon her, suggested a drink. Freddy declined.

'If Miranda is ready we'll get along. The Radizlos and Mara are waiting in the car.'

He rather wished the words unsaid as he saw the look in his friend's eyes, the momentary contraction of Charles's disciplined mouth. Poor devil; the girl he loved down there below—and he must stay up here with this ghastly wife. But for all his sympathy Freddy, like Mary Willison, was losing patience with Charles.

'I'm quite ready.' Miranda caught up a long, wide stole, wrapped it around her slim little silk frock, one end tossed over a shoulder.

'You wear a shawl like a Portuguese or Spanish girl,' Sybil informed her.

'I know.' Miranda spoke in her airiest fashion. 'It's an art.'

Sybil sniffed.

'In my opinion, British people should look British.'

'They generally do, poor pets. Goodnight, Sybil. Goodnight, Charles.'

'Got your key, poppet? And your money?'

'Yes, darling. And a clean hanky with scent on it.' She flashed him a smile, thinking, as Freddy had thought—'Mara down there, so near—and what is *she* feeling, looking up at our lighted windows, knowing that Charles is behind them—'

189

Her troubled glance met Freddy's as Charles, having seen them into the lift, went back to Sybil. Freddy shrugged, not unsympathetic but saying, in effect, that there was nothing to be done about it.

They went out to the car, Count Radizlo descending as they appeared. Instinctively, Miranda made for the seat beside the driver's and saw it was occupied by the countess. She was handed into the back, the count followed, Tamara in her pink frock sitting between them.

'How lovely that you were able to come, Miranda,' Tamara said in the tone of brittle gaiety she had employed yesterday at Mrs Sangster's.

'A pleasure, indeed,' Bela supplemented politely.

'It's a pleasure for me.' Miranda made an effort to speak in her normal cheerful manner, acutely conscious of the tense girl at her side whose secret she must pretend not to know. 'I haven't been to the Casino since we were all there together at Freddy's other party. I lost every stake that time but you and Mara couldn't do wrong, could you, Count Radizlo? Do you feel this to be another lucky night?'

He replied that he did, at which Olga uttered a trill of laughter that seemed to Miranda, if not quite mocking, at any rate mirthless. Once again she felt what she called a vibration, a subtle something disturbing the air. She wondered whether the count and countess, always pleasant to each other in public, were privately on bad terms. She devoutly hoped not; she liked the Radizlos and, heaven knew, there was sufficient unhappiness among them all as it was.

She continued to make conversation with her two companions, her veiled gaze fixed upon the figure at the wheel, the easy pose of the broad shoulders, the

190

alert head; visualizing to herself the strong hands so light and sure, the dark eyes intent upon the road as she had seen them so many, many times when her place, by right, had been beside him. Freddy— Freddy—

It was a relief to reach the Casino where the Ashwins and Freddy's other guest, a naval commander from a visiting cruiser awaited them. These three were in the best of spirits, unconscious of cross currents, the Navy man charmed by the sight of two pretty girls, Louise Ashwin delighted to meet again her favourite Bela and that fascinating princess child.

They found places at one of the tables; Tamara had been provided by the count with a modest sum to stake.

'But go small-small,' he instructed her. 'Do not risk all and lose all.'

Her fair head went up.

'I shall not lose. At gambling, I am lucky.'

Freddy grinned.

'Sweet innocent. Just because you had beginner's luck—'

'No, you shall see if I am not right.'

Miranda sent her a quick, curious look, wondering if the princess knew and were ironically applying to herself the old adage; unlucky in love—poor Mara.

The princess's luck held and Miranda, to whom the adage equally applied was also fortunate tonight. None of them was indulging in serious gambling and after an hour or so their host suggested adjourning to the Wonder Bar to dance and have supper. As they left the table and threaded their way among the people clustered behind the chairs the monotonous voice of the croupier was raised again. *Make your plays—*

Tamara caught at Miranda's arm.

'Wait with me—just once more—'

'Very well.'

Tamara placed her stake, the ball spun, her number came up.

'So; I am satisfied.'

'How much have you made?' Miranda asked as they hurried to overtake the others.

'Not like last time; this evening I go very small-small. But I think I may have what would be five pounds in here.' She swung her pink bag and, characteristically, dropped it; the clasp opened and a number of coins scattered about her feet.

'Oh—my—' she stood staring down and was about to stoop and gather them up when a man stepped swiftly forward, collected and put them into the bag and handed it to the princess with a respectful little bow.

'Thank you—oh, it is you, Jenks.' Like all the frequenters of the famous at-homes she knew Mrs Sangster's quiet efficient major-domo.

Freddy, who had turned and come back at the sound of Tamara's familiar cry was now beside them.

'What happened? Good evening, Jenks. Been having a go at the tables?'

'Just putting in time sir, watching the players, until Madame is ready to leave.'

'Is Mrs Sangster here?'

'Madame has been dining with friends at their villa. I am on my way to call for her now.'

'I dropped my bag,' Tamara explained, 'and some of my money fell out and Jenks picked it up for me.'

'If I may say so, I think the clasp of the princess's bag needs adjusting. It shouldn't have sprung open like that.' With another respectful inclination of his head the man went on.

'Your *bête noire*,' Freddy said to Miranda.

'Oh, no. I am used to Jenks now.'

Miranda took a sip of her wine, set down the glass, and with her fingers still curled around its stem gazed abstractedly at the sparkling contents. At a table on the edge of the dancing floor she was seated between the Commander and Count Radizlo, both of whom for the moment were engaged with their other companions. She thought of that earlier party of Freddy's of which this could be called a replica on a smaller and less formal scale. A replica upon the surface, but how different beneath.

She remembered Tamara, joyous, the brown eyes limpid as sunlit pools; enslaving Fergus, glancing from time to time at Charles with the happy confidence of a young girl in a kindly, older man whose sympathetic presence reassures her. And Charles with his indulgent, amused smile, calling her Alice in Wonderland, looking upon her as no more than an enchanting child. Now they were tragically in love with each other and Tamara's eyes tonight were clouded and a little wild, her youthful joyousness replaced by a false vivacity, exaggerated and jarring.

As for Miranda—ruefully she recalled her uncomplicated state on that former occasion. True, there had existed the disconcerting situation between herself and Frederick Clayton but the first shock had subsided, the initial awkwardness was eased and the affair assuming a certain piquancy. It had been amusing to come to his party, playing her role as he played his. He had meant nothing to her; she had talked with him, danced with him, serenely unmoved. Now the sound of his voice, the sight of him, filled her with restless pain, while her heart stood still at the recollection that, in the very near future, she would no longer see or hear him.

'Well, Miranda?'

She started, and saw Freddy looking quizzically down at her; the band was playing again and everyone was getting up to dance. She blushed, and hastily rose from her chair; he drew her out to the floor, his arm went about her and they slid into a slow waltz.

'Such a brown study,' he said. 'Where were you?'

'Right here,' she answered in her deliberate, attractively flat tones. 'I was neglected for the time being and just sort of relaxed.'

'Are you tired? Finding the evening dull?'

'Fishing, Freddy. You know you are giving us a delightful evening.'

'You are enjoying it?'

Miranda nodded briefly.

'And you don't like to talk while you're dancing.'

Her dimple flickered.

'No good dancer does.'

He laughed, and drew her more firmly to him.

'Relax again, then, Miranda. I'm a good dancer myself.'

Too good, she thought. We go too well together. I can't bear this, I wish I could stop—I wish I could go on for ever and ever and ever.

In the salon of a pink villa on the outskirts of Estoril Mrs Sangster was taking leave of her hosts, an Argentine consular official and his wife.

'It has been so pleasant, and I am more than grateful for your interest in my young couple. You think I can rely on their obtaining their visas?'

'I think you may safely rely upon it. Their credentials, as you have given them, sound entirely satisfactory. They will, as a matter of routine be checked, but I foresee no difficulty.'

'And as a personal favour to me, you will do your best to cut the preliminaries as short as possible?'

The Consul, who knew Mrs Sangster well and was fully aware that if the preliminaries were protracted she would allow him no peace, replied that he would make every effort to expedite matters.

'A formidable woman,' he remarked to his wife when their guest had departed. 'Thank heaven, in this instance there is no obstacle; people of standing, the man an expert breeder and trainer of bloodstock, possessed of the required means and with friends already established in the country. You remember, Pilar, the case of the Zilowskis and several others—what our department went through with their determined sponsor—yes, a truly formidable woman.'

CHAPTER SIXTEEN

COUNT RADIZLO and the countess were seated in Mrs Sangster's study facing their hostess who sat at her great square desk.

'So you can take it,' she was saying, 'as settled.

and I have made an appointment for you at the Consulate tomorrow morning. You should be able to sail next week.'

'Madame—' the count looked dumbfounded. 'You have taken my breath away. We had, of course, hoped eventually to obtain permission to settle permanently in the Argentine but we had not intended to rush matters—not that I don't sincerely appreciate your kindly intervention—'

'Wait, Bela.' The countess laid a retaining hand on her husband's arm. She had gone very pale, her fine eyes fixed upon the elder woman with an expression of hatred and fear. 'I think Mrs Sangster has more to say.'

'I have. A great deal more. I have been making certain inquiries and received most shattering information.'

'Inquiries? Of what nature?'

'That is what I am about to tell you. As you know, I was aware of your circumstances, that you still had some meagre capital but were living chiefly upon disposing of jewels. I knew, as well, that you were entrusted with a small sum paid monthly by a Swiss bank, on behalf of the Princess Tamara.'

'Naturally, you knew. There was no secret—'

'One moment. Let me continue. It struck me as odd that the princess should not also possess some valuables since that Princess Obelatski her mother, had lived comfortably during her years abroad and had saved sufficient from her resources to leave this income for her daughter. Tamara herself, one evening, casually mentioned that her mother had had beautiful jewellery deposited in that bank. It could, in the end, have been sold, but for some reason I doubted it. I pondered the situation, her complete lack of any such possessions, your own apparent fund of them, and at last my suspicions were aroused. I determined to investigate.'

'You pious meddler,' Bela exploded. 'What business was it of yours?'

Mrs Sangster regarded him sternly.

'It was very much my business. I had assisted you, trusting your integrity. Moreover if, as I suspected, a young girl was being robbed, my duty was plain. I went to Geneva where I have affiliations with various welfare organizations, obtained the introductions I required, and had one or two confidential interviews. I learned, Count Radizlo, that the income left for Tamara is very much larger than the amount she receives from you, and that the Princess Obelatski had *not* disposed of her jewellery but had entrusted it to your safe keeping for her daughter.'

For a breathing space the count and countess sat rigidly silent, then Bela said hoarsely:

'If you intend to bring up these charges—'

'I have no such intention. What is done, is done. You and your wife will go to Argentina; the princess remains here. You will sign a document resigning your trusteeship in favour of the Swiss Bank; Tamara's income will henceforth be paid by them into one with which they are affiliated in Lisbon. As for the jewels— those you have not already made away with—I suppose they are at present in some safe deposit in your name?'

The count, through set teeth, murmured yes.

'Then I will go with you and you will withdraw and hand them over to me, to be deposited for the princess in the bank that will now deal with her affairs. For the rest—no case will be brought against you and I shall not expose you. You have behaved infamously but that,' said Mrs Sangster in her old-fashioned phraseology, 'lies between you and your Maker. Perhaps He will take into consideration your cruel adversity and terrible temptation.'

'Do you mean,' the countess said, brushing aside this edifying peroration, 'that you will not inform—Mara?'

'I shall not. It could serve no good purpose and would deeply shock her.'

'What is to be said to her? What explanation made of our—desertion?'

'You will find no difficulty there. The princess would have bitterly opposed accompanying you. She does not want to leave Lisbon; she has made friends of whom she is very fond. Tell her you came to the conclusion that she would be happier here; she will accept it without question. Nor will she question her sudden rise in income and the fact, which will later be made known to her, that a portion of her mother's jewellery is intact and has been transferred from Switzerland. This, too, she will accept, thankfully but without a second thought.'

'It is true. She has the brain of a bird, the little one.'

Miranda and Charles were doing a crossword puzzle, seated side by side. Sybil, coming in from her club, eyed them with disfavour. She was always obscurely annoyed to see the brother and sister congenially absorbed in this favourite diversion of theirs.

'So you're at *that* again. Can't you find anything better to do?'

'We like it,' Miranda smiled.

'Well, I don't. You're always at it—I mean, it absolutely gets on my nerves—'

'We'll stop, then,' Charles said. 'As a matter of fact, I must be off; I'm meeting Freddy at half past six.'

Miranda's uncontrollable heart gave a little twist. 'Is Freddy back?' He had been for a few days' jaunt to Madrid.

'He got back a couple of hours ago and rang me at the office.'

'You can pour us a drink first,' Sybil directed. She took off her linen jacket, seated herself and continued, 'I'll give you some news for Sir Frederick; if he's just back I expect he hasn't heard it. Those phoney Hungarians of his are leaving for the Argentine.'

'Leaving for the Argentine,' Miranda echoed amazedly. Her eyes flashed to her brother. 'When? Who told you?'

'I heard Mrs Raymond telling someone that her husband had met Count Radizlo in the street and he said they were off in a day or so. Charles! Look what you're doing—' he was pouring tonic water into a glass already full. 'All over the tray—if ever there was a messy man—'

'Sorry. It's only a few drops.' He repaired the damage with a folded handkerchief and brought his wife and sister their drinks. 'That's news indeed, and a lucky break for the count. He ought to do well out there. I'll tell Freddy—' Miranda's eyes followed him as he left the room. Poor Charles—he had been badly shocked—but it was the best thing that could happen. . . .

Charles, his handsome eyes once again strained after a bad night, was saying the same thing to himself as he walked along the Avenida da Liberdade on the following afternoon. Freddy had not heard the news when the two friends met on the preceding evening and, like the Rendles, he had taken it for granted that if the Radizlos were leaving the princess was naturally accompanying them. He, too, had reflected that this was the best solution for the unhappy lovers since Charles would never swerve from his rigid—in Freddy's opinion absurd—standard.

But although Charles was thoroughly agreeing now, the ache in his heart was scarcely to be born. Never to see again that fair head, those deep brown eyes, the lovely smile. Never to hear the quick voice, the adorable way of speech—Tamara gone—for ever. . . .

He was walking idly, disinclined as yet to go home and listen to Sybil, absorbed in his painful thoughts. He came to the café where he and Tamara had sat on that other afternoon—and saw her, alone, seated at a little table. She saw him, started, flushed, then waved a hand.

They had met during the previous weekend at Mary Willison's delayed picnic and Tamara, as if at last accepting the inevitable, had preserved appearances and behaved towards him with casual friendliness. She was keeping up the same role today, and he crossed to the table; to pass by with merely an answering wave would be too churlish.

'May I join you for a moment?'

'If you wish. You will have a sherbet?' Her tone was light and cool.

'Not today.' A waiter scurried to them and Charles ordered a coffee. 'I have just heard your news, Tamara. That you are leaving Portugal.'

'*I?* Oh no. It is Bela and Olga who leave. I remain here.'

'Remain here!' He stared at her in stupefaction. 'But why? What has happened?'

'Nothing has happened except that Bela and Olga have got visas for the Argentine where they have wished to go. I do not wish to go. So.' She thrust out her small expressive hands.

'You refused? How can they dream of allowing it?'

'Allow? They have no authority over me.'

'But I understand that the count is your trustee—'

'Was an arrangement. Now we make a new arrangement. My money will come to me through the bank.'

'But you can't stay in Lisbon by yourself, no one to look after you—'

'I am not a child, Charles. I am nearly nineteen. And I shall be in the hostel with all the others. Many girls of my age, girls earning their livings, are quite alone.'

They were, of course, but those girls had background, families, roots; they weren't homeless, exiled, peril-besought castaways—

As for the others in the hostel, he knew too well that Tamara would find no shelter or support from that irresponsible lot.

'Tamara,' he began hesitantly, for it wasn't an easy thing to say, 'are you staying because—'

'Of you, Charles? *A quoi bon?*' She gave him a bright hard smile, very different from the one he knew and loved so well. 'No, do not flatter yourself. I am staying because here I have found kind friends and I cannot once more go away to a new country among strange people. I have travelled far enough and long enough.'

Charles set his lips together, gazed down at his

coffee cup. For the first time since childhood he felt the pressure of tears behind his eyelids.

He looked up again, the momentary weakness overcome.

'Your friends will be glad not to lose you,' he said. 'And there is one in particular—I hope you are going to be kind to Fergus, give him a chance—'

'I do not wish to hear any more of that, Charles.'

'But you can't go on drifting—you must think of the future—'

The princess drew herself up.

'My future is no affair of yours. Nor will I permit you to dictate to me.'

'I didn't mean to dictate, only advise you—'

'I have already had the benefit of your advice.'

'Very well, I will not—presume—again.'

A sudden breeze blew in across the flower-studded avenue, bearing a sharp sweet scent. Tamara caught a breath, her face changed, the brown eyes widened and met his with a stricken look.

'Do you smell it, Charles? It's jasmine. You remember?'

'Yes, I remember.'

She placed her hands on the table, pushed back her chair.

'I go, now.'

'Wait, Tamara—'

'No.' She shook her head; he guessed that she was struggling with tears of her own. 'I have not paid for my ice-cream—'

'That, at least, is my affair.'

'Thank you. Goodbye.' She ran across the terrace, hailed one of the ever-available passing taxis and was driven away.

Within the next twenty-four hours it had become generally known that the princess was not leaving with the count and countess for Argentina. Freddy, when he heard the news, cocked an eyebrow and said to himself that the obsessed child still failed to grasp that Charles Rendle was not for her. Miranda, wholly in accord with this view, was filled with dismay. She had every sympathy for Tamara—she herself, if one came to that, was in much the same boat—but it was too hard on Charles. Sybil observed acidly that the girl had evidently not yet given up hope of snaffling Sir Frederick or, failing him, the unfortunate young Seton; Sybil knew nothing about young Seton's proposal and rejection.

'And no doubt,' she said, 'the Radizlos are glad to get her off their hands. There's probably more to it than meets the eye; I mean, if you ask me, that wretched girl will come to no good.'

'We aren't asking you,' Mary Willison retorted. Sybil laughed, bright-eyed and malicious.

'Oh, of course, you won't hear a word against her. She's a princess, isn't she?'

Mrs Sangster who, with half a dozen other ladies was having tea with Mrs Willison, said in her authoritative manner:

'There is nothing to give rise to gossip or speculation. The facts are quite simple; the princess has made a niche for herself here and prefers remaining. To drag her off to the Argentine against her will would be unreasonable.'

'Especially,' Lady Brewster said, 'when such a good prospect is opening for her. It won't be a case of snaffling—' she cast a glance of distaste at Mrs Rendle.

'I understand that Fergus Seton is making all the running himself, very much in love with her.'

Mrs Sangster nodded.

'You are right. And I fancy she will soon cease her girlish coquetry and accept him.'

The ensuing days, for Miranda, were a period of stress. At the weekend Jim Morland came down again and, a young man who knew his own mind and never wasted time, asked her the question she had foreseen. Gently, but with a finality that left him under no delusion, she gave him her answer. He took it very well, without rancour, and returned to the home that would always come first with him.

For her part, she had said the only thing she could, but she wondered whether she were not the most foolish girl in existence. Giving up the substance for the shadow, flinging away a happy, interesting, worthwhile life—at Santa Joana—with a man she so thoroughly liked and respected. Flinging it all away—for what?

'But I couldn't—I couldn't—I can't marry Freddy but so long as he is in the same world as myself I can't marry anyone else.'

The weather turned sultry and oppressive with a threat of storm that would not break. Miranda became increasingly restless. Each passing day brought nearer the time when Freddy would go back to England, a time beyond which she saw utter blankness. In addition to this was her concern for her brother and the difficulty of her intimacy with Tamara. Impossible to drop the friendship, yet to continue it, in the circumstances, seemed ill-advised and no true kindness to either of those two.

It was on one of these troubling days when she was alone in the flat, Sybil playing bridge as usual and the two maids enjoying a few hours' outing, that she was startled by the violent ringing of the bell.

Hurrying to open the door, she discovered Mrs Sangster's little maid, obviously in a state of frantic excitement.

'Oh, Mees Rendle—I come to tell you—you will know what to do, who to inform—'

'Elita!' Miranda looked electrified. She drew the girl in and shut the door. 'What has happened—'

'Oh, Mees Rendle—we were so right—but there is more—much more— Never will you believe what I have to say but it is true, true!'

CHAPTER SEVENTEEN

IN THE sitting-room of a service flat at the top of a tall modern building Sir Frederick sat at his writing table, his chin cupped in one hand, the fingers of the other beating an abstracted tattoo upon the polished wood.

A frustrating business, this. He had got so far, but still lacked the required evidence. 'And how the devil I'm going to get it—'

His musings were interrupted by the ringing of the telephone that stood at his elbow.

'Clayton here—'

'Freddy—thank goodness, I was afraid you'd be out—it's Miranda.'

'And how is Miranda?'

'I'm fine but—listen, Freddy. I've got to see you—at once if you can possibly manage it—I have something to tell you—'

'Another problem?'

'Wait till you hear! I can't say anything on the telephone—'

'Right. I can manage it. Are you alone? Shall I come round?'

'I'm alone just now but Sybil might arrive at any moment—'

'You'd better come over to me, then. You know where I hang out?'

'Yes.' She had never been to his flat but she knew where it was. 'I'll be there in about twenty minutes.'

Miranda rang off. Freddy, wondering what new crisis had developed, whether Charles and Mara, to put it bluntly, had done a bolt, set a cherry decanter and glasses on the writing-table and took his stand by one of the high windows. Presently he saw the little car draw up at the entrance below and Miranda descend. A few moments later he heard her light step and opened the door to her before she could ring the bell. She was hatless, her hair ruffled as if she had run distracted fingers through it, the pupils of her eyes enormous.

'Sit down and get your breath,' he said.

She sank into a deep armchair, conscious even in her extreme agitation of a thrill, half pleasure, half pain, at being here alone with him in his eyrie. The small flat occupied one of the two towers that topped the building; the sitting-room was octagonal, like a room in a lighthouse, an effect carried out by lamp standards and candle brackets of finely wrought iron.

The furniture was unobtrusively luxurious and typical of the present tenant; Freddy always did himself well.

He poured the sherry, gave her a cigarette and took the chair facing her across the screened fireplace.

'Well, Miranda,' there was a note of indulgent amusement in his tone, 'what's it all about? Charles taken the bit in his teeth?'

'No, no. It's nothing to do with Charles. I had a visit from Elita this afternoon.'

'Elita? Who is she?'

'You must know—Mrs Sangster's maid—she always presides at the tea table—'

'Mrs Sangster's maid!' Freddy was all attention now. 'What on earth—'

'She came to tell me she had overheard a most frightful row between Jenks and her mistress. It was Elita's afternoon off and she had already left the house when she discovered she'd forgotten her handkerchief. She went back, and heard voices in the study, and crept along to listen. The door was shut but she could hear perfectly well; the cook had gone out, too, and they naturally imagined they were alone in the house. They were quarrelling—you won't believe your ears, Freddy—quarrelling about the princess's—Mara's—jewels.'

Freddy uttered a sharp ejaculation. Miranda nodded.

'No one knew Mara had any, she obviously doesn't know it herself. But Mrs Sangster has got hold of them, from Count Radizlo. Jenks was demanding his share and she was refusing—I couldn't believe my own ears when Elita told me. *Mrs Sangster*. It's simply fantastic—and yet it sort of bears out—'

'One minute, Miranda.' Freddy put a hand up to

stem the excited flow. 'I want to get this straight. Let's begin at the beginning. Why did the maid come to you, of all unlikely people, with this tale?'

'Because she and I were in it together.'

'*What?*'

'I distrusted that man from the first,' Miranda explained. 'And I had the queer feeling about the house. Then one day I met Elita who was in a bit of trouble; I fixed it for her and she was very grateful and we made friends. I found she didn't trust Jenks either; she couldn't bear him although he was perfectly civil to her. We compared notes and she told me, for one thing, that he constantly goes to a certain café on the river front—not the sort of place a respectable butler-chauffeur would be expected to go. Elita got that information from friends in the quarter; she was as curious as I, and felt the same way; that Jenks was leading a double life.'

Miranda paused and took a sip of sherry.

'Go on,' Freddy prompted. 'What else did you two young self-appointed investigators find out?'

'Nothing, really. Except that for my part, I saw him at the Casino both times I was there and it looked as if he might be a gambler or perhaps a go-between for people who wanted to sell a diamond or something.'

'None of these activities being necessarily crooked—'

'No. But we were sure he *was* a crook and was doing Mrs Sangster down. It wasn't our business, of course, and we just sort of speculated about it; we never expected to find out the truth—or what Elita discovered today. She was horrified, and frightened, and came at once to me.'

'Tell me exactly what she overheard.'

Miranda did so; Jenks had learned from Count Radizlo that Mrs Sangster had taken charge of the princess's jewels; Elita had definitely heard the man say this. Then he demanded his cut, in terms that proved to the appalled young girl that these two were no employer and employee but colleagues in a most nefarious activity. While the ensuing quarrel was at its height she had slipped out of the house and rushed to Miranda.

'Where is the girl now? Has she returned to Mrs Sangster's?'

'I persuaded her to go back and she has promised not to breathe a word of this until she has heard from me. It's been an awful shock; I didn't know whether I was on my head or my heels. I knew I must tell someone, and by the time Charles came home Sybil would be in too and she'd start one of her scenes if I tried to get him alone; accuse us of talking behind her back and keep on and on. So I rang you; I thought you'd know what to do.'

'Good girl. You did exactly right. You and that excellent little eavesdropping maid have given me the one thing I wanted and was in despair of getting.'

"Given *you*—'

'Played straight into my hands.'

Miranda's mouth opened and stayed open as she stared at him, dumbfounded. Freddy smiled.

'I'm in your debt, so I'll let you into the secret. I can trust you to keep it—'

'Yes,' she answered dazedly.

'I have been working on the same case. I suspected the man Jenks but couldn't get anything on him. What you have told me warrants our taking him into custody for questioning, which is all we need. The rest will follow. I take it the girl will be ready to testify, swear to what she heard?'

'I am sure she will. But, Freddy—*you*—I can't understand—'

'I did a lot of undercover work during the latter part of the war,' he said, 'and until I was demobbed. Happened to have a flair for it, and knowing several languages was an asset. Since then, the civilian authorities have found me useful from time to time. I'm not attached to any official body, just do it because it interests me. What you could call my hobby.'

He explained that in this instance he had been requested to undertake an investigation concerned with the increasing traffic in jewels which was causing various European governments grave concern. The British authorities in Lisbon strongly suspected that one at least of these traffickers was someone in the employ of a member of the circle with whom Freddy had affiliations.

'That's why my chief here, Colonel Wylie, asked me to come. But I didn't agree with his theory. I had got a hunch—'

Miranda brushed a hand across her eyes.

'My head is spinning again. I thought you only—played around—that you had come to Portugal simply to have a good time—had wangled it—'

'That, my dear, was what you and everyone were intended to think.'

'Oh—' she laughed, shakily. 'Of course you had to pretend—how stupid of me. And all the time you have been trailing Jenks?'

'Yes. I secured plenty of information but I had to get something on which to base an interim arrest. Thanks to you, I've got it.'

'And got more than you bargained for, haven't you. *Mrs Sangster*. It's the most incredible thing—but now I know why I felt that room of hers was all wrong. People said it was so typical of her, and in a way it was, yet to me something just didn't fit. I couldn't analyse what I did feel, it was a sort of intuition. You remember my saying so to you?"

'I do.'

'And that was the day I saw Jenks in the garden and felt *he* was wrong. You looked out of the window, too, and saw only his back. Did you get your idea then and there?"

'No. I had got it some time before.'

'But surely that was the first time you had seen him?'

'It was. But my idea concerned someone else. Jenks was merely what you could call the—pilot fish.'

'*Someone else.*' Again she stared, wide-eyed and openmouthed. 'Not—not—'

'Yes. Mrs Sangster.'

'Freddy! You suspected her—but why, when—'

'When I was introduced to her on board ship.'

'But how—what made you—'

He grinned.

'Intuition, Miranda. I felt what you felt; something just didn't fit.' Freddy stood up. 'And now I must push along and report. Don't say anything about this to a soul, not even to Charles. I'll get in touch with you; I shall probably want your help. But we'll leave that for the moment.'

She rose obediently, wishing she could stay longer with him in this intimate small room but thrilled by his saying he might need her again. A foolish elation;

the less she saw of him the better for her peace of mind, but Miranda thrilled none the less.

'I'll do anything,' she began, then stopped.

'What is it?' he asked, looking down into her suddenly troubled face.

'It's the thought that, through me, Mrs Sangster is being—caught out.'

'Are you fond of her?'

'Oh, no. I don't think anyone could be really fond of her; she's not an endearing type. And I know she deserves whatever is coming to her; not so much on account of the smuggling—that always leaves me pretty cold—but stealing Mara's jewellery—she is a bad woman. And heartless, which is worse.'

'Well, then—'

'I have been to her house,' Miranda faltered, 'accepted so much hospitality, and when I think of the awful exposure—all my doing, and it honestly was none of my business—it sort of goes again my grain. You'll think me very silly—'

'I don't think you silly at all,' Freddy said in the gentle tone he so seldom employed. 'And you are not responsible; the girl Elita would certainly have told her story to someone.'

'I suppose she would.'

'And it isn't likely that the person she told would have acted so sensibly and discreetly as you, Miranda. We may be able to do something about the—exposure. So don't fret, as I said before, you have done exactly right.'

Freddy, seated in the office of his chief, finished his report. For a long moment the elder man sat in stunned silence.

'I know it is hard to believe, sir,' Freddy said.

'Hard,' the other echoed forcibly. 'Never, in the entire course of my career—' he laughed shortly. 'A damned clever woman. What a camouflage. And you have actually suspected her all along?"

'I thought she might repay a bit of scrutinizing the first time I set eyes on her.'

'I can't grasp it. What occurred, at your first meeting, to arouse your suspicions?'

'They were aroused by her appearance and by certain remarks made by John Willison who introduced me.'

'I should have thought her appearance the very last to give rise to doubt. The essence of dowdy respectability.'

'Her dress, yes. But I looked at the woman. That heavy, muscular throat, the stout freckled arms, eyes like gimlets and big pale mouth—to my way of thinking they didn't altogether tally with the naïve, rather old-fashioned dress.'

'I must confess that seems to me far-fetched. Many excellent women have features of the same kind. Well —and John Willison's remarks?'

'He mentioned that Mrs Sangster was exceedingly interested in the refugees, an indefatigable worker on their behalf. Remember, I was coming out on a jewel investigation; naturally, it was uppermost in my mind. Many refugees have diamonds to dispose of. Incidentally, that was my object in furthering my shipboard acquaintance with the Radizlos and the princess; charming people, of course, but of particular interest to me on this account. I guessed—and later found I was correct—that the count had jewellery to dispose of, and hoped to get a lead there. As for Mrs Sangster, she was represented as altruistic and benevolent; the impression I received was of a woman hard, astute and occupied with the main chance.'

'And so—'

'And so, I got a—signal. A mere vibration, as a young friend of mine would call it, and decided to follow it up. I was taken to one of Mrs Sangster's at-homes—and saw the drawing-room—and learned more of her general activities; her frequent trips to and fro on ostensible welfare work, for instance. I also heard, by chance, that she and Count Radizlo had been seen in earnest conversation in a most secluded and unlikely spot. And when I presently made the acquaintance of her devoted henchman I added it all up and had small doubt that I was on the right track. Janco was a pure gift; cleared the way for me.'

'You never gave me a hint about her—'

'No. You would have scoffed at the idea and there was no point in my doing so. I'm not at all sure that I should ever have managed to trap the good lady herself but I knew that if I could get hold of the man for questioning he was bound to squeal. A perfect specimen of the rat type. Luckily, the young maid overheard more than enough to justify the police, on our representations, roping him in.'

The Colonel nodded.

'Your hunch came off. I was afraid you were wasting your time, and ours; I haven't much faith in vibrations but I'm an old hand trained in the old school.' He smiled rufully. 'I feel completely flabbergasted. I remember being greatly concerned on her account when you told me your idea about Jenks, as we knew him then; such a shock for Mrs Sangster if you were proved right, such a painful position—that unconscionable woman! Pulling the wool over all our eyes—'

'A neat piece of work,' Freddy contributed.

'Decidedly. She must have made a tidy sum—that astonishing collection of hers—it is high time she was brought to book.'

'Nevertheless,' Freddy said shrewdly, 'I believe you have a sneaking regret.'

'I don't in the least regret her Nemesis having caught up with her. But Mrs Sangster was an institution; Lisbon won't be the same without her.'

CHAPTER EIGHTEEN

PEDRO, THE Willison's major-domo, opened the library door and announced a caller.

'O Senhor Rendle.'

'Ah, here you are, Charles.' Willison laid aside some typed sheets of writing paper and removed his reading glasses. 'Sit down, my boy. I have had a letter from Brewster; he asks me to have a talk with you since he himself won't be back for some time.' Mr Willison, among other interests, was a director of the big firm and a close friend of Sir Robert Brewster. The latter had left for England shortly after the weekend they had all spent at Santa Joana.

'It's about that post which was suggested to you,' he continued. 'They have decided to appoint someone older with more executive experience. I'm afraid you were counting on it—'

'No, as a matter of fact I wasn't,' Charles replied, with truth. 'And I quite agree; I haven't the necessary qualifications.'

On the contrary, the other observed silently, you have sufficient qualifications but you also have an impossible wife.

'I am glad you see and take it like that,' he said. 'Now, they are putting forward another proposition they hope you will consider. There isn't much future for you in this branch, you have gone about as far as you can go.'

This was not strictly the fact but Charles made no comment. Mr Willison outlined the new proposal.

'It's a far cry from representing the firm and being based on London,' he finished. 'Out in the blue—but you'll be able to get into civilization occasionally, by air. Very different from the old days. Well, what do you think of it?'

There was a momentary pause, a barely perceptible stiffening of the muscles in Charles's face. Then he said:

'It sounds a wonderful opportunity.'

'And appeals to you?'

'On the whole, yes. Much more in my line and something I can get my back into.'

'With a chance to exercise your practical engineering talents. After all, it seems a pity to let them lie fallow; there are plenty of years ahead for soft executive jobs. I am not asking for an answer today, however; you'll want a breathing space to think it over. If you decide to accept, they'll expect you to leave within a month or six weeks. That should give you ample time to arrange your affairs.'

'I have already decided,' Charles said in his quiet,

steady way, 'and I shall start arranging my affairs immediately.'

'My dear boy,' Mr Willison looked oddly moved. 'I believe it is a wise decision; you'll gain invaluable experience. But we—we'll miss you, Charles.' With a sudden bustling movement he got up from his chair. 'Come along to the drawing-room; Mary has some people in for cocktails.'

Charles hesitated; he was not in the mood for any social effort. But his host was opening the door, motioning him forward, and he could only accede.

In the drawing-room, a charming apartment opening on a walled garden, a cheerful company were collected. Mary Willison, standing by a buffet table which had been placed near the wide french doorway, waved a welcoming hand.

'Hallo, you two. Is the conference over?' Her eyes flashed a question at her husband who responded by a significant gesture. 'Come and mix yourself a drink, Charles.'

As he made his way to her he saw, in the garden beyond, a number of young people among whom was Tamara. She was looking into the room and could not have failed to see him but she gave no sign.

'Whisky?' Mary said.

'Whisky, please,' he answered with his slow, pleasant smile. 'I'm gate-crashing your party, Mary.'

'I feel rather guilty about my party, not asking Miranda—and Sybil—but Adelaide Morland is here and I thought it might be awkward for her and Miranda to meet so soon.' Mary did not add that she had resolved, in any case, not to have the occasion marred by the obnoxious Sybil.

'You know what has happened, then?' Charles

asked. 'Miranda confided in me but we haven't informed Sybil or anyone else.'

'Adelaide has told me. She is sadly disappointed. So am I; it did seem the ideal match for Miranda.'

'I should have liked to see the child so happily established, myself,' Charles confessed, 'but since she feels otherwise—'

'Foolish girl.' As Mary spoke, Tamara's voice came from outside, raised on a note of hilarity. 'And there's another one; she could have been happily established, too, and her position is very different from Miranda's. Precarious, to say the least. I can't understand her refusing Fergus Seton.'

'It's early days—she may come round—Fergus moved too fast,' Charles said jerkily.

Mary shook her head.

'The princess has lost her chance. Fergus has gone—'

'Gone?'

'Didn't you know? He's been transferred. Left yesterday. It was very hurried; he's replacing someone as Second Secretary. A nice step up for him. He rang us to say goodbye; obviously it is all off between him and Mara.'

'I hadn't heard. Miranda probably knows.'

Tamara's high young voice rang out again.

'I've got some of the officers from the cruiser here,' Mary said. 'I hope they haven't been giving that excitable girl too much to drink; she takes very little as a rule. A pity the Radizlos have gone off and left her; not that one can blame them for going and I must say they didn't pay much attention to her when they *were* in Lisbon. But it's a bad thing for a girl of that age to be so utterly unprotected.'

'Yes, it is a very bad thing.' Charles set down his glass.

'Have another, Charles.'

'No, thanks. If you'll forgive me for drinking and running I think I will get along. I have one or two things—'

She gave him a quick glance, her heart tightening as she noted the strained young face, the troubled eyes. Damn that wife of his. If it had been for her there would have been no question of this new post.

'I'll forgive you,' she said, 'if you really must go.'

As he left her she wondered whether he had any conceptions as to why, in effect, he was being removed. He always seemed so blind . . .

Charles, however, was under no illusion. He had seen it coming, just as Mary had. Sybil dropped by everyone, himself of necessity fading out—in a community so small and closely knit it would be a most uncomfortable and embarrassing situation for his friends. An impossible situation.

Meantime, Miranda had arrived home to find her sister-in-law there. Sybil was not in a good temper; she had heard that Mrs Willison was giving a cocktail party.

'Entertaining the officers from that British ship,' she informed Miranda. 'And Mrs Morland is staying with her for a few days—she never told me—and now she has this party and leaves me out. It's jealousy, of course.'

'Jealousy,' Miranda echoed, faintly.

'She's always looked on the Morlands as her special preserve and can't get over my having been to Santa Joana. It's as plain as the nose on your face.'

What *is* plain, thought Miranda, is that even Mar
is revolting; she wasn't going to inflict you on Mr
Morland or anyone else. Poor Sybil; it was beginning
there had been two or three other affairs to which she
had not been invited, much to her surprise and chagrin
She had laid the blame at Charles's door, as usual. I
would not be long now before all invitations ceased, a
Miranda had for some time become increasingly aware
'They have borne enough—and who can blame them'
But what sort of life—poor Charles—'

At this juncture Charles himself came in. Sybil a
once regaled him with her wrongs, Mary's jealous be
haviour.

'I mean, if this sort of thing continues I'll have it ou
with her. There's no use expecting you to do anything
about it, stand up for your wife as any other husband
would—'

'There'll be no necessity for either of us to take ac
tion,' he replied. 'We are leaving Lisbon.'

Sybil's jaw dropped.

'What do you mean? Oh—have you got that post,
the one Sir Robert wrote about?'

'No. I have been offered, and accepted, something
else.'

Miranda sat silent, gazing at her brother. He was
speaking as she had never before heard him. Not un-
civilly, but with a curt finality. Like a man, she thought,
at the end of his tether.

'What sort of thing?' Sybil demanded. 'Where?'

'Construction. In Alaska.'

'*Alaska*. Are you out of your mind, Charles?'

'Not at all. It is an excellent job—' he explained the
nature of it. A great dam and hydro-electric installa-
tion for which his firm had secured the contract. He

was to be in charge of a very responsible part of the undertaking.

'If that isn't you all over,' Sybil shrilled. 'They suggest that other marvellous job—travelling, meeting high-up people, headquarters in London—you could have had it if you'd stirred a finger. I did my best, talked to Sir Robert—he was very much impressed with me—but you make no effort, just go muddling on, and I suppose they decided you wouldn't make the grade. So they offer you this as a sop and you spinelessly accept—behind my back—well, you can withdraw your acceptance. I won't hear of it.'

'I am not withdrawing, Sybil, and we leave within a month, or six weeks.'

'*We.* Do you imagine I'll consent to grubbing in a tent or a log hut in a savage wilderness?'

'It isn't as bad as that. There's an airport and a sizeable little town five miles from the camp where, John tells me, you'll find provision shops and a cinema and even a Women's Institute. The company have put up a number of prefabricated houses there, for the personnel and such wives as accompany them. Plenty of heat, and light—you'll be quite comfortable.'

'Comfortable. You expect me to live in a prefabricated house in a makeshift town with the wives of sub-engineers and clerks and—'

'You will have to live in the town. There is nowhere else—'

'That's what you think. I happen to think otherwise. It's an absolute insult to ask a woman like me to do such a thing. I'm not going. Nothing on earth will induce me.'

'It is for you to say, Sybil. If you would rather go back to England—'

'I'm not going to England. I'm staying in Lisbon. And what's more—' the frog-like head raised itself from the high, choking collar of her Italian designed jersey, the small truculent chin thrust forward. 'What's more, I shall give up this flat and take a house and live properly. I'll show Mary Willison—and Mrs Morland —and you can jolly well foot the bill. You owe me that much; you've done this without the slightest consideration for me—'

'I'll foot any bill in reason,' he returned, 'but I strongly advise you not to remain here. It will be better and happier for you to be among your own people while I am abroad. You can take a place at home, live as you choose—'

'And show all your old friends *there*,' Miranda could not resist adding.

For an instant a speculative gleam lighted in Sybil's round eyes, then the tiny mouth tightened obstinately.

'I'm not going to be dictated to as to where I shall live.'

'As you will.' Charles wearily passed a hand back across his hair. 'I think you are making a mistake, but it's up to you.'

'Sybil.' There was a vibrant ring in Miranda's voice. 'You can't stay in Lisbon by yourself. You'll be utterly miserable—'

'On the contrary, I'll have a far better time. Charles is no joy to me; I mean, cramping my style in every way, an absolute millstone—'

'You won't have any sort of time at all, without him.'

'Why not? I know everybody in the place worth knowing—'

'You do, thanks to your husband. If it weren't for him—no, Charles—' as he was about to interpose, 'let

222

me speak. It is time she heard the truth, for her own sake. You know perfectly well what will happen if she stays here. Listen, Sybil. The only reason people have put up with you as long as they have is because they are so fond of, and sorry for, Charles.'

'Sorry—'

'Desperately. Everybody pities him—'

'Be quiet, Miranda.'

'Be quiet yourself, Charles.' She flashed him a lightning glance. 'You aren't going to shut me up. Apart from your treatment of him,' she swept on, 'you have antagonized every blessed person you have met out here. The awful things you say; ill-bred things, rude things, catty things—it's beyond me what satisfaction you get out of it, what possesses you.'

'You're talking a lot of rubbish, Miranda. I don't let people put anything over me, if that's what you're getting at.'

'Well, whatever it is, people are tired of it and they aren't taking any more. Even if Charles were still here, you'd find everyone except his most intimate friends dropping you. It has started already; the Sinclairs, the Mayhews, the Sayers—they've cut you out, you have seen this for yourself. And if you insist on staying, alone, no one will have anything more to do with you. Not even Mary Willison. You'll be left flat; I know what I am talking about—'

'You have said enough, poppet.'

'Maybe too much. And Sybil can send me packing if she likes. But it was time *someone* spoke.'

'Why should I send you packing, silly girl? You are Charles's sister and think he's a little tin god and naturally side with him. I don't take any notice of that; I mean, I couldn't care less what a kid of your age says.

As for the rest, I see it all. Someone has been making mischief, setting people against me. Mary, of course. She has always resented Charles's marrying me; wanted to keep him for herself, a young man in her pocket. Now she is getting back at me in this sly way. I've seen through her from the beginning.'

Miranda stared, fascinated. Fully as Sybil deserved it, she had felt a twinge of compunction for having made so harsh an attack. But it hadn't penetrated; nothing ever did or ever would penetrate this thick and egoistic skin.

'All the same,' Sybil continued, 'if you know this for a fact, Miranda, that Mary *has* set everyone against me—'

'I know for a fact,' Miranda answered, 'that you are going to be dropped, Sybil.'

'Very well.' The small chin was thrust forward again. 'Then I'll drop them first. I mean, I'll shake the dust of this place off my feet. And no loss to me, either, I'm sick of Charles's adoring friends. I'll go home and take a smart house and enjoy myself while Charles grubs away in his camp. I've always hated Lisbon, anyway. So now you know.'

CHAPTER NINETEEN

'Do you think the girl Elita can be trusted to keep it up?' Freddy was saying. 'It is rather a lot to expect— and she's little more than a child—'

'I think we can rely on her,' Colonel Wylie replied. She is a good girl and an intelligent one and has given her word. Besides, she has a very strong incentive.'

The two men were threading their way along the narrow street in which Mrs Sangster's house was situated. Arriving at the doorway, Freddy pulled the great iron bell chain; the door was opened by Elita who, on the preceding day, accompanied by Miranda had had an interview with Freddy and his chief.

'Is Mrs Sangster at home?' the Colonel inquired.

'Yes, Senhor.' Elita spoke breathlessly, looking up with wide eyes. He smiled reassuringly.

'It is all right; just carry on as arranged—'

'Yes, Senhor. If you will enter—' she led them into the drawing-room and went off to inform her mistress.

'Good afternoon.' Mrs Sangster came briskly in. 'How nice of you to call, Colonel, and Sir Frederick too; I hope this doesn't mean Sir Frederick is leaving us and has come to say goodbye?'

'I shall be leaving in a few days.'

'Your friends will miss you. Do sit down—' they seated themselves on the little round-backed chairs in the centre of the room. 'You are just the person I want to see, Colonel Wylie,' Mrs Sangster continued. 'I am very worried about my man, Jenks.'

'Indeed?'

'Yes. He went out last evening to spend an hour or so in recreation as he usually does when I don't require him, and has not returned. The maid discovered this morning that his bed had not been slept in. I thought he had stayed somewhere with friends, and although greatly annoyed—for it is his duty to see that the house is safely locked and make a round of inspection last thing at night—I was not alarmed. Now I 'am beginning to fear that he has met with an accident or been molested.'

'As it happens,' the Colonel replied, 'it is on this very matter we have come to see you. Your man Jenks was taken into custody last night and is being held.'

'Into custody! Why? What is he supposed to have done?'

'He has been under suspicion for some time, of being implicated in smuggling and the jewel traffic generally. Clayton, who came to Lisbon to make some investigations—'

'*Sir Frederick,*' Mrs Sangster exclaimed. 'Do you mean to tell me—'

Freddy nodded.

'I'm by way of being a free-lance investigator. The Colonel asked me to come and have a look-see, and your major-domo interested me at sight. I followed his trail and eventually obtained sufficient evidence to procure a warrant for his arrest.'

'I can't believe—there must be some mistake—'

'There is no doubt whatsoever, Mrs Sangster. I am afraid this is a great shock for you.'

Mrs Sangster's large face had paled, the brown freckles standing out against the pallid skin.

'I have never had such a shock in my life! Jenks! I trusted him as I trust myself. To think that he could so deceive me, take advantage of his unquestionable position in my household, abuse my confidence—dear, dear, how true it is that we know nothing of the inner man, even those closest to us. You, too, Sir Frederick—' she regarded him with pained severity, 'coming among us on what I can only call false pretences— one understands, of course, that you had to disguise your mission, but in my day one did not expect a gentleman—however, that is just my old-fashioned code of etiquette. Times change, and standards with them—'

'Yes, well—' Colonel Wylie interposed, 'the point is, Mrs Sangster, that Jenks has already undergone a gruelling by the police and I need hardly tell you they don't use kid glove methods here. He has admitted his own misdoings and, doubtless with some idea of getting off more lightly, has made accusations against yourself.'

'What an infamous thing. Surely, Colonel, you don't find it necessary to ask me whether these accusations, whatever they may be, have any foundation? That is really nonsensical.'

'So it appeared to us,' he agreed suavely. 'But in the interests of all concerned I find it imperative to clear the air. The man Jenks declares that you, also, are implicated in this traffic, a charge which, depending solely on the word of a thorough-paced rascal is inconclusive to say the least.'

'I should hope so, indeed,' Mrs Sangster rejoined indignantly.

'But he has made one specific accusation; namely, that you have appropriated jewellery belonging to the Princess Tamara Obelatsky.'

'I have done nothing of the kind. This is outrageous.'

'Will you tell me exactly what has happened concerning these jewels? They exist, I suppose?'

'Certainly they exist. Count Radizlo entrusted them to me before leaving Portugal. Tamara knew nothing about them; he was holding them for her as her trustee.'

'Where are they now?'

'Here in this house. In the secret wall safe where I keep my valuables.'

'It is some little time since the count left, and the

princess has her own banking account. Why did you not deposit them in her bank, and inform her?'

'At the time of the count's departure the princess's account had not been opened.' Mrs Sangster was breathing rapidly but she spoke with undiminished indignant vigour.

'But since it has been opened,' the Colonel persisted, 'why are they still in your possession, and why have you said nothing about them to the princess?'

'I have been intending to take them to the bank but I am a very busy woman, Colonel Wylie, and saw no reason for any great haste; the jewellery was quite secure here. As for telling the princess, I used my own discretion. She is a very young, irresponsible girl; I happen to know that she has a passion for gambling. I considered it wiser to leave her in ignorance for the time being. I believed, as all her friends did, that she would shortly marry young Fergus Seton; when this occurred, I should have informed her. The responsibility would then have been her husband's.'

'Well done,' Freddy applauded silently.

'I see,' the Colonel said. For an appreciable moment he and she measured each other, eye to eye. 'Your motive was unexceptionable but you will forgive me if I say it was altogether too high-handed. Frankly, you had no right; there is no legal justification for what you have done.'

'My conscience is clear, I was acting in the girl's best interest.'

'Quite. I am not disputing that. Nevertheless, you have, unfortunately, placed yourself in an invidious position. Jenks is making these charges; it is, of course, only the word of a self-confessed criminal against yours, but if the matter is pursued—' he paused.

Mrs Sangster's face was suddenly mottled with dull colour.

'We don't want this to happen,' Colonel Wylie went on. 'Neither we nor the Portuguese authorities with whom I have been in touch want any sort of scandal in connection with a highly respected British subject like yourself. At the same time, it will be difficult to avoid unless—' he paused again.

'Unless—' she echoed, sitting rigidly upright.

'If you were to leave the country, on an extended visit, I think it would be the solution. Can you do this immediately?'

Mrs Sangster exhaled a long breath; the stout figure in the black silk dress with its white cuffs and collar, relaxed. Freddy, watching her, said to himself, 'She's got it. Caught the lifeline.'

'If you think it best,' she said, 'I can do so. I certainly don't want any unpleasant publicity, my name bandied about by every vulgar tongue in the city. I had been considering, in any case, making a trip to South America where I have a small property left by my dear husband; he was born in Brazil, you know. I can put my affairs here into the hands of my solicitor, the house, and so on. Yes, I see no reason why I should not be able to get off in a day or two.'

'Good. Now, as to the jewellery, will you let me have it? I will give you a receipt, and deposit it for the princess.'

'Very well. But you'll have a cup of tea first—Sir Frederick, if you would be so kind as to pull that bell—'

'Thanks very much,' the Colonel said, 'but I'm afraid we shall have to run along.'

'Must you? I don't like my friends to leave my house

without refreshment. However, if you cannot wait—' she bustled away, and returned with a large jewel case, fashioned of fine morocco leather and embossed with a gilt coronet. Colonel Wylie opened it with the gold key, studied the contents, took his pencil and a slip of paper from a pocket and wrote the receipt.

'There we are. I'll put it in the bank at once and they can inform her; she need only be told that it has been transferred from Switzerland.'

Out in the street, when they had made their bland adieux, Freddy grinned at his chief.

'You've got to hand it to Mrs Sangster.'

'You have,' the other smiled. 'In character to the last.'

'And what a role. Was it all assumed?'

'Not a bit of it. She's a born organizer and busybody and was simply following her bent in taking up welfare work. She liked the prominent position it gave her, both here and among affiliated organizations, and thoroughly enjoyed playing fairy godmother.'

'And the at-homes?'

'She revelled in that, dispensing old-fashioned hospitality and making her house a centre. So far, she was genuine enough.'

'She's getting off darned lightly—'

'It would be a difficult case to prove, and not worth the attendant—' the Colonel, who disliked coarse expressions, made a little grimace.

'Stink,' supplied Freddy, who was less inhibited.

'Exactly. All we and the Portuguese want is to be rid of her and stop that particular leakage.'

'She won't reappear—'

'Never. She has completely grasped the situation She'll settle down in Brazil where, I strongly suspect e "property" consists of what she has prudently salted away in that country. No doubt she has for some time envisaged the possible necessity of making a quick get-away and has made provision accordingly. Hello, here's Miss Rendle.'

Miranda was watching them from the corner of the street leading to the car park, smiling the composed little half smile that just lifted her cheekbones and deepened the silly dimple. Characteristically she did not move as they approached her.

'What are you doing here?' Freddy demanded.

'I had to come, I couldn't resist, I want to hear how it went.'

Colonel Wylie eyed her with amusement and approbation.

'You deserve to hear at once. I'll leave Clayton to tell you all about it.' He went off to collect his car; Freddy said:

'Suppose we go to that churchyard of yours, Miranda. We can talk in peace there.'

They crossed the road and made their way to the quiet enclosure and sat down side by side on a secluded stone bench.

'Now—' Miranda said.

He told her of what had taken place, the duel between the Colonel and the lady, the former's suavity, the latter's righteous indignation.

'She's a quick thinker,' he commented when the tale was told. 'Her explanation of why she had held on to Mara's jewels was pretty well hole-proof. But when Wylie made his veiled threat of taking her into court she was obviously shaken and realized the game was up.'

'And she's going to South America, right away?

What will happen to her house and all those things of hers?'

'I expect she will send instructions for the house to be sold and the furniture shipped out to her. I don't see Mrs Sangster parting with her collection.'

'Freddy, how *do* you imagine she and Jenks ever teamed up together?'

'I can tell you that. I've been into Spain a couple of times, ferreting out her record. It appears that Jenks was an associate or in the employ of the late Mr Sangster. He, Sangster, had an export-import business and was proconsul for one of the South American states. Great scope for an enterprising man who isn't over-scrupulous.'

'So she and her husband were crooked—from the beginning—'

'It looks remarkably like it.'

'I wonder what she'll do in Brazil. Start again, organizing charities?'

'Bound to. And make a good thing of the pickings. There are plenty to be had, if one can get away with them. But that's up to the Brazilians now; their pigeon.'

'And none of her friends here will ever suspect—'

'That's the idea. Her going off at a moment's notice won't surprise anyone, she's always trotting here and there and will probably give out that she has had word concerning some trouble about the Brazilian property. Later on, she may inform her friends that she has decided to remain there. Or let them gather it for themselves.'

'I'm glad she isn't going to be exposed. A lot of people would be terribly shocked and it wouldn't do any good.'

'None at all. And so long as Elita doesn't talk—'

'She won't talk. She has promised. And, as she said, if her parents knew she had been in the house of such a woman they'd never let her take another job in Lisbon; she's Lisbon mad. They were very much opposed to her coming in the first place and Mrs Morland persuaded them, saying she would be so safe with Mrs Sangster. Jim told me about it.'

Freddy cast her an inquisitive look but forebore to inquire whether Jim, on his recent trip down from Santa Joana had told her something else and what her response had been.

'Oh—' Miranda exclaimed, 'I have some news for you; I hadn't a chance to tell you yesterday when we were with Colonel Wylie. Unless you have seen Charles and know already—'

'I haven't seen him for several days.'

She told him about the Alaska post and Sybil's refusal to accompany her husband.

'She'll live in England while he is out there. She was furious with him and packed right up and is flying home tomorrow.'

'What a break for Charles.'

'Yes, it is a respite, but poor Charles. It doesn't *solve* anything.'

'She may fall under a bus or get knocked on the head in the meantime,' Freddy said cheerfully. 'And you, Miranda? Will you stay on until your brother goes?'

'Yes.' Her heart stirred as the thought crossed her mind—Freddy and Charles are such friends—with Sybil gone he'll come to the flat—

'I'll see Charles off,' she said, 'and then go to Mary for a week or two.'

He gathered from this, that her affairs were still un-

233

settled; young Morland had not as yet declared himself or, if he had, she was taking time to consider her reply. But the outcome was hardly in doubt; once again Freddy felt that extreme dissatisfaction with what, on the face of it, was so excellent a marriage for Miranda.

'How much longer will you be here, Freddy?' she asked.

'I'm pushing off next week.'

Her heart went very still then.

'So soon?'

'I've finished my job and want to get back.'

'To your farm? They'll be harvesting soon, won't they.'

'I'll have a look at the farm but I rather think I shall make a trip to America. I have friends in New York who want me to come out; I may spend the autumn with them.'

He had not, until this moment, been contemplating any such thing but an obscure restlessness had assailed him, a sudden disinclination to resume his normal life at home. Hitherto that life, free from all ties, pleasantly filled with the social activities of a well-to-do and popular young man, and spiced from time to time by some undercover adventure had wholly satisfied him. Now it seemed pointless, leading nowhere. . . .

'How—nice,' Miranda said. 'I believe autumn is a beautiful season in New York.' She spoke with difficulty; to her dismay she wanted to cry. She pressed her eyelids tight against the threatening sting of tears and got up from the bench.

'Shall we go? Have you got your car or did you come with the Colonel? I can drive you home—'

'I came in my car.'

They walked back, pausing an instant to gaze at the blank grey façade of Mrs Sangster's old mansion.

'No more tea-parties,' Miranda said. 'They'll be missed—'

'I feel a distinct sense of loss, myself,' Freddy smiled, 'when I think that I shall never again see that fantastic drawing-room.'

'So do I,' Miranda responded, remembering the times she had met Freddy in that incredible room. She had always gone with the unacknowledged hope of finding him there and he had never failed to appear. It had surprised her that he should so punctually attend the at-homes; now she knew the reason.

They reached the car park and he put her into the little Citroën.

'We'll see you before you go, Freddy?'

'Certainly. I'm all tied up for the next few days but I'll look in to say goodbye, if I may.'

'Any time. Give us a ring and come in for a drink.'

'I will do that.'

He shut the car door, lifted his hat and Miranda drove away.

When she entered the flat she found her brother, alone, standing by the window from which Tamara had once promised not to throw herself, gazing soberly down across the roofs.

'Charles!' Miranda's voice was edged. He turned swiftly around.

'Anything wrong, poppet?'

'Nothing. But—is Sybil in?'

'No, she hasn't come back yet. Having a final session at her hairdresser's.'

'Then—' she ran forward, put her hands on his

shoulders and looked up at him with urgent, appealing eyes, 'Listen, Charles. I want to go with you. To Alaska.'

'With me,' he echoed amazedly. 'My dear child—'

'Why not? If it's a fit place to take your wife it is fit for your sister.'

'That isn't the point. What would you do in such an isolated spot? A gay young girl—a little social butterfly—'

'I'd do what the other women do. Keep house, and look after my man. Wouldn't you like to have me?'

Charles smiled.

'I'd like to have you, my sweet, but it's unthinkable.'

'No, it isn't. Listen, Charles, I want to go, to be with you, and I want to see that marvellous country; lakes and mountains and snow and dogs and things—it's a *chance* for me. I've never been anywhere except the Riviera and Ireland and here. I don't want to go back to London yet, to the same old round. Please say yes; if I get tired of it I can come home. You said yourself one can fly in and out—I wouldn't have to be stuck there for two years—'

'Two years! I should think not. Two months is more like it; or weeks. I don't know what to say, poppet; I agree, it would be a fine trip for you—there's nothing actually against it—you took my breath away for a moment.'

'Then you *will* take me?'

'If you are so set on it, we can think it over. There's plenty of time.'

'I'm going,' she said.

From the landing outside came the familiar grunt of the lift.

'That's Sybil,' Miranda whispered. 'Don't say a word

236

to her; if she knew I were going with you it would be just like her to change her mind and insist on coming too.'

Sybil, frizzed and flushed, came in; Miranda slipped away to her bedroom.

The idea of accompanying Charles to his construction camp had no more entered her head than had that of spending the autumn in America entered Freddy's until this very afternoon. He was somewhat at a loss to account for his own abrupt decision; she was entirely clear as to hers.

She had repeatedly warned herself that, once at home again, her path and his would cease to cross. Nevertheless, her foolish heart had refused to profit by the warning. She had thought—at least we shall be in the same city, Freddy will be *there*—she knew he maintained his bachelor flat in town and spent most of his time there. And perhaps—perhaps— But today she had learnt that, for some months, he would not even be in the same country.

The hope had been finally extinguished then and the prospect of returning to London seemed unutterably dreary. She couldn't bear it; not yet, not after Lisbon where on any day, at any moment, she had known she might encounter him.

'I can't—' But what else could she do?

As she sat there on the bench at his side, terrified lest she should begin to cry, the alternative had flashed upon her. Alaska. A wonderful unknown country—a new exploration—it wouldn't cure her, nothing would ever cure her of Freddy, but it was infinitely better than wearying in London while he enjoyed himself in New York.

CHAPTER TWENTY

ON THE following day Sybil, expensively and, for once, becomingly dressed in a button-through frock and matching dust coat and minute hat of deep anchusa blue, the exact colour of her round, thickly lashed eyes, was driven to the airport by her husband, Miranda with them. Sybil's outfit was new, and so were the air-travel suitcases in linen covers of the same shade.

'She's really very pretty,' the young sister-in-law reflected, 'when she doesn't get herself up like an over-dressed frog. Poor Sybil. If only she weren't so ugly underneath.'

'I hope you'll have a smooth trip,' Miranda dutifully kissed the unresponsive cheek as they parted in the waiting-room. 'And thank you, Sybil, for having me and all you've done for me.'

'That's all right, you weren't any trouble. Goodbye, Miranda. I hope you'll get Jim Morland in the end but I shouldn't count on it. I mean, if he doesn't come up to the scratch soon—Goodbye, Charles. I expect the next time I see you, you'll be wearing a beard and have forgotten how to wash.'

The brother and sister watched the small blue figure as it crossed to the plane. Sybil turned to wave, then mounted the steps and disappeared. Charles said briefly:

'Come along, poppet.'

They drove back and Miranda, feeling a celebration in order, suggested stopping at a café for ices.

'And I have something terrific to tell you, Charles. I'm simply bursting—'

'We must prevent that. Where shall we go?'

'To my pet one in the Avenida da Liberdade.'

Charles's face tightened a little but he nodded assent and drove to the café where he had twice been with Tamara.

'Freddy didn't want me to tell you,' Miranda said when they were seated on the terrace, until everything was finished but there's no reason why you shouldn't know now.' She unfolded the tale of Mrs Sangster, and Freddy's part in it, and the part she and Elita had played, her brother listening in stupefaction.

'Could you ever have believed it, Charles?'

'None of it. Mrs Sangster—good heavens! And Freddy, of all people—'

'And me—'

'And you, you inquisitive child. I'm staggered by the whole thing.'

They discussed the astounding affair while she consumed her ice and he drank his coffee. When they had finished and were walking to their car they saw Tamara coming along the pavement towards them. She caught sight of them, hesitated for a split second, then came on.

'How nice to meet you, Miranda, and Mr Rendle. Is some time since I see you.'

She spoke gaily but she was pale and heavy-eyed, with shadows below her eyelids. Impulsively Miranda said:

'You look tired, Mara. Are you having that migraine again?'

'Oh no. It is just again hangover. Not that I drink so much but I am at Estoril last night with some girls and the naval officers and we dance and are very late—such a party. We drive somewhere—and have breakfast—was very gay. And what have you been doing, Miranda?'

She might as well know first as last, Miranda thought, and told her they had just been seeing Sybil off at the airport.

'So?' Tamara's eyes flickered to Charles. 'Mrs Rendle is gone for a holiday?'

'She's gone to stay with her people at home for a time,' he replied. 'I'm leaving Lisbon—it's all rather sudden—'

'You are leaving? For how long? Where do you go?'

'He's off to build a dam and things in Alaska,' Miranda explained. 'A new job.'

The princess did not move but the elder girl received the same impression as once her brother had done; Tamara seemed to shrink, like some young animal beaten to final despair.

'Is a long way,' she said.

'It is,' Charles returned, 'but a very good job and engineers must go where they are sent.' He too was pale, now, the familiar lines of strain etched about his eyes and mouth.

'I'm not letting him go alone,' Miranda went on, speaking more quickly than usual, giving them time to pull themselves together. 'I have coaxed him into taking me with him. It's frightfully exciting—a marvellous trip—Charles says once I get there I won't last a

fortnight but I know I'll adore it. Sybil couldn't face
it; too rough and crude for her, she hasn't the pioneer
spirit. Or maybe she just has more sense. Anyhow, I'm
risking it.'

Tamara had herself in hand now.

'Is wonderful opportunity for you, Miranda,' she
said in the gracious, mature fashion she assumed at
times; the manner Louise Ashwin, who greatly admired
her, called the prince's daughter speaking. 'And how
nice for Mr Rendle to have his sister with him. I shall
miss you, and always remember our pleasant drives together.'

'We aren't leaving at once, Mara. Not for a month
at least.'

'No? But you will have much to do, I think, and
many friends to see and say goodbye to. So, if we do
not meet again—*bon voyage, mes amis, et bonne
chance.*'

She gave them her hand to each in turn, gave them
her enchanting smile and walked on, the fair head very
erect.

We are dismissed, Miranda said silently. Well done,
Mara; I shouldn't have thought she had it in her. Her
heart's broken; I saw it break right here under my eyes.
I suppose she had still been hoping against hope—as I
have been doing. Oh, Freddy, just as I have.

As they got into the car and drove off, Charles, following a train of thought of his own, said abruptly:

'Of course those naval types are all decent chaps.'

'Of course,' she agreed. 'But Mara might get in with
some men who were less decent. I'm sure Mary and the
others will more or less keep an eye on her but there's
no one who really *cares* or has any authority over her

241

—Charles!' her voice quickened. 'Can't you—won't you—it seems so utterly senseless, in the circumstances—'

'You know, do you?' he returned quietly.

'I'm not an owl. I've known all along. It isn't as if Sybil cared twopence about you; if you ask me she hates and resents you because you wouldn't conform to her vulgar ideas. She's made you utterly miserable and you don't owe her a thing, but you do owe it to Mara. You're responsible, Charles; I'm not implying that I think you have ever made love to her, but all the same—'

'If you are suggesting that I should take Tamara away with me—'

'Why not? I understand your feeling about that sort of thing in general but this is a special case. Let Sybil divorce you, settle plenty of money on her—'

'That's the main point, my dear. Sybil would never divorce me. She would refuse from sheer spite, to punish us both.'

Miranda drew a breath.

'I suppose—yes, you are right. She'd do exactly that. But even so, Mara would be happier—with you—'

'I couldn't do that to her. It is out of the question. And when I am gone, for good, Tamara will recover. She isn't nineteen yet; she'll find someone else. She may reconsider and recall young Seton. And now, poppet—' Charles spoke in a tone his sister recognized and knew better than to oppose, 'we'll say no more about it.'

CHAPTER TWENTY-ONE

FREDDY CLAYTON entered the ancient lift and
slowly ascended. He had telephoned to ask whether he
could come in between half past six and seven for the
starting drink. Miranda had replied that he could.

It was a heavily overcast evening and the lamps in
the drawing-room were lit; as he was ushered in he saw
her standing there alone, as she had stood on the evening of his first visit, wearing the same soft, full-skirted,
amber coloured frock. He was reminded of his former
shock of pleased surprise at the sight of the delightful
room, and how he had thought, involuntarily, that it
was the perfect setting for dark-haired Miranda. The
shock was repeated, less pleasurably, tonight; the dress
and the setting became her too well. But he said, easily:

'You are looking very charming.'

'We're going to a supper dance later on. Sit down,
Freddy. What will you drink? Charles will be a little
late, he had to see one of the managers in his department.'

Freddy said he would like a whisky and she poured
it and a sherry for herself. They sat down in two little
chintz-covered armchairs, the glasses and a dish of
olives on the small table beside them.

'Happy days—' he lifted his glass.

She lifted hers in response, setting it down again
with a bump and he put out a quick hand to steady it.

'How clumsy I am.' Her own hand was unsteady because of the uneven beating of her heart; the last time I shall see him, it was crying, the last time.

'On the contrary,' Freddy retorted, 'you are quite the least clumsy person I have ever known. And the least fidgety. Your capacity for keeping still was one of the first things I noticed in you.'

'Was it?' Miranda was glad of the deeply shaded lights as she felt herself flush. 'I didn't know I was stiller than other people. It's probably my convent training.'

'No,' he smiled. 'It is just—Miranda. Have you heard from your sister-in-law? The plane didn't crash?'

'Freddy—you really shouldn't—she got home safely. We've had a cable.'

'When do you give up the flat? Are you having a sale of the furniture?'

'The man replacing Charles has taken over the lease of the flat and wants to buy most of the furniture. He is letting us stay on until the last moment.'

'And then you go to Mary.'

'Not to Mary.'

'I understood—' Freddy's tone was suddenly stiff.

'Yes, but my plans have changed.'

'I see.' And at this precise instant he knew the reason for his extreme reluctance to her marrying young Morland. Miranda belonged to him; she had belonged to him ever since the evening of her nineteenth birthday when he had looked across the ballroom and seen her standing beside Charles in her white tulle frock, gardenias pinned to her dark hair, looking at himself with shining star sapphire eyes. The fact that for two years he had been blind to this simple incontrovertible

ct did not alter it; she was his, and it was preposter-
s for any other man to lay claim to her.

Preposterous or not, however, another man had
aimed her; his own awaking came too late. There
as only one thing now to be said and Freddy wryly
id it.

'Congratulations, Miranda.'

'Congratulations?'

'You are going to Santa Joana of course.'

'Santa Joana! I'm going with Charles. To Alaska.'

'What?' He looked dumbfounded.

'I've persuaded him to take me. Isn't it exciting?
n so thrilled.'

There was a slight quaver in her voice as if, he
ought, she were not really very much thrilled.

'But what has happened, Miranda? I thought—'

'That I was marrying Jim? Oh, no.'

Freddy's dark eyes regarded her intently.

'Are you going to Alaska on his account? Because
ou have found that he doesn't, after all, intend to ask
ou?'

'He *has* asked me.'

'And you refused?'

Miranda nodded.

'You aren't in love with him?'

'No, Freddy.'

Something in her tone, in her suddenly averted face
aused him to look at her with still sharper attention.
nnerved by this close scrutiny she said hastily:

'We'll both be on the other side of the Atlantic this
utumn. When do you plan to go to New York?'

'I am not sure,' he replied, 'that I shall go at all now.'

'Oh.' She put out a hand towards her sherry glass

245

and again, by some mischance, nearly overset
Freddy cocked an amused eyebrow, but he had se
the tremor in the slender fingers.

'Can't you cope with your glass, Miranda?'

'It appears that I can't. I don't know what's got in
me—'

'If it's what I hope it is,' he said, 'you aren't goin
with Charles. You're coming home with me.'

The grey eyes dilated; she sat transfixed.

'Is it that, Miranda?'

'Yes,' she breathed.

'You'll come back with me?'

'If you—want me to.'

He rose from his chair and drew her up from her
The russet brown head bent down over the dark on
he kissed her lowered eyelids, her mouth, and the ble
sed, adorable dimple that he had called absurd.

'Lovely girl, my lovely Miranda—'

'Freddy, I can't believe it. You've fallen in love wi
me again—'

'And you with me.'

She smiled up at him, her head cradled in the ho
low of his shoulder.

'I'm beginning to think I've never been *out* of lov
with you.'

'I'm beginning to think,' he mimicked, 'that I hav
been in the same case.'

'And when we met on the ship, and for a long tim
afterwards, we thought we hated each other.'

'That was a very good sign.'

Miranda laughed, then a shade crossed her face.

'What is it?' he asked.

'Charles. I'll have to tell him I won't be coming wit
him now. He'll have to go all alone—'

'Charles,' a voice said from the doorway, 'has already deduced that and is taking it on the chin.'

CHAPTER TWENTY-TWO

SOME FOUR weeks later Miranda drove into the courtyard, put her car away and went up to the flat. Freddy had gone back to England, reluctant to leave her but agreeing that she should stay to keep her brother company while he wound up his affairs and initiated his successor into the ways of the department. Meantime, Freddy would be making his own arrangements for the reception of his future bride.

'Get the house ready for you, Miranda.'

'Shall we really live in the heavenly old house?'

'Where did you expect to live?'

'But I thought you didn't take any practical interest in the farm—'

'I wasn't interested in living there in solitary state. Now that I'm going to have a wife—'

'You'll settle down? And we'll be *real* farmers?'

'Well—' Freddy's strong white teeth showed in the incorrigible graceless grin. 'I don't say we'll never take our hands from the plough. But for the most part, yes. I'll settle down; with you, Miranda.'

The month had not seemed long to her for there was much to do. Shopping for a basic trousseau—she was to be married almost immediately upon returning home—arranging for the sale of such furniture as the

new tenant did not require, taking final sentiment.
drives and walks about the beloved city, attending t
the housekeeping.

She had seen nothing of Tamara during this inte
val. Mrs Sangster, in whose hospitable room the
might otherwise have met, was gone, her departur
causing no surprise or comment, as Freddy had for
seen. And a number of other people in whose house
Tamara might have been encountered had departe
for home, on leave, or to the Mediterranean coast fo
a change of air. Mary Willison was still in town bu
Miranda had taken upon herself to confide in Mar
and the princess was not invited to the Willison's whe
she and Charles were to be there.

It distressed her to cut Tamara out from her ow
friendship but it was the only thing to do and Tamar
for her part, had shown plainly that she neither ex
pected nor wished the friendship to continue. Th
brother and sister never spoke to her; Miranda didn
dare. Charles was his cheerful kindly self but the loo
of strain deepened daily in his eyes. Miranda's hea
was torn for him; there were times when she found he
self thinking, shocked by her wickedness but unable t
resist—'If only Sybil *would* fall under a bus or ge
knocked on the head.' But things like that didn't hap
pen to people like Sybil; their bad angels always looke
after them.

As she opened the door on this present afternoo
her brother called from his small study.

'Miranda? Come here.' There was an indescribabl
note in his voice; she hurried to him.

'Read that.' He handed her a letter.

The letter was from Sybil, couched in vindictive an

triumphant terms. It began with a diatribe against Charles for forcing upon her the alternatives of spending two if not three years in the wilderness or occupying the same period by twiddling her thumbs as a grass widow, waiting until it pleased his lordship to come back. It simply proved that she and her happiness meant less than nothing to him and if she had found a chance of happiness elsewhere he should be the last to complain.

Miranda, at this point, gasped.

'Charles! Does she—is she—'

'Read on,' he said.

The letter went on to say that a few days after arriving at home Sybil had met an old friend, Joseph Lester, who had gone to Australia years before and done exceedingly well. *Joe always had initiative and ambition,* Sybil wrote, *he didn't plod along and let everyone else get ahead of him.* Now, however, he had done more than well; like so many others he had made a killing in wool during the last few years. *I mean, he could buy and sell you Rendles twice over and never miss it.* He had, she continued, the added merit of knowing how to spend, make a showing; in addition to his fine ranchhouse he had bought a grand place in Sydney. He was a widower, happily childless, and wanted to marry again; *someone who can be a credit to him, who knows how to make a show of herself; his wife couldn't make the grade at all. He's fallen for me and I've fallen for him; I mean, we are exactly suited in every way. Joe wants things settled as quickly as possible so we're giving you the evidence, Charles. Any man but you would give his wife evidence, but you're so high and mighty and self-righteous you'd be sure to say you couldn't do a thing like that. And if you did consent, you'd only make a muddle of it. I mean, you simply can't do anything properly.*

Miranda finished the letter and flopped inertly into a chair. 'She wants you to free her—you're rid of her—oh—' she began hysterically to laugh. 'How marvellous—what a letter—poor Joe. She's trapped him as she trapped you—how *does* she do it? But of course she *is* pretty—'

'Very. And I am inclined to think this marriage may turn out well. The good man is obviously much impressed by her, which is just what Sybil needs. He sounds to me a simple sort of chap—'

'Joe,' Miranda returned, 'may be simple, but a man who has made a fortune, sheep ranching, must be tough. He'll probably beat her if she doesn't behave and *that's* what Sybil needs. She'll realize it, too, and know better than to play up with him.'

'I dare say you are right.'

'I'm always right,' Miranda affirmed without false modesty. 'And now—you and Mara—we must let her know at once—shall I call up and say you want to see her? Or you call her—'

'I can't baldly announce that my wife has asked for a divorce and now it is her turn. I've got to think this out, treat the princess with the respect due to her—or to any other girl in like case.'

'Charles—' Miranda spoke in the forcibly controlled tone of one who is on the verge of tearing her hair. 'I love you very much, more than anyone in the world except Freddy. I respect you, more than anyone in the world, including Freddy. But there are times—honestly, Charles, there are times—when I almost sympathize with Sybil.'

'Poppet—'

'Listen,' she swept on. 'You are madly in love with Mara and she with you. You're leaving Lisbon the day after tomorrow. Are you going to leave *her*, still believing it is all finished, brokenhearted, unprotected, just because you feel it is too soon, disrespectful to her, not quite the thing to do? Of all the wrong-headed, rigid, muddling—yes, I know that's Sybil's word, but—'

Charles was broadly smiling, such a smile as his sister had not seen in the harassed young face for many a day.

'Give me time to breathe, I only got that letter by the late post, a few minutes before you came in. I have no intention of going away without seeing Tamara but I've got to have something concrete, some plan for her—put it to her decently and ask if she will consider it—'

'I've made the plan,' Miranda said. 'Mara will go home with me and we'll look after her until you are free to take care of her yourself.'

'If you would—but you and Freddy won't want a third person—'

'Darling, where are your wits? She'll go to Aunt Mollie; Aunt Mollie would welcome any girl for your sake, and you know it, but she'll be charmed with Mara, her pretty manners and everything. As for Grumps—' it was thus that his affectionate, irreverent niece referred behind his back to her uncle, the eminent Mr Justice Rendle, 'Mara'll have him eating out of her hand. Now, are you satisfied?'

'I'm satisfied.'

'Then you'd better call and see if she is in and ask her to come over. There's no place to talk in that Hungarian beehive. You have only tomorrow and she might be going off for the weekend or something—tomorrow's Friday—'

'Will you call her, poppet? She might refuse to speak to me.'

'Very well.'

Miranda went off, returning shortly to say that she had spoken to the princess.

'I said I wanted to see her about something urgent. She didn't ask any questions, just said in a funny little voice that she'd take a taxi and come.'

The two Portuguese maids had been installed in other households some days earlier; Miranda answered the bell of the flat when it presently rang. Tamara, very pale, said:

'You wished to see me?'

'It's Charles who wants you. In here—' Miranda led the way to the open drawing-room door, then ran and shut herself into her bedroom.

'Charles?' Tamara stood on the threshold. 'You have sent for me?'

'Only because there is no privacy in your hostel, Tamara. Otherwise I should have come to you.' He bent down and took her hands in his. 'I have something to tell you, and to ask you—'

She gazed up at him, her eyes wide and dark in her pale face. Then she went whiter still, her eyelids came down and the red lips parted on a breath of such utter, almost sick rapture that Charles, for a second time, felt the smart of tears behind his own eyelids.

'My darling—'

'I must not die,' Tamara said, 'but I think I am going to.'

'You mustn't die now, and leave me.' The strong,

gentle arms came around her; with another rapturous sigh she lifted her face to his.

'Charles—I have ached for this—for you to hold and kiss me—'

'So have I, Tamara. And now I must tell you—explain—'

'Is enough for me that you say I am not to leave you. Are you asking me to—to go with you—'

'Not that. Not that way.'

'I would come, Charles. I love you—so much—'

'And I love you—too much. I am asking you to go home with Miranda and wait for me there until I can come for you. I have had a letter from my wife—' he hesitated. Tamara was wearing the remembered flax blue skirt and little sleeveless top that made her look so young and fresh and sweet. He didn't want to speak to her of Sybil, it was all too sordid, a dark smear on something fair and lovely.

Tamara, watching him, seemed intuitively to grasp what troubled him. She had not scrupled to speak of Sybil in former days but to his surprise and relief she said:

'I think I understand. You have had a letter that asks you to set her free. Is it not so?'

'Yes.'

'Then that is all I need to know. We shall forget her. Already I forget her.'

Some time later Miranda, deciding that she had given them sufficient time, appeared in the doorway.

'Well, is it all fixed up?'

'Dear Miranda. It is all fixed. I am to go home with you—I do not know how to thank you. I shall try in all ways to please your aunt—'

'You'll please her,' Miranda smiled. 'I am so glad, Mara, so happy for you and Charles—'

'And I for you, Miranda. Charles tell me—you and Freddy—everyone is happy—' she made a joyous, all-embracing gesture and the sunset light, streaming in through a window flashed upon the ring she was wearing.

'What a beautiful diamond,' Miranda exclaimed, with a sideways glance at her brother.

'Oh—I forgot my diamonds in all my happiness. Charles, Miranda, what do you think? Mama's jewellery was not sold, it was still in the bank in Switzerland, for me to claim, and I could not claim it because I do not know and would never have known if it had not been for that wonderful, good Mrs Sangster. She thought it strange that I had nothing and she made inquiries and find this out and now the jewels have come to the bank here. She telephoned and told me about it before she went away. Is it not like her? So thoughtful for everybody, taking trouble always—'

'How—splendid,' Miranda said.

'Yes. And now I do not come to you without a *dot*, Charles.'

'I'm delighted for you,' he replied, 'but if you think it enhances your value in my eyes—'

'I do not think that. But—' she spoke with the sudden access of dignity that sat so charmingly upon her, "it enhances me in my own eyes. I shall not go to your aunt as a—a waif—'

'I see,' he said gently.

'I am so grateful,' Tamara continued. 'And I beg Mrs Sangster to meet me at the bank and we look at the jewels there and then I ask to be allowed to present her with something as a remembrance of me and to express my gratitude. She did not wish—but I insist—'

'And she gave in?' Miranda inquired.

'Yes. I am able to persuade her to accept a brooch and earrings.'

'Diamonds?'

'Naturally. I tell you this because I would not like you to believe I could owe such a great debt and say only thank you. But she did not do this to be thanked; only from the great goodness of her heart. Dear Mrs Sangster.'

1-74